ILLUSION TOWN

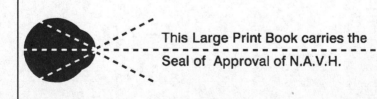

This Large Print Book carries the
Seal of Approval of N.A.V.H.

ILLUSION TOWN

JAYNE CASTLE

THORNDIKE PRESS
A part of Gale, Cengage Learning

GALE
CENGAGE Learning·

Farmington Hills, Mich • San Francisco • New York • Waterville, Maine
Meriden, Conn • Mason, Ohio • Chicago

GALE
CENGAGE Learning®

LIBRARY OF CONGRESS CATALOGING-IN-PUBLICATION DATA

Names: Castle, Jayne, author.
Title: Illusion town / by Jayne Castle.
Description: Large print edition. | Waterville, Maine : Thorndike Press, 2016. |
 Series: Thorndike Press large print core
Identifiers: LCCN 2016023724 | ISBN 9781410492715 (hardcover) | ISBN 1410492710
 (hardcover)
Subjects: LCSH: Large type books.
Classification: LCC PS3561.R44 I45 2016 | DDC 813/.54—dc23
LC record available at https://lccn.loc.gov/2016023724

Published in 2016 by arrangement with The Berkley Publishing Group,
an imprint of Penguin Publishing Group, a division of Penguin Random
House LLC

*This one's for Virgil: Tell Arizona Snow
I said hello.*

A NOTE FROM JAYNE

Welcome back to my Jayne Castle world — Harmony. A new adventure begins in Illusion Town. This is Las Vegas on Harmony but way more weird. The local slogan says it all: *The thrills are real.*

Turns out the town sits right on top of the latest Underworld discovery, the mysterious ruins known as the Ghost City. The Coppersmith Mining Company won the contract to open up the potentially lucrative new territory. They've set up headquarters just outside of Illusion Town. Coppersmith outbid the competition to get the rights but could be looking at a bad case of buyer's remorse. This is Harmony, after all.

There are Alien mysteries and dangers lurking around every corner, both aboveground and in the Underworld, but, as usual, the real trouble is caused by humans.

CHAPTER 1

TO: E. Coppersmith
SUBJECT: It's late
FROM: Finder

You're up late again. More problems with the Ghost City project?

Sincerely,
Finder

TO: Finder
SUBJECT: It's very late
FROM: E. Coppersmith

The Ghost City project is presenting the usual challenges, most of which fall into one of the following two categories: SNAFU and FUBAR. (Sorry for using technical terms.) And it looks like I'm not the only one who is up late. It's one

9

o'clock in the morning. Am I interrupting anything?

> Sincerely,
> E. Coppersmith

TO: E. Coppersmith
SUBJECT: Nope
FROM: Finder

You're not interrupting anything. A
dream woke me up. I decided to do
some work online. What's your excuse?

> Sincerely,
> Finder

TO: Finder
SUBJECT: Your dreams
FROM: E. Coppersmith

Working here, too. I'd like to talk to you
about your dreams. And I'd like to do
that in person. Will you have dinner with
me tomorrow night?

> Sincerely,
> E. Coppersmith

TO: E. Coppersmith
SUBJECT: Dinner
FROM: Finder

Thank you for the invitation to dinner. It is a very nice gesture but entirely unnecessary. I am glad that I was able to find your heirloom ring. You paid my fees. You don't owe me anything else. Really.

Sincerely,
Finder

TO: Finder
SUBJECT: It's not about the ring
FROM: E. Coppersmith

I'm an engineer. I do not make very nice but entirely unnecessary gestures. I am no longer a client. This is personal. I would like to take you to dinner.

Sincerely, but not nicely,
E. Coppersmith

TO: E. Coppersmith
SUBJECT: Bad dates
FROM: Finder

I have found that dates with clients

11

generally don't end well. Sooner or later it turns out that the client wants an off-the-books favor.

Cautiously,
Finder

TO: Finder
SUBJECT: What the hell?
FROM: E. Coppersmith

This isn't about the damn ring. I told you, I'm no longer a client. Off-the-books?

Curiously,
E. Coppersmith

TO: E. Coppersmith
SUBJECT: Bad dates
FROM: Finder

Off-the-books, as in finding antiquities on the black market or missing-persons work. I never do the former and I try really, really hard to avoid the latter. Never ends well. Like dating clients.

Clarifying,
Finder

TO: Finder
SUBJECT: Just dinner
FROM: E. Coppersmith

I do my own black-market searches, and no one I know has gone missing. I just want to take you out to dinner tomorrow night.

Sincerely not a client,
E. Coppersmith

TO: E. Coppersmith
SUBJECT: Just dinner
FROM: Finder

Thank you. I would like to have dinner with you. My address is 15 Midnight Lane, Dark Zone, Illusion Town. I live in an apartment above my shop, Visions. Finding a specific address in this zone can be tricky. GPS and the mapping programs don't work well. I can meet you at the restaurant, if that would be easier.

Sincerely,
Hannah

TO: Finder
SUBJECT: I'll find you
FROM: E. Coppersmith

I'm an engineer. I'll figure it out.

Good night,

Elias

The Coppersmith Mining headquarters of the Ghost City project was located several miles outside Illusion Town. The narrow two-lane highway cut through empty desert for the entire distance. Roadside signs promising flashy casinos, high-payout slot machines, and sexy shows appeared every couple of miles.

At the posted speed limit the drive took about forty minutes. A man behind the wheel of a Cadence could cover the distance in half an hour. A man driving a Cadence who was looking forward to an evening with an intriguing woman could do it in twenty-five minutes.

Elias Coppersmith was driving a hot, enhanced Cadence and he was making very, very good time because he was looking forward to meeting Hannah West in person.

For the first few weeks of their online connection he had known her only as the Finder. She specialized in locating missing,

14

lost, or stolen antiquities in the murky underground world where secretive collectors bought and sold powerful relics and crystals. She dealt in hot crystals and he was a crystal engineer. He figured they had a few things in common.

When he contacted her two months ago, he hadn't expected much. She was just one in a long line of experts he had consulted. But she had located the long-lost Coppersmith family heirloom within days. He had known then that she possessed some very powerful psychic abilities. It hadn't taken him long to figure out that she was a dreamlight talent.

Dreamlights were not uncommon. After all, everyone dreamed and, to some extent, everyone possessed some psychic ability. But most dreamlight psychics ranked at the lower end of the paranormal scale.

Powerful dreamlight talents were scarce and he was pretty sure he knew why. Parapsych researchers were convinced that strong dreamlights possessed unstable, fragile para-psych profiles.

Given the general consensus of the research community it seemed perfectly reasonable that very strong dreamlights would keep the extent of their abilities to themselves. No one wanted to be labeled unstable or fragile.

He knew a lot about keeping paranormal secrets. His family had kept a few for generations.

The online connection with Hannah had evolved quickly from a business relationship into something that he hoped was about to become much more personal.

Night fell fast in the desert. The glittering lights of the opulent casinos and hotels of Illusion Town had just come into view when Elias got the call. He would have ignored it but it was coming in on the frequency reserved for emergencies.

By the time the call from headquarters ended he knew that all of his carefully laid plans for the evening had just gone up in smoke.

So much for assuring Hannah West that their relationship was no longer a business affair.

Another sign came up in his headlights.

WELCOME TO ILLUSION TOWN.
THE THRILLS ARE REAL.

CHAPTER 2

The dream walk started the way it always did . . .

She rose from the bed and stopped to look down at herself. Over the years she had become familiar with the weirdness of an out-of-body experience but it always sent a psychic shock across her senses. She had been dream-walking since the age of thirteen, yet the sensation of being in two places at the same time was still disorienting, at least in those first few seconds. She was both the dreamer and the doppelgänger — her very own double.

The dreamer was curled on her side, asleep on top of the cheap, faded bedspread. The doppelgänger was relieved to see that she was still wearing the new, pricey little red dress that she had saved for a special occasion. The skirt of the dress was hiked up high on her thigh but at least she wasn't flashing the room. Her high-heeled evening sandals were on the floor beside the bed.

The crystal necklace that she had worn earlier in the evening was gone.

"Not good," the doppelgänger said in the silent language of dreams.

"I know," the dreamer replied in the same soundless whisper. "Need to find it."

"Finding things is what we do."

"Careful with the 'we,' pal. Remember, 'we' were recently diagnosed as having a para-psych personality disorder. Our goal is to try to pass for normal."

"Grady Barnett is a lying, cheating bastard. We aren't going to pay any attention to his diagnosis."

"Yeah, yeah. Speaking of finding things, let's try to stay focused here."

"Right."

The light filtering in around the blinds was a familiar eerie green.

"We're near the Dead City ruins," the dop-pelgänger said. "Probably better than being stranded somewhere in the desert."

"That's right. Think positive."

The doppelgänger surveyed the shadowed space, searching for something that was important. She was dream-walking so there had to be a reason. There was always a reason for a lucid dream.

The doppelgänger considered the black

evening bag sitting on the room's only chair. It looked as if it had been dropped there just before the dreamer collapsed on the bed.

"My necklace," the dreamer said. "What happened to it?"

"Check the evening bag," the doppelgänger said to the dreamer. "It's important. Answer is inside."

"Okay. Is that all you've got for me?"

For the first time the doppelgänger looked at the man standing by the window.

"He's important, too," she said.

"I know."

There was a dust bunny perched on the windowsill. Like the man, his attention was focused on the scene outside the window.

But the dreamer recognized the dust bunny. He was a friend. In her world that made him family.

It was the man who was a mostly unknown factor. His dreamlight prints were all over the room — the floor, the window blinds, everything he had touched. They shimmered with strong, controlled paranormal energy.

His prints were on the bed beside the dreamer, too.

"He slept next to you," the doppelgänger said. "That's interesting."

"Drugged or psi-burned, probably. No other explanation."

19

Men did not sleep well when they slept next to the dreamer. No one did. The few brave souls who had attempted to do so over the years usually awoke on the currents of a panic-driven nightmare. When the dreamer dreamed normally, the currents radiating from her aura were so strong they had a disturbing effect on anyone in close proximity. When she went dream-walking, no one who had physical contact with her could tolerate the waves of dreamlight for long. It made for a limited love life.

The man at the window gripped a narrow boxlike object in his hand. Even in her dream-state the dreamer recognized that the device had been shaped for a human hand. It wasn't Alien tech. It looked like a remote control.

"It's a weapon," the doppelgänger said.

"I know," the dreamer said. But she did not remember how she had come to know that.

As if he had heard the silent conversation, the man turned his head to look at the dreamer on the bed. He did not see the doppelgänger. No one else ever saw her, which was, of course, one of the reasons why powerful dreamlight talents got saddled with labels like "fragile" and "unstable."

"Wake up, Hannah," the man said. The voice was dark, masculine, and infused with a lot of control. It suited the power in his aura. "We need to get moving. It's almost dawn. We have to assume they're looking for us. No way to know how much time we've got before they find this place."

Elias Coppersmith. His name was Elias Coppersmith.

A rush of relief swept through her. At least he was not a complete stranger. He had been an online client for about two months. Yesterday evening he had walked through the door of her shop, Visions, for the first time. Assuming yesterday was actually yesterday. How much time had she lost?

Okay, so she hadn't awakened in a cheap motel room with a total stranger.

"So much for the good news," the doppelgänger said. She started to fade, slipping back into the dreamer's physical body.

"Wait," the dreamer said. "I've got more questions."

But the dream walk was ending.

For a heartbeat or two the dreamer experienced the usual but always unnerving shock of transition.

And then she was awake.

Hannah West took a deep breath and came back into her normal senses. At least she hadn't screamed the way she still did sometimes when she woke up in an unfamiliar location. She liked to think she had developed good control over her talent but there were still times when she awakened in a semipanic.

She opened her eyes, trying to orient herself. Her dream-walking doppelgänger had been right; the radiant acid green energy at the windows told her that they were near some of the Dead City ruins. The fact that the glow was fading also indicated that dawn was approaching. The natural illumination of the green quartz that the Aliens had used to construct most of their cities and many of their artifacts was barely visible in daylight.

Virgil chortled a cheery good-morning greeting and vaulted off the windowsill. He landed with a thump on the bed and scurried toward her.

She sat up slowly and reached out to give him a quick hug. "Good morning to you, too, pal."

"How do you feel?" Elias asked.

She tried to summon up the facts she could be sure of. She was in a strange room with a man who had, according to the dreamlight evidence, slept next to her on a lumpy, rock-hard mattress.

And her necklace was gone.

But Virgil was there and he seemed to approve of Elias Coppersmith. So there was that.

"Disoriented," she said. "I feel very, very disoriented. I can't remember anything after you walked through the front door of my shop yesterday."

"Same here after I first woke up. But I'm starting to get a few flashes of memory, so hopefully the effects will wear off."

"Do you think we were drugged?"

He shook his head, his jaw set in a grim line. "I don't know. But we were running from someone. I recall that much."

She examined him carefully. He looked as if he had used his fingers to rake his dark hair straight back from a sharply defined widow's peak. His face was all hard planes and angles and covered with the dark shadow of a morning beard. His eyes were a dangerous shade of amber.

He wore a crewneck T-shirt, expensively tailored dark trousers that showed signs of having been slept in, and a pair of low, recently polished boots. There was a crumpled white dress shirt and a tie draped over the back of the chair and a dark gray sports coat.

He had navigational amber set into his belt. She was willing to bet that there was more concealed in the heels of the boots.

He also wore a ring on his right hand. It was unusual in several respects. The first was that it was a simple Old World design, made of some strong black metal and set with a green crystal. There was nothing particularly attractive about the ring. It looked functional, not decorative. She assumed that Elias could use the strange crystal to focus his talent — whatever that was.

She knew something about the ring because she was the one who had tracked it down for him in the underground market, where powerful crystals and gemstones with a paranormal provenance were bought and sold by collectors, most of whom preferred to remain anonymous.

"My necklace," she said. She touched her throat. "It's gone."

Elias frowned. "I noticed that earlier after I woke up. Must have lost it on the way here."

"No." Panic rushed through her. "No, that can't be possible. The clasp was specially designed to be very secure."

"I'm no judge of fashion when it comes to jewelry but I do know crystals. No offense, but the ones in your necklace didn't appear to be particularly valuable."

She stiffened. "It was a family heirloom.

Pretty much my only family heirloom."

His mouth tightened. "Sorry. I under-stand."

"Under the circumstances, it's a good thing I know who you are," she said. "Oth-erwise I might be very concerned."

Grim amusement came and went in his eyes.

"Don't worry. There's still plenty of reason to be worried," he said. "I can't remember much of what happened last night but my gut tells me that someone is hunting us. We need to find out what's go-ing on, and fast. That means we need to get moving."

"Right."

First things first. Get out of the damn bed.

Layers of dreamlight had soaked into the old mattress as well as the sheets and the bedspread. A lot of the paranormal residue was infused with the added heat of sexual energy.

She hated old beds. She hated sleeping where others had slept. And motel room beds were the worst.

She swung her feet to the floor, trying not to think about the bed.

She grabbed the stilettos and slipped into them, squelching another wave of anxiety with an effort of will. Then she got to her feet.

She suddenly remembered what the doppelgänger had said about the answer being in the evening bag. She hurried to the chair, picked up the clutch, and unfastened it. There was the usual paraphernalia inside — her cell phone, some spare navigational amber, a packet of tissues, and a lipstick. There was also a small, square piece of paper.

But there was no necklace.

"Damn," she whispered. She was afraid she might actually burst into tears. "It can't be lost. I just found the missing crystal a couple of weeks ago."

"It's okay," Elias said. He came toward her and patted her somewhat awkwardly on her shoulder. "I'll help you look for it."

She pulled herself together. She could have a nervous breakdown later, she told herself.

She was about to close the bag when she noticed the slip of paper again. She took it out, thinking it was a receipt of some kind that might give them a clue about what had happened.

It wasn't a receipt.

"Weird," she said.

"What is it?"

"It's a fortune," she said.

"What the hell?"

"You know, the kind you get at a fortune-teller's booth. You put in a few coins and out pops a fortune."

"I have never, in my entire life, bought a fortune at a fortune-teller's booth."

"Well, evidently I did last night," she said.

"What does it say?"

She read the words and winced. "Just the usual generic stuff."

"Read it to me. Maybe it will help point us in the right direction."

She braced herself. *"You will find true love soon."*

He considered that briefly. "You're right. Not very helpful."

She took a deep breath. "Well, it does indicate that we visited a fortune-teller last night."

"Good point."

She started toward the bathroom but paused as another thought occurred.

"What day is it?" she asked.

"Tuesday," Elias said. "We checked in here very early this morning — shortly after one a.m. I paid cash."

"We get a lot of cash business here in Illusion Town. Some people don't want to leave an electronic trail when they patronize

27

places like this."

Elias shook his head. "I wasn't trying to hide the room from a wife or a girlfriend. I'm sure of that much."

That news lifted her spirits somewhat.

"As soon as I woke up, I left Virgil here with you and took a look around," Elias continued. "I had to find out just what we were dealing with. The night clerk is still on duty downstairs. He remembers checking us in. He also said no one showed up asking questions about us."

"Well, that sounds like good news. Sort of. I guess."

"Yeah, that's my take on it. Assuming he wasn't lying, of course. But I'm inclined to believe him."

"Why?"

"Because we're still here and there's no indication that anyone has tried to get into this room." Elias angled his head toward Virgil. "Also, your dust bunny pal doesn't seem to be concerned."

Hannah looked at Virgil. He was fully fluffed. You could hardly see his ears or his six paws, and only his baby blue eyes were showing. When things got serious, his second set of eyes — the ones he used for hunting — popped open. He was in full cute mode at the moment. That was reassuring.

28

"Good point," she said. "But why are we dressed up? It looks like we went out on the town."

"A date, I think."

"I never date clients."

"First time for everything."

"Let's start with the basics," she said. "Where, exactly, are we?"

"The Shadow Zone Motel." Elias plucked an old brochure off the nightstand and handed it to her. " 'A luxurious retreat and spa in the heart of the Shadow Zone. Every amenity designed with your privacy in mind. Honeymoons are our specialty.' "

"Honeymoons, hmm?" She surveyed the room, taking in the shabby furnishings, yellowed walls, and worn carpet. "Looks like a hot-sheet kind of place."

"Yeah, that pretty much describes it. But it seems clean. Probably why we chose it."

She started toward the bathroom. The room shifted on its axis and then settled back into place. She stopped abruptly and massaged her temples, trying desperately to recover some memories. The harder she tried, the more elusive the fleeting images became.

"Damn it, what happened to us?" she asked.

"I don't know." Elias went to the window.

He used the barrel of the strange weapon to ease the curtains aside. "Best guess is that we got psi-burned sometime last night. Somehow we found this place, checked in, and crashed."

Psi-burned. That was not good. She tried to remember what she knew about getting burned. The effects were notoriously unpredictable and could vary from temporary amnesia to serious trauma or even complete destruction of the paranormal senses. A really bad psi-burn could kill.

"We're not dead," she said.

"There's that," he agreed.

She groped for memories and got only fleeting, meaningless flashes. *A dark street. The full-throated roar of a big motorcycle engine. A cupcake iced with white frosting.*

A cupcake?

Another little rush of panic flickered through her, tightening her breathing. Maybe she was hallucinating. She told herself to process things slowly.

"I need to wash up," she said. "Maybe some cold water will clear my head."

"Good luck with that. Didn't do much for me. Just make it quick."

"Who, exactly, do you think is after us?"

"I have no idea," he said.

"Oh, hey, don't try to sugarcoat your answer."

"Sorry. Figured you'd want the truth."

"I do." She paused. "I think."

She started toward the bathroom again, automatically rezzing a little talent. Overwhelming relief snapped through her when she felt her para-senses stir in response. Between one breath and the next the room was suddenly illuminated in a range of colors that she had not been able to perceive using her normal vision.

Not that the place looked any more attractive when viewed in light from the paranormal end of the spectrum, she thought. It was still a hot-sheet motel.

"Yeah, I've still got my talent, too," Elias said. "Whatever burned us didn't wipe out our para-senses, just our memories of last night."

She stared at him. "You could feel me rez my senses?"

"Sure. Hard to not notice. You're strong."

That was true. But it took a powerful talent to sense that sort of thing from across the room.

Well, she had known that he was a high-end talent, she reminded herself. She hurried toward the bathroom.

"I'll be out in a minute," she said.

31

"By the way, one more thing you should know about our current situation."

She paused in the doorway and looked back at him. "How bad is this *one more thing*?"

"Depends on your point of view. We're married."

CHAPTER 3

"What?"

Up until that moment she thought she had been coping quite well with the whole waking-up-in-a-low-rent-motel-room-with-a-man-who-was-virtually-a-stranger thing. But now she felt as if she had stepped off a very high cliff.

"Found the license in my wallet when I woke up," Elias said. "I wasn't able to get online with my phone to access the official records."

"They call this side of town the Shadow Zone for a reason," Hannah said. "It's hard to get a connection." She sounded oddly numb, she realized. It was the shock. She was having a very hard time trying to wrap her head around the word *marriage*.

"The desk clerk let me use his computer," Elias said. "A Marriage of Convenience was recorded for Hannah West and Elias Judson Coppersmith forty-seven minutes after midnight at the Enchanted Night Wedding Chapel here in the Shadow Zone. The desk clerk says it's just down the street."

"I can't believe it."

"I was a little surprised myself." He did not smile. "Your first MC?"

"Well, yes. Yes, it is."

"My first, too."

"Good heavens." She clenched her fingers around the doorjamb. "What happened to us last night?"

"That's what we're going to find out just as soon as you get moving."

He sounded as if he was losing patience. She reminded herself that he couldn't be any more thrilled by the situation in which they found themselves than she was.

She made it into the bathroom and closed the door. One glance at her image in the mirror was enough to make her wonder if she was still asleep — maybe trapped in one of her own dream-walking dreams.

Grady Barnett's words slammed through her. *"Your profile is extremely unusual, so unusual that I'm afraid it's borderline unstable. You must be careful to avoid stress."*

Grady had said something else about her, as well, but not to her face. He had made the comment to his research assistant. *"It's no wonder she's single and lives alone. Her dreamlight patterns would give any normal man the creeps. Thinks she's having out-of-body experiences on a regular basis."*

"Go to hell, Grady Barnett," she whispered to the mirror.

She pushed thoughts of Grady aside. He was old history, and bad history at that. She had walked out of his lab and she had no intention of ever returning. There were other para-psych profilers in Illusion Town.

She focused on her image in the mirror and concluded that she looked like she'd been caught outside in a thunderstorm and zapped by lightning. She had a vague memory of her hair being done up in a flirty little twist the last time she had checked a mirror. But now it was down around her shoulders in a tangled mane.

She was sure she had not been wearing a lot of makeup yesterday morning — she never put on much for daytime. But at some point she must have spent some time with a mascara wand and an eyeliner pencil. The results were now badly smudged.

She looked like she had spent the night in a low-rent nightclub before letting a really bad boy take her back to the kind of hotel that rented rooms by the hour.

Scratch the bad-boy thing. Elias Coppersmith might be bad — the jury was still out

— but he was definitely not a boy.

For the past two months he had remained simply *E. Coppersmith* in her files. That, in itself, was rather unusual. It was not uncommon for serious collectors to go to great lengths to protect their identities. Those who traded at the deep end of the hot rocks market — crystals, quartz, and amber — usually preferred to keep a very low profile. But Elias had been up front about his identity right from the beginning. Then again, he hadn't had much choice. He had asked her to find a long-lost family heirloom — his ring — so it had made sense to tell her as much as possible about the family that had lost it.

But until very recently he had known her only by her online name — Finder. She owned a storefront shop, Visions, but for the most part, the relics, rocks, and small-time antiquities and collectibles she stocked there were unremarkable. Her real business was conducted anonymously in the murky underground market. It was a market that attracted eccentrics and, occasionally, dangerous people. It was only common sense to protect her identity.

Her online business was built on confidentiality and anonymity. She worked by referral only. By the time a would-be client got to her online, she was reasonably certain that he or she had been thoroughly vetted.

But not long ago she had taken the rare step of identifying herself to an online client. Elias had asked her out to dinner. She had a long-standing policy of not dating clients but she remembered breaking her own rules for Elias. The email correspondence of the past two months had evolved from a business relationship into something much more intimate — at least on her end. She had accepted his invitation.

And given the way she was dressed now, it looked as if they had gone out on a date. But the invitation had been for dinner. How had she ended up in a Marriage of Convenience? Not only that, but the two of them had evidently spent their wedding night passed out in a cheap motel in the Shadow Zone. That was definitely intimate, but not in a good way.

What happened to us?

She grabbed the thin rag of a washcloth and got busy scrubbing the smeared makeup off her face.

She felt somewhat better when she emerged from the bathroom a short time later, but the thought of facing the unknown in a pair of stilettos and the very short, very battered dress was daunting.

Virgil raced toward her across the floor. She scooped him up and tucked him under one arm.

She looked at Elias, who was buttoning his white shirt.

"I'm as ready as I'll ever be," she said. "Where, exactly, are we going?"

He held up his copy of the Marriage of Convenience license. "We'll start by retracing our steps. We need to find out why we got married last night. There must have been a logical reason."

She wasn't sure how to take that, but he was right about one thing: There had to be a reason for their tacky Marriage of Convenience.

"Of course," she said coolly. "It's not like either one of us is the type to get swept away by the kind of passion that makes two people run off to the nearest wedding mill."

She could be logical, too, damn it.

Elias gave her an odd look. She could have sworn that he was irritated by her perfectly *logical* observation.

"Right," he said.

He yanked open the door and moved out into the hall.

"Stairs are at the end," he said.

They went quickly along the dimly lit corridor, heading toward a burned-out sign

38

that read EXIT.

"The Shadow Zone is quite a ways from the Dark Zone," she said. "I don't own a car so did we drive here in your car or come in a taxi?"

"The guy at the front desk said we didn't arrive in a car or a taxi. Apparently we walked here from the wedding chapel. He also said we looked like we were ready to collapse. Figured we had been flying high on some illicit substance and were about to crash."

"If your car isn't in the motel parking lot, it must still be sitting in the street out in front of my shop. Or maybe you drove us to dinner in it?"

"Wherever it is, I'm not worried about the car. It can take care of itself."

"Good locking mechanism, huh?"

"Straight out of a Coppersmith lab."

"Like that gadget you had in your hand when I woke up?"

He touched his jacket pocket, as if reassuring himself that the odd piece of tech was still inside. "It's called a silencer. Temporarily neutralizes the frequencies used in most small firearms like handguns and flamers, but only at very close range."

"Cool. Can it neutralize a mag-rez pistol?"

"Yes, if it's within a radius of less than

39

twenty feet. The technology is still in the testing phase. Got a few bugs to work out. Ultimately, we plan to market it to law enforcement agencies."

She smiled.

He glanced at her. "What's so funny?"

"Nothing. You just sounded, well, proud, I guess is the right word."

"The company's labs are good."

A faint memory pinged like a tiny ray of light into the darkness of her missing memories.

"You're a para-crystal engineer," she said. "I remember you told me that your official title was director of the Coppersmith Research and Development Labs."

His eyes tightened a little at the corners. "I told you a little about my work over dinner, didn't I?"

A few more memories trickled back. Her spirits sank deeper as she pulled up some scattered details.

"You invited me out for dinner," she said. "That's why I'm dressed the way I am. But I remember cancelling my reservation at the Glass House restaurant in the Amber Zone. We went to the Green Ruin Café, instead. At least I think we did."

"That fits. I've got a receipt from the Green Ruin in my wallet."

"It's just a fast-food place a few blocks from my shop," she said. "We would have walked."

He glanced back over his shoulder, eyeing her stilettos. "With you in those shoes?"

"I'm an Illusion Town girl. I can walk for miles in high heels."

Okay, that was a bit of an exaggeration, but still. In Illusion Town, dressing up for an evening out was a competitive sport for women. And it was not about looking demure and refined. The dress code in Illusion Town was all about showcasing one's assets, and that generally called for very high heels. It was, after all, a city that prided itself on being the number one destination for those seeking the excitement of casino gambling, spectacular shows, and shadowy nightclubs. Visitors came from all over the four sprawling city-states with one goal — to take a walk on the wild side. As the signs said: *Welcome to Illusion Town. The thrills are real.*

She snapped her fingers. "That's right. You said you wanted to hire me for a job at the new Coppersmith operation outside of town — the Ghost City project. Some kind of emergency, you said."

"Yes." He rubbed the back of his neck, frowning in concentration. "On the drive to

Illusion Town to pick you up for our date, I got a call from headquarters. Several members of the advance exploration team are trapped inside the ruins at the portal site. A dreamlight gate closed without any warning. Nine people got caught inside a cavern. They've got enough supplies to last for a few days but there's a lot of unknown radiation in that cave. We need to get the people out as soon as possible."

Yep, that was when the hot date had started to go downhill, she thought. Hard to forget that magic moment. That was when cold reality had finally struck and she had realized that the fantasies she had been indulging about E. Coppersmith were probably just smoke and mirrors.

Really, she should have known better, she thought. After all, she had been raised by two magicians. She knew all about smoke and mirrors. *The audience sees what it expects to see* might as well have been the family motto.

"I agreed to take the contract," she said. "But we couldn't do anything last night because the portal is in the underground Rainforest."

"Can't travel in the jungle at night. We decided to have a quick meal at the Green Ruin and then you were going to go back to your place and pack your field gear. We planned to drive back to headquarters last night so that we would be ready to descend into the Rainforest at dawn."

She looked down at her red dress. The delicate fabric was crushed and ripped in various places. What a waste.

"So much for Plan A," she said.

"I remember working on logistics at the restaurant while you finished your sandwich and coffee," Elias said.

"Logistics. Of course."

He seemed blithely unaware of the sarcasm in her voice. He went quickly down the stairwell steps.

She tried to string a few facts together, hoping something would jar loose another memory.

"I suppose we could have come here by cab," she ventured. "But I don't remember a cab ride."

"Neither do I." He paused. "I remember guys on motorcycles."

"So do I. At least I think I do."

"There was also some very hot psi at some point," Elias said. "I'm sure of it. I think we got burned. We knew we were going to crash."

Something in his tone prompted another

little ping in the shadows of her lost memories.

"Do you think that whatever happened to us, it's connected to the problem at your company's jobsite? Maybe someone doesn't want you to get that gate open."

"Given what facts we've got, that explanation has the highest probability of being correct," he said.

"So why is my necklace missing? And what's up with the fortune in my purse?"

"I don't know. We need more data."

She cleared her throat. "Okay, let's say someone is after us and somehow we got psi-fried last night and decided that we had to go into hiding before we blacked out. That doesn't explain why we got married. It makes no sense. After all, it's obvious now that our relationship was — is — strictly business."

"You're not much of a romantic, are you?"

She glared at him. "Is that supposed to be humorous? Because if so, I have to tell you that your timing is lousy."

"You're not the first person to mention that."

They reached the ground-floor stairwell. To her surprise, Elias paused, as though listening intently. But she could feel energy rising in the atmosphere. The stone in his ring heated.

After a few seconds, Elias nodded, satisfied.

"The good news is that I don't think there's anyone waiting to ambush us on the other side of this door," he said.

She looked at his ring. "You can tell that with the crystal in your ring?"

"It's pretty accurate when it comes to picking up the vibes of high-tech devices."

"Is that all it can do?"

"I don't know." He smiled a little and pushed open the door. "I just got it recently, remember?"

"I know, but are you telling me that you don't know much about its properties?"

"It's a family heirloom but apparently not many of my ancestors could figure out what to do with it," Elias said. "There's hardly any data in the Coppersmith archives. I'm still on a learning curve. Still conducting experiments. Until now, the only use I've been able to discover is its ability to detect the frequency of other crystals. That's handy in the lab but hardly unique. We've got lots of other instruments that do just as good a job."

"I don't know about that. You said it alerts you to the fact that someone might be waiting for you with a high-powered weapon.

45

That sounds very useful to me. Especially at the moment."

"True," he agreed. He hesitated, glancing down at the ring. "I think that may be why we escaped whoever was gunning for us last night. We had some warning. Not much, but evidently enough to get away."

"So why didn't we run straight to the cops?"

"Good question. Maybe we didn't have a chance. If we got chased into the tunnels we would have just kept going until we lost whoever was chasing us."

They walked out into a mostly empty parking lot illuminated in the dull light of a fogbound dawn. The weather was hardly a surprise. The Shadow Zone was always locked in psi-infused fog.

The fog was something of a mystery. After all, Illusion Town was a vast, sprawling city in the middle of a desert. Theoretically, it shouldn't experience a lot of fog. But the normal meteorological rules didn't apply whenever there were a lot of Alien ruins in the vicinity. And in the case of Illusion Town, the ruins were underground as well as on the surface. And those ruins were weird, even by Harmony standards.

The city consisted of eight zones, each corresponding with one side of the vast octagon-shaped wall that enclosed the aboveground ruins. Each zone had its own unique characteristics. Two of the zones — the Storm Zone and the Fire Zone — were considered virtually uninhabitable due to the intense paranormal radiation that infused those regions.

Most of the upscale, opulent casinos and nightclubs were located in two of the so-called gem zones: the Amber Zone and the Sapphire Zone. The lower-rent gambling establishments and the racier shows and entertainments were found in the other gem zones — Amethyst and Emerald.

The Dark Zone, where Hannah had been raised, was more of a neighborhood community. There were plenty of small gaming establishments and a smattering of clubs, but it was where many of the people who worked in the big gem zone casinos, hotels, and clubs made their homes.

The Shadow Zone, however, was the least prosperous side of a generally prosperous town. Whatever glamour it aspired to project was only evident after dark. By day it looked almost deserted. The casinos and clubs were dingy and unwelcoming. Most were actually closed during the daylight hours. A closed casino was unheard-of in the gem zones.

The oppressive, paranormal fog of the

Shadow Zone gave people a significant buzz, especially after dark, but few visitors hung around after sunrise, not if they could afford to take their business into the brightly lit gem zones.

"According to the desk clerk, the Enchanted Night Wedding Chapel is just a block away," Elias said. "He said to turn left when we got to the corner. 'Can't miss it,' he said."

"Slow down. I'm carrying Virgil, remember? He's heavier than he looks. All muscle."

Virgil chuffed at the sound of his name.

"Here, give him to me." Elias plucked Virgil from Hannah's arms and plopped him down on his shoulder.

Virgil was thrilled with the higher perch.

"How did you and the dust bunny find each other?" Elias asked.

"He just showed up at my back door one evening." Hannah smiled at the memory. "I thought maybe he was hungry so I put some of the quiche I had made on a plate and set it on the step. He ate the quiche and disappeared. The next morning I found a lovely little piece of green amber on the step. He came back the following evening and I fed him again. Things went on like that for a few days and before I knew it, he had moved in with me."

48

"My brother's wife, Ella, has a dust bunny companion. Her name is Lorelei. No question but that they've got some kind of psychic bond."

"I think that's what happened with Virgil and me. I admit I felt a certain connection with him right from the start."

"That fast?"

"We had something in common. He showed up on my doorstep pretty much the same way I showed up on my aunts' doorstep. Well, technically, they aren't my aunts, and he wasn't wrapped in a blanket and he wasn't in a basket, but you get the picture."

Elias looked at her, evidently fascinated. "Someone left you on a doorstep?"

"My mother. She was a friend of my aunts. They were all working in a show in the Emerald Zone. My mom was in love with a magician. They were in an MC. Anyhow, shortly after I was born, Mom left me on Clara and Bernice's doorstep with a note saying she and my father had to take care of some important business. The note said that they would come back for me. Only they never did."

"Do you know what happened to them?"

"They were found shot to death in a cheap hotel room. The police declared it a drug deal gone bad."

49

"Did your aunts try to find any of your blood relatives?"

"Yes, but they gave up after a while. Mom and Dad were alone in the world. So Clara and Bernice made a pact to raise me themselves. It was either that or put me into the foster care system."

"That is an amazing story," Elias said softly. "No wonder you're worried about losing that necklace."

"It's all I've got left from my mother. In her note to my aunts she said that it was important and that if anything happened to her and my father, they should hide it until I was old enough to understand that it was my inheritance."

Elias nodded but he didn't say anything.

"I know what you're thinking," she said. "You're thinking it was just a cheap crystal necklace. But you're wrong."

"Yeah?"

"It turned out to be exactly what my mother wrote in her note — the key to my inheritance. The problem was that it was missing a single crystal. Two weeks ago I finally found that stone. A week later it led me to my inheritance."

He gave her a considering look. "Something in the Underworld?"

"Yes. Naturally, I kept quiet about it until

50

I could file a claim on the sector where it's located. But the paperwork was completed a few days ago." She smiled with satisfaction. "My inheritance is safe. I plan to sell it to the highest bidder."

Elias startled her by coming to a sudden halt. He turned to face her, eyes narrowed. "How many people know about this discovery of yours?"

"Just Aunt Clara and Aunt Bernice." Belatedly she started to wonder if she had made a serious mistake — make that another serious mistake. "And now you, of course. But you're a Coppersmith. My inheritance is penny-ante stuff compared to your family's mining empire."

"You're sure you've only told three people?"

"Positive. Why do you ask? You're starting to make me nervous."

"Good. Because if you're nervous, you'll be careful. Take some advice from a man who grew up in the mining business. Don't tell anyone else about your claim until you've figured out exactly how you're going to sell it. And then move very, very fast to close the deal."

"I told you, I filed a claim. It's all signed, sealed, and legal."

"In the Underworld, a claim is only a

strong as the person who files it. Why do you think they invented the term *claim jumping*? And why do you think Coppersmith employs a very large and very well-equipped security team? There will always be claim jumpers and pirates, so keep your secrets close."

A chill of dread whispered through her. Elias sounded unnervingly knowledgeable about the security issues.

"Okay," she said. She took a breath. "I'll be careful."

"Good. When this is over, I'll check out your claim if you'd like. Set up some good security for you."

She chuckled. "Don't worry. For now, it's safe enough. Locked up nice and tight and I've got the only key."

"The necklace? But you lost it."

"No. The necklace was a map. It led me to my inheritance. Technically, I no longer need it, but it has sentimental value."

Elias glanced at his ring. "I understand."

"Enough about my inheritance. It's safe for the time being. We've got more immediate problems. Like why did we get married last night?"

"I've been thinking about that," he said. "I can't be sure but it occurs to me that there is one very plausible reason why we

52

stopped off at the Enchanted Night Wedding Chapel long enough to file an MC."

She looked at him, startled. "What?"

"We knew or strongly suspected that we were going to crash. We would have realized that we might wake up with amnesia, temporary or otherwise."

"So?"

"So we had to come up with a plan that would ensure that we would stay together, at least long enough to figure out what was going on," Elias said. "What better way to do that than file a Marriage of Convenience? Waking up married was a surefire way to force us to try to figure out what happened last night."

"Seems a bit drastic."

"We must have been desperate," he said. "And if we were psi-burned and heading for a crash, we may not have been thinking clearly."

Somehow, that sounded vaguely insulting but she couldn't decide how to respond so she kept quiet.

There was only one vehicle in the foggy street, a newspaper delivery van with the *Curtain* emblazoned on its side. It was just pulling away from the curb. The notorious tabloid catered to a niche market that could not get enough of conspiracy theories, scandals, and rumors about Alien abductions. It was one of those newspapers that most people denied reading but that nevertheless enjoyed an extremely high circulation.

Hannah considered herself a loyal subscriber, so when they walked past the vending machine, she automatically glanced at the headline.

Shock brought her to a standstill. "Elias, we may have a very big problem."

He did not stop. "Put it on our list."

"Take a look at today's edition of the *Curtain*."

"Why? Nobody reads that rag."

"I do, but before you decide to continue insulting my reading taste, I suggest you look at the damn headline."

He stopped, turned around, and retraced his steps.

"I didn't mean to insult your taste in newspapers," he muttered.

"That's not the point."

She waited in silence while he absorbed the implications of the lead story.

COPPERSMITH MINING HEIR MARRIES IN SECRET MC WEDDING

Underneath the headline was a photo

showing Hannah and Elias emerging from the Enchanted Night Wedding Chapel. There was something very furtive about the scene, Hannah thought. In the picture she had Virgil clutched under one arm. He was the only one who appeared cheerful, probably because he had a cupcake slathered in bridal white frosting clutched between two front paws.

"The happy couple," Elias said.

"We look like we've just attended a funeral," Hannah said. "Good thing nobody reads that rag."

"Yeah. Good thing."

CHAPTER 4

"I'm very sorry if you two woke up with a case of buyer's remorse, but I'm afraid we don't do refunds here at the Enchanted Night Wedding Chapel," the receptionist said.

According to the little sign on her desk, her name was Mrs. Henderson. She was middle-aged, comfortably proportioned, and endowed with a warm, solicitous, vaguely maternal air that no doubt put nervous couples at ease. But Elias could see the steel beneath the surface. She was in charge of a business that was supposed to turn a profit. She knew her job.

The Enchanted Night Wedding Chapel was typical of the cheap-and-fast Marriage-of-Convenience operations that were found scattered around the Old Quarters of all the city-states. But in Illusion Town they were as common as slot machines. The MC mills did a steady trade, drawing customers from the nearby nightclubs, taverns, casinos, and other shady businesses that flourished in the dark.

Although he knew that they both had a good idea of what to expect from a twenty-four-hour wedding factory, he was very aware that Hannah was vaguely horrified by the Enchanted Night Wedding Chapel. She was doing her best to conceal her dismay, but it didn't take a psychic to pick up on the vibe. Maybe the fake flowers, the dingy drapery, and the illuminated arch looked more romantic at night.

"We're not here for a refund," Elias said. "We just want to talk to you."

"You're not the first couple to return here the morning after, wanting to make it all go away." Mrs. Henderson sighed. "But cheer up. Remember, it's only an MC. You are, of course, free to terminate the marriage today, but, as I'm sure you're aware, there is some paperwork involved. You'll have to go to the proper office at City Hall and file the appropriate forms. An MC is a legally binding contract after all. There are a few rules."

But not many, Elias reflected. A Marriage of Convenience was easy to get into and almost as easy to terminate — unlike a formal Covenant Marriage, which was a legal and financial nightmare to dissolve.

The costs of getting out of a Covenant Marriage were not just of a financial nature. The social price paid by both husband and wife was huge. Careers and reputations were badly damaged or even destroyed by a CM divorce.

Everyone knew that Marriages of Convenience were a polite fiction designed to lend an air of respectability to an affair. Nevertheless, it did provide both parties with certain legal protections, and if a child was born to a couple who were in an MC at the time, the marriage was automatically converted to a full-blown Covenant Marriage.

"We just want to ask you a few questions," he said, going for what he hoped was a soothing tone.

At that moment Virgil rumbled enthusiastically and leaped off Elias's shoulder. The dust bunny dashed across the room and vaulted up onto the table that held a tiered tray of cupcakes.

Mrs. Henderson shrieked and leaped to her feet. "Stop him. Those cupcakes are for the customers."

"Virgil." Hannah rushed toward the table. "No."

Virgil had already selected a cupcake. He clung to it with his two front paws. Hannah scooped him up and put him on her shoulder. He perched there and happily munched his prize.

"I'll pay for the cupcake," Elias said. He fished his wallet out of his pocket and extracted a few large bills. "Did you perform the ceremony for us, Mrs. Henderson?"

She sniffed but she seemed somewhat mollified by the cash. "My goodness, you can't even remember your own wedding? You both must have been flying high on something last night."

"Something," Elias agreed. "It's all a blur. Would you mind answering the question?"

Hannah smiled a bright little smile. "You know, in case we want to recommend your services to others."

"Oh, I see." Mrs. Henderson relaxed. "No, I was not the person who officiated at your wedding. That would have been Joe. He had the graveyard shift last night."

"Do you know where we can find him?" Elias said.

"You just missed him. He was on duty until five this morning. I expect he'll be having breakfast. He usually stops at the Fog Café before he goes home to bed."

"Is that near here?" Hannah asked.

"Just down the street."

"Thank you," Elias said.

Outside on the sidewalk Hannah took a

tissue out of her clutch and used it to wipe white frosting off Virgil's furry face.

"At least Virgil has fond memories of our wedding," she said. "Good to know one of us does."

For some reason Elias found that observation depressing.

"I don't think we were so badly burned that we'll have permanent amnesia," he said. "We're both strong talents. That will help us recover our memories. Hey, we're already getting bits and pieces, right?"

"I think so."

And when she did recover her memory of their hasty midnight wedding, would she be horrified all over again? he wondered.

He considered his first impressions of her yesterday when he had walked into her shop: smart, powerful, mysterious. Somehow she was exactly how he had known she would be.

He had never seen a picture of her. She guarded her identity well. But the moment he saw her he was certain he would have recognized her anywhere. Her dark hair had been caught up in a cute twist that went with the flirty red dress and the very high heels. She had a striking face with intelligent, watchful green eyes. The heat and power in her aura warned him that she could be passionate or dangerous or both.

Definitely his kind of woman.

It dawned on him that he might have some trouble convincing her of that now.

They walked in silence for a time. The Shadow Zone was in the process of waking up to a new day and it gave every indication that it was starting the morning with a decades-long hangover. The last of the ambient green light had disappeared from the fog. The seedy storefronts, garbage-strewn alleys, and grimy, barred windows were spectral shadows in the mist.

In some of the districts around the Dead Cities, including Illusion Town, serious gentrification was taking place. The Colonial-era buildings put up by the First Generation colonists were being remodeled and marketed to homeowners and shop-keepers who sought locations infused with the psi-laced atmosphere of the Alien ruins. But the effects of modernization had not yet come to this section of Illusion Town. It looked as if no one was in a hurry to institute the process.

But you could still sense the energy in the atmosphere, Elias thought. You always knew when you were near Alien ruins. The para-normal vibes seeped up from the quartz catacombs belowground and leaked out of the green-quartz walls that surrounded the ethereal green towers. Even in daylight the atmosphere gave most people a tingle. The rush was always more intense after dark, even for those with minimal talent.

But Illusion Town was different. It had a unique vibe — several different vibes, actually, depending on which of the eight zones you happened to be in at any given moment. The engineer in him was intrigued.

"Something happened here a long time ago," he said.

He wasn't aware he had spoken out loud until Hannah responded.

"The experts agree with you," she said. "We get a lot of para-researchers who show up with their instruments. They're always running experiments in an attempt to analyze the hot psi in the various zones. But so far no one has come up with an explanation for the weirdness. The locals don't worry about it too much because it's good for business."

"Could have been some sort of explosion in the heart of the ruins that released a lot of unusual para-radiation."

"If that's the case, the researchers haven't been able to find the epicenter of the blast."

"Fascinating. Any indication that the radiation might have had an effect on people born and raised in the zone?"

Hannah shot him a quick look and then just as swiftly looked away.

"Nope," she said a little too smoothly.

That amused him. "It wouldn't be a big deal if the local currents have created a few interesting variants in some people's parapsych profiles. At least, it wouldn't be a big deal to anyone in my family."

She eyed him warily. "Is that so?"

"A long time ago, back on the Old World, one of my ancestors — the one I'm named for, the first Elias Coppersmith — discovered some unusual crystals with paranormal properties. There was an explosion. He was hit with some unknown radiation. Let's just say the Coppersmith gene pool was seriously affected."

"What happened after your people settled on Harmony?"

"What do you think happened? We're still in mining. Still messing around with hot crystals. The family para-genetics are as unpredictable as ever."

She was silent for a moment.

"Must be nice to be able to trace your family history all the way back to the Old World."

The wistfulness in her voice bothered him.

"It's interesting," he said, choosing his

63

words carefully. "But not particularly useful. What matters is the present and the future, right? Those are the only two things that we can change."

"I know. But the past is a lot like ancient para-energy, isn't it? The currents continue to resonate with the energy of the present, and in that way they affect the future. That's why it would be useful for a person to know her own personal past history."

"Maybe. But only if the person in question is willing to use the information to change her own present and future in a positive way."

"I suppose so," she said.

"Look, I'm an engineer, so I'm not always real intuitive or insightful when it comes to conversations of a personal nature, but I'm going to take a stab in the dark here and guess that we're talking about you."

Her mouth kicked up faintly at one corner. "Good guess."

"Ever gone looking for your own past?"

"Sure. Several times over the years. Wasted a lot of money on so-called professional genealogists. I spent hours and hours of my own time trying to find my family roots. And I'm good at finding things. But until recently I've always come up with dead ends."

"What happened?"

"A couple of months ago I came across Dr. Paxton Wilcox. He specializes in using para-genetic theory to create family trees for dreamlight talents. He's a retired professor who used to teach para-genetics at the University of Resonance. Now he does private searches for clients."

"How did you find him?"

"The usual way — I found him online. He's got a website. His office is in Resonance City but all of his work is done on the rez-net so it doesn't matter that he's a few hundred miles away. He has access to the Arcane Society's files as well as other genealogical records databases."

"How's that working out for you?"

"Well, I hit a stumbling block recently." Hannah made a face. "Not surprisingly, Wilcox requested a full para-psych profile. He sent me to a para-genetics researcher here in Illusion Town to get the workup. Since my talent is linked to dreamlight, part of the testing required me to try to sleep in a lab for a couple of nights while I was hooked up to various monitors. After the first night I discovered that Dr. Grady Barnett is a lying, cheating, hypocritical dumbass."

"I hear there are a lot of those around."

"Sure, but usually I can spot them early on. In this case it took me a while — probably because I wanted the para-psych profile very, very badly. Anyhow, long story short, I told Barnett to go to green hell and walked out of the lab. I won't be going back. Which means I've got to find another para-psych profiler and start all over again. Turns out profiles are very, very pricey."

He wondered what Barnett had done to earn the title dumbass.

"You are one tough lady," he said. *And I do like that in a woman,* he added silently.

She gave him a startled glance. Then she smiled. It was a real smile, the kind that warmed her brilliant green eyes.

"Thanks," she said.

"You look surprised."

"Well, I didn't get my full para-psych profile from Grady Dumbass Barnett because I stopped the testing. But he did make sure to inform me that the data he had collected on me indicated that I was quite fragile, psychically speaking."

Elias opened his senses a little, savoring the sensation of her aura. "Dumbass was wrong."

"You sound very certain."

"I'm a para-engineer, remember? Assessing paranormal currents is what I do. Yours are strong and steady."

"I thought you were an expert with crystal energy."

He shrugged. "Paranormal energy is paranormal energy. I can usually sense it quite clearly, regardless of the source."

"My aunts insist I'm strong and stable, too. But, you know, they're my aunts. They love me. What else are they going to say?"

"Yeah, well, I'm not your aunt. And I am an expert."

"Good to know. Thanks." Hannah chucked the used tissue into an overflowing garbage can. "I've been thinking. We must have been in very bad shape last night."

Elias glanced at her. "To end up at the Enchanted Night Wedding Chapel, do you mean?"

"Uh-huh."

"Probably knew we didn't have much time before we crashed." He stopped and looked at the broken neon sign overhead. "This is it, the Fog Café. With luck, Joe, the night guy, will still be eating breakfast."

He opened the door and did a quick reconnaissance of the establishment. It looked exactly as expected. There were a couple of patrons sitting on stools at the bar. Either they were early risers or they had never left last night.

A bored-looking waitress was pouring coffee for the lone diner who occupied a booth. The place smelled of spilled beer, decades of greasy food, and whatever powerful disinfectant had been used to mop the floor the last time someone had bothered to clean.

He kicked up his senses again, probing for the subtle vibes that warned of danger. He got nothing.

"All clear," he said.

He stood back to usher Hannah inside but just as she moved across the threshold, Virgil chortled and jumped out of her arms.

"Virgil," Hannah said. "Come back here."

He ignored her to dash across the dingy room and vault up onto the one occupied table. The lone diner was a portly middle-aged man dressed in a white jumpsuit studded with crystals and styled with a high collar open at the throat. His hairpiece was a sleek, shiny black pompadour. There were some gold necklaces around his throat. A white cape embellished with more crystals was thrown over the back of the booth. Although the room was dark and there was a lot of fog on the other side of the window, he wore a pair of slick, wraparound sunglasses.

He chuckled when he saw Virgil and offered a bite of what looked like fried potatoes.

"Hey there, little guy," he said in a deep, resonant voice. "How are you doing? Didn't expect to see you again."

Virgil chortled and graciously accepted the fried offering.

"Something tells me that's Joe, the night guy," Elias said.

They walked toward the booth. The waitress narrowed her eyes.

"Restrooms are for customers only," she said.

"Coffee, please," Hannah said politely.

It occurred to Elias that he was hungry. "And maybe some eggs."

The waitress relaxed. "You got it."

She disappeared into the kitchen.

Elias followed Hannah across the room. They stopped at the booth where Virgil was holding court.

"Joe from the Enchanted Night Wedding Chapel?" Elias said.

"That's me. My stage name is Elvis, though."

"Stage name?" Elias said.

"Yeah, Enchanted Night hires me to put on a real nice show for couples who want a quickie MC. I take pride in my work. So, when I'm on the job, I'm Elvis. You can call

69

me Joe, though. I'm off duty now."

"Thank you," Hannah said.

"Look, I'm sorry, but Enchanted Night doesn't do refunds," Joe said. "To be honest, I'm real surprised that you changed your minds so soon. You two were sure set on getting married last night. You could hardly wait. I would have bet good money that you knew what you were doing."

"You don't understand," Hannah said.

"Sadly, I do understand." Joe shook his head in a world-weary way. "You're not the first couple to have morning-after regrets. But you're gonna have to do what everyone else in your situation does. Go file the proper termination papers."

"We're not looking for a refund," Hannah said gently. "We just want to ask you a few questions. Do you mind if we sit down?"

She slipped into the booth before Joe could respond. Admiring the slick move, Elias sat down beside her.

"What kind of questions?" Joe asked. There was deep suspicion in his eyes but he fed Virgil another bite of fried potatoes.

Elias folded his arms on the table. "To be honest, my wife and I are having a little trouble remembering what happened last night."

Joe snorted. "That's no surprise. When

70

you came through the door you looked like you were both exhausted. But I'm pretty sure neither of you had been drinking. Figured you'd hit the wrong nightclub or gone down a bad street and run into some hot energy. The vibes get weird around here after dark."

"What, exactly, did we say?" Elias asked.

Joe waved his fork. "Not much. You just insisted on getting married as fast as possible. I went through the usual routine. Asked which song you wanted me to sing. I gave the lady the list of titles. She made her choice and I performed the service. You were in and out in under fifteen minutes."

"We wound up at the Shadow Zone Motel," Elias said. "Was that your idea?"

Joe shrugged. "You asked for directions to the nearest motel. I suggested the Shadow Zone on account of it's cleaner than most of the short-stay places around here. Figured your wife would appreciate that."

Hannah smiled. "That was very kind of you."

"Sure. Part of the job." Joe went back to his food.

"You gave Virgil a cupcake," Hannah added. "He remembers you fondly."

Joe's expression softened. He looked at Virgil. "The cupcakes were delivered yesterday morning. They were getting a little stale. Figured the dust bunny wouldn't mind."

The waitress emerged from the kitchen with two heaping platters of scrambled eggs, fried potatoes, and greasy sausage.

"Oh, good," Hannah said. "I'm really hungry for some reason."

"So am I," Elias said. He forked up a healthy bite of eggs and looked at Joe. "Did we arrive at Enchanted Night in a cab?"

"Nope." Joe drank some coffee. "You just showed up at the front door demanding to get married."

Elias ate some eggs and then slathered butter on a slice of toast. He really was hungry, he thought. So was Hannah. She was making big inroads into her eggs and potatoes.

Elias took a large bite of the toast. "Did we mention where we were before we arrived at your door?"

Joe shrugged. "You said something about having had a real thrill ride."

"A thrill ride," Hannah repeated softly. She set her fork down very suddenly and reached into her purse. She took out the slip of paper with the fortune on it and handed it to Joe. "Do you know what that is?"

He frowned at it. " *'You will find true love*

soon.' It's one of those fortunes you get from a machine. You know, like the kind they have at carnivals and amusement parks."

"A carnival," Hannah whispered. She fixed Joe with an intent look. "Is there a carnival around here, by any chance?"

"No," Joe said.

Elias could have sworn that Hannah looked relieved at that news. He turned back to Joe.

"Did we give you any indication of where we had been just before we landed here?"

Joe shrugged again. "You said something about having just come from a restaurant that was closed but still hotter than a Saturday night special. Figured maybe you'd wandered into Burning Street by accident."

"Burning Street?" Elias repeated carefully.

"It happens now and again," Joe said. "Tourists get too close to the scene of the old disaster and get singed. There are signs up everywhere on Burning Street but there's always folks who don't believe them."

"What kind of old disaster are we talking about?" Elias said.

"It happened during the Colonial era," Joe said. "There was a big explosion and fire underground — the paranormal kind.

73

Happened at one of the entrances to the tunnels. No record of what caused the explosion but the fire burned for months. The place is still red-hot. The locals all stay clear but like I said, once in a while a tourist takes a wrong turn and ends up in Burning Street. In the old days no one worried about the occasional fried tourist, but a couple of decades ago the authorities decided to clean up the zone's reputation. A special hazardous-psi team was brought in to install heavy mag-rez steel-and-glass doors to contain the para-radiation coming out of the tunnel entrance. Place is all locked up now. Hardly ever get a fried tourist."

"Can you give us directions?" Elias asked.

"Sure, Burning Street is only a few blocks from here. But I'm telling you, you don't want to go near the place."

"It's important," Hannah said.

Joe heaved a sigh. "Okay, but be careful. It's not what you'd call one of our local scenic attractions."

He rattled off the directions.

"Appreciate it," Elias said. He pulled out his wallet. "You've been very helpful. Breakfast is on us."

"Hey, thanks." Joe relaxed. "You were real generous with the tip last night, too."

74

"You're welcome," Elias said. He finished the last of his eggs in a hurry, got to his feet, and looked at Hannah. "Ready?"

She swallowed the last of her toast and slipped out of the booth. She plucked Virgil off the table and looked at Joe.

"Just one more question," she said.

"What's that?" he asked.

"Which song did I choose?"

" 'One Night,' " Joe said.

"Really? That's a surprise."

"Not really," Joe said. "It's an Old World classic."

Elias took Hannah's arm and steered her across the café and out into the misty street.

"What was so surprising about choosing 'One Night' for our wedding song?" Elias asked.

"I love the Old World classics, but that particular song is not one of my favorites," Hannah said. "I always thought it was sort of depressing. Then again, I probably wasn't in a real romantic mood last night. Or maybe —"

She broke off.

"Or maybe what?" he prompted.

"Maybe I was trying to send a message to myself."

"What kind of message?"

"That the marriage wasn't real. That it

75

was never meant to last. You know, good for one night only."

"Wow. And they say engineers aren't romantic. You want to tell me why you were so shocked when Joe mentioned that your fortune might have come from a fortune-teller's booth in a carnival?"

"That Underworld find I told you about? The one I filed a claim on?"

"Yeah?"

"It's a carnival. For a moment there, I was afraid that someone else had found it."

"Explain. Why would an old carnival be valuable?"

"It's not just any carnival. How much do you know about the Arcane Society?"

"Some. Not a lot. The Coppersmiths and the Joneses have been friends for generations but my family never joined the Society."

"Ever heard of the Midnight Carnival?"

He started to say that he hadn't but his sleeping memories stirred and then awakened with such force he stopped in the middle of the street.

"Damn," he said softly. "That's how we lost them last night."

"Lost who?"

"The motorcycle gang. Remember? They were waiting for us when we left the restaurant to walk back to your place. There were at least four, maybe five. They were on motorcycles. Probably ex-Guild men because they tried to trap us in an alley using heavy ghost light. I think they intended to knock us unconscious with the ghost. We ran for a hole in the wall that you knew about and escaped into the tunnels."

"Yes. *Yes.*" Hannah brightened. "I remember now. We thought we would lose them once we were underground but they followed us."

"Must have had the frequency of your tuned amber. We grabbed your sled. That allowed us to stay ahead of them but we couldn't shake them. They kept coming after us."

"That's when I came up with the plan to lose them by ducking into the Midnight Carnival," Hannah said. "I knew they couldn't follow us through the dreamlight gate."

"You got us inside," he said. "And you were right. They couldn't follow us. But we also knew we couldn't exit by that gate because the gang would be waiting on the other side."

"We escaped through another gate but we ran into a terrible psi-storm," Hannah said. "We had to turn back but we got burned in the process. We knew then that we were going to crash. Found a third gate and made it out."

"By then we knew we were headed for a very hard crash," Elias said. "So I came up with the plan to get married first."

She looked at him. "I need to get back inside the Midnight Carnival."

"Why?"

"Because I remember what I did with my necklace."

Elias felt the last of his memories click into place. "Oh, yeah. Right. There's just one problem. We were having a hard time holding it together by the time we hit that third gate last night. We weren't thinking clearly. We didn't record the coordinates."

CHAPTER 5

The dark energy seeping out around the edges of the thick mag-steel-and-glass barrier stirred the hair on the back of Hannah's neck. Perched on her shoulder, Virgil muttered softly.

The old tunnel entrance was a small, windowless Colonial-era structure that resembled a short, squat stone tower.

The faded green sign above the entrance read HIGH-PSI LOCATION. DO NOT ENTER.

"Obviously we didn't come up from the Underworld through this exit," Hannah said.

"No, but I think this is the first route we tried," Elias said. "This is where we got psi-fried. I remember the energy."

"I'll bet it was the original entrance to the Midnight Carnival," Hannah said. "I don't think the explosion and fire was an accident. It was probably set to block the above-ground route that led directly to that particular gate."

"Joe said the fire dates back to the Colonial era." Elias shook his head in awe. "That means someone back in the day knew a hell of a lot about paranormal energy."

"That someone was a Jones," Hannah said.

"Okay, that explains the expertise."

"After we were forced to turn back we found a third gate," Hannah said. "Virgil led us to it, remember? It dumped us out in this very same street."

"Which means the other tunnel entrance has to be around here somewhere," Elias said.

They both looked at Virgil. He fluffed up, basking in the attention.

"Hmm," Hannah said.

Elias glanced at her. "What?"

"You and I don't know where the third dreamlight gate is located but Virgil does," she said. "He led us out of the catacombs last night."

Upon hearing his name Virgil blinked his baby blues.

"Can you actually communicate well enough with him to ask him a question like that?" Elias asked.

"I can't expect him to understand a complicated question but he loves to play games like hide-and-seek."

She took Virgil down off her shoulder and held him in the crook of her arm. With her free hand, she took the fortune out of her evening bag and held it up directly in front of his face.

"Where did I get this?" she asked. "Can you find the fortune-teller? *Find*, Virgil. Please."

She tried to infuse a psychic plea into her words.

Virgil chortled gleefully, sensing a game. He sleeked out a little. His ears appeared out of his fur and his second set of eyes snapped open.

She put him down on the pavement. He immediately took off, dashing across the lane to a doorway vestibule.

Hannah and Elias hurried after him. Virgil stopped in front of a door and bounced up and down impatiently.

Cautiously, Elias pushed the door open. Shadows seethed in the unlit interior. The windows had been boarded up long ago.

Virgil zipped inside.

Hannah followed Elias into the space. She picked up a whisper of disturbing energy.

"It's hot in here, too," she said.

"But not nearly as hot as whatever is behind those steel doors across the street,"

Elias said. "This place was close to the scene of the explosion and fire, though, so it absorbed some of the paranormal radiation. It's safe enough. I'm pretty sure we came through here last night."

He moved deeper into the darkness. Hannah followed close behind.

The darkened space looked as if it had once been a fast-food restaurant. There was a long counter topped with some old-fashioned cash registers and a number of plastic tables and chairs.

"No one bothered to salvage the tables and chairs," Hannah said. "I guess they weren't valuable enough to make someone push through this hot zone."

A muffled chortle sounded from the kitchen area. Hannah moved around the end of the sales counter. Elias followed. They were both rezzed now, using their talent to suppress the surrounding currents of energy so they could continue to move deeper into the restaurant.

They went through an opening into an even darker space. Thanks to her other senses, Hannah could see the objects around her but the scene was bathed in an eerie, spectral light. The place looked as if it had been abandoned in a hurry. Pots and pans were scattered across the floor. The fryer

basket was tipped on its side. Large knives and other utensils had been tossed aside in a chaotic manner.

"Looks like they didn't get any warning," Elias said. "They just ran for their lives." He paused. "I think we were running, too."

"What do you mean?"

"Take a look at the floor."

She glanced down. There was a thick layer of grime and dust on the tile flooring, but in the ghost light she could make out two sets of murky footprints that appeared to be fresh. Familiar dreamlight burned in both tracks.

"Those are our prints, all right," she said. "And we were really burned. I can see it in the dreamlight currents. It's a wonder we lasted long enough to get to the wedding chapel and the motel."

"The good news is that no one followed us up from down below," Elias said. "There aren't any other prints."

Virgil chortled to get their attention.

They followed him down a flight of cracked concrete steps that clearly dated back two hundred years to the Colonial era. At the foot of the steps they crossed a basement to a jagged hole in the stone wall. Familiar green energy illuminated the opening.

"Tunnel entrance," Elias said. "This must be where we exited the catacombs. Check your amber."

It was standard procedure before entering the disorienting maze of the ancient catacombs. The amber was for navigational purposes. There was no need for flashlights. The Aliens had vanished a few thousand years earlier but their network of underground, psi-infused tunnels still glowed endlessly with the energy of the green quartz that had been used to construct them.

No one knew what had caused the ragged holes in the almost indestructible green quartz. The stuff was certainly impervious to human machines. The theory from the scientific community was that the openings had, at least in some cases, been made by the Aliens themselves. Others suspected that the occasional rips and tears in the quartz walls had been created by major seismic and geothermal forces.

Hannah touched her earrings and rezzed her talent a little. She felt the familiar resonance and nodded.

"I'm good," she said.

"Same here," Elias said. "At least we didn't burn out our amber last night."

They followed Virgil through the hole in

the wall and were immediately enveloped in the senses-disturbing currents of para-normal radiation. Turn a single corner or go through an arched entranceway into another section of the catacombs and you were im-mediately lost unless you had navigational amber.

"There was no need to block this entrance with psi-fire," Hannah said. "It didn't lead directly to the Midnight Carnival. It's just another hole in the wall. There are thou-sands of them in the Underworld. Once you enter the catacombs you're in a maze. If you don't know the coordinates of your destination, you'll never find it."

"Unless you have a dust bunny," Elias said.

Virgil was already several yards ahead. Hannah and Elias went after him.

He wove a complicated path through a series of hallways and chambers before finally turning one last corner and disap-pearing.

Elias and Hannah rounded the corner and stopped short at the waterfall of seething nightmares that blocked the tunnel.

"Oh, yeah," Elias marveled softly. "I remember this part."

Hannah knew a flicker of relief. "So do I."

They were several feet away from the torrent of pounding energy, but even from a distance, Hannah could feel the rush of raw power that roiled her senses.

"A dreamlight gate," she said. "I've run into smaller ones from time to time. My talent has a way of drawing me to them when I'm in the Underworld. But the gates that seal the entrances to the carnival are special. They're psi-coded. Only someone with a certain para-profile can de-rez them."

Elias gave her a knowing look. "That would be you."

"Yep."

The nightmare energy crashed and churned. The currents that sealed the tunnel were composed of heavy waves of paranormal radiation that emanated from the darkest end of the spectrum. It was the energy of dreams that had haunted humankind since primordial times, the energy of nerve-shattering nightmares.

Hannah smiled. "What a rush."

Elias looked at her. "Speak for yourself."

"Right. I know dreamlight isn't everyone's cup of tea."

"It's like looking into a mini universe of nightmares."

"Is the gate you want me to open at the Ghost City jobsite as powerful as this one?"

"Yes."

"Then you came to the right dreamlight talent," she said. The buzz of energy off the gate was making her feel cocky. She looked around. "Where's Virgil?"

At the sound of his name he appeared out of the hot dreamlight, or, rather, half of him did. His fur stood on end. He chortled encouragingly and disappeared back into the nightmares.

"Obviously, dust bunnies don't have a problem with human dreamlight," Elias said.

"Nope. Are you ready?"

"Sure. Not like I've got anything better to do. Might as well sample a few nightmares."

She reached for his hand. "Physical contact helps. Stick with me and enjoy the ride."

"Just like last night."

She was oddly pleased when he did not hesitate. He grasped her hand, his fingers tightening firmly, confidently, around hers.

"Here we go," she said.

She rezzed her talent. Together they walked closer to the cascade of nightmares. Elias's grip on her hand tightened abruptly. Out of the corner of her eye she saw the stone in his ring suddenly blaze with paranormal light and energy.

The dreamlight stirred her hair, lifting it into a cloud around her face. The dark energy called to her senses, sending wave after wave of intoxicating thrills through her. She wanted to laugh and scream with delight.

She glanced at Elias and knew from the heat in his eyes that he sensed some of her own exhilaration.

She focused intently, searching for the psi-lock frequencies. When she identified them she went to work, deftly de-rezzing the currents until they flatlined.

The gate winked out of existence.

Hannah walked through the opening and swept out a hand. "Welcome back to my inheritance, the Arcane Society's legendary Lost Museum, otherwise known as the Midnight Carnival."

CHAPTER 6

The Midnight Carnival looked as if it had been trapped in time and preserved in another dimension. The rides, booths, and concession stands — all garishly illuminated in lights that generated colors from across the spectrum — were spread out around a vast green-quartz chamber. Here and there were entrances to halls and tunnels that held still more attractions.

Although the carnival was lit up, thanks to the paranormal crystals used to decorate the attractions, nothing moved. There was a great stillness, a dreamlike quality about the scene.

"Isn't it amazing?" Hannah said. "It's as if the crowds and the behind-the-scenes workers just walked out a few minutes ago and left the lights on. None of the paint has faded and there's no dust anywhere."

"Thanks to the paranormal forces down here," Elias said.

Hannah walked to a nearby concession stand illustrated with a picture of a giant slice of pizza.

"There's no garbage or rotting food, either," she noted.

"That would be thanks to the paranormal forces here, as well," Elias reminded her. "The tunnels are self-cleaning, remember. Food and other organic garbage would have disappeared over time." He whistled softly. "This is an incredible find. No wonder you rushed to file your claim on this sector. It's going to be worth a fortune to the Arcane Society."

"I know. But I want to do a full inventory first to figure out exactly what I'm selling so I can come up with the right asking price. That's why I've held off notifying the Society."

"Do you know who built this place?" Elias mused.

"I'm still researching the history of the Lost Museum. But I did find out that it was created by a First Gen colonist who was a member of the Arcane Society. His name was Aloysius Jones. He was in charge of the artifacts that the Society brought through the Curtain. Essentially, he was the director of Arcane's first museum here on Harmony. But when the Curtain closed and life got hard for the colonists, he was afraid the artifacts would be lost, stolen, or destroyed."

"According to the history books, life was tough for the colonists after the Curtain closed. Most of their Old World technology failed within months and there were no replacement parts coming from Earth. The First Generation was focused on survival while they figured out how to use rez amber in place of the Old World technology."

"Exactly," Hannah said. "So they didn't have time for civilized luxuries like museums. Aloysius Jones had every reason to believe that not only would the Arcane treasures be lost, but the Society's history as well. He built the Midnight Carnival to preserve both. And then he asked a powerful dreamlight talent to lock the entrances with a gate that could only be opened by someone with a similar para-psych profile."

Elias smiled. "And that turned out to be you."

"I'm sure there are others who could unlock the gates."

"But not many."

"I don't think so."

"Okay, why a carnival?" Elias asked. "Why didn't Aloysius Jones just hide the artifacts down here and lock the entrances?"

"I think it was because he had no way of

knowing how much of the historical records would be lost in the chaos of those first few decades. He was a student of history himself, of course. It was his passion. He knew that the best way to preserve the historical record is to embed it in a story. That's also the easiest way to make sure it gets passed down to the next generation. Each of these objects and attractions embodies a piece of Arcane history."

"History books and archives get lost but legends and myths have a way of hanging around. Makes sense. Aloysius Jones created a legend for the Society."

"I think that was the whole point of this place. He did an amazing job of it, too."

"It looks like a working carnival, right down to the pizza and hot dog stands," Elias said. "Was it ever open to the public?"

"No. Jones wrote in his diary that he never intended to create a working carnival because some of the relics in here are actually quite dangerous. But he wanted his museum to look and feel like an actual carnival. The various attractions are designed to portray the historical significance of the artifacts to future generations who might have forgotten the Society's history. The man had a passion for his creation. He wanted it perfect in every detail."

"It was genius," Elias said. "If nothing else the design of the attractions would force future scholars to at least ask the right questions about the significance of each artifact."

"Like our midnight marriage. It forced us to start asking the right questions this morning." Hannah paused. "It was probably the carnival that gave you the inspiration for that idea."

Elias shot her an unreadable look. "Uh-huh."

She was not sure how to take that. She realized she had been hoping for a different answer. *Be careful what you wish for,* she reminded herself.

He walked to a carousel that featured several elegantly painted figures and objects. The statues were dressed in ancient, Old Earth costumes. One wore a sparkling crown. The animals were all Old World, as well. Some had proudly arched necks, flaring manes, and hooved feet. Hannah could not remember the name of the creatures but she was certain she had seen pictures of them in history books. Some of the sculptures were in the shape of wheeled vehicles pulled by the prancing animals.

Elias stepped up onto the platform.

"What are you doing?" Hannah asked uneasily.

"There was no time to look around last night. I just want to check something."

He disappeared into what looked like a control booth. Hannah followed and stopped beside the carousel.

Virgil appeared from behind a concession stand and chortled excitedly. He dashed to the carousel and hopped up onto the platform. He scurried through the various figures, and finally chose his ride. He vaulted up onto the driver's seat of one of the carriages. The vehicle was harnessed to a pair of the hooved creatures and looked like something out of an Old World fairy tale. The cab was enameled in white and trimmed with gilt. The windows looked like they were made of dark mirrors.

Something about the mirrors worried Hannah.

"Be careful," she said.

She wasn't sure if she was speaking to Virgil or Elias. Both, she decided.

"This is crystal-based tech," Elias said from inside the control booth. "I think I can rez it."

"Probably not a good idea," Hannah said.

Elias ignored her. A few seconds later, music sounded through hidden speakers. The carousel began to rotate.

Virgil bounced up and down on the driv-

94

er's seat of his carriage, chortling madly.

"Oh, for pity's sake," Hannah said. "This is so dumb."

But this time she was speaking to herself. Neither of the males was paying any attention to her.

The carousel went faster. The glass eyes of the sculptures started to heat with an energy that Hannah knew intuitively came from the dark end of the spectrum. The queenlike figure turned its head, eyes darkly flashing. Hannah got the feeling the clockwork mechanism was searching for a target.

Virgil whirled past, clinging to the carriage seat. He was high on dust-bunny adrenaline.

The queen shot by again, this time her glass eyes locked on Hannah for a couple of beats. A chilling energy turned Hannah's insides cold for an instant before the motion of the carousel carried the figure out of range.

"Elias, that's enough," Hannah said. "Stop that thing. It's dangerous."

"Hang on." He spoke from inside the control booth. "Give me a minute to figure out how to shut it down."

"You got it going," Hannah said. "Please tell me you can stop it."

"No problem. Just need a little time to get

a handle on the tech."

The carousel was spinning faster now. Virgil was whizzing around on his fairy-tale coach at what seemed a dangerous rate of speed. Not that he appeared the least bit alarmed, Hannah thought.

The music got more intense. It was carrying paranormal vibes now, the kind that made Hannah's senses stir, and not in a good way.

"Elias," she called, raising her voice to be heard above the strange music. "You need to stop this machine."

"Working on it," he called back. "It's a little tricky."

"No kidding," Hannah muttered.

In hindsight, it had probably been a mistake to bring an engineer and a dust bunny to the carnival, she concluded.

Virgil flew past again. Hannah could see that he was clinging to the vehicle seat with all six paws now. His fur was plastered back by the wind the moving platform created. The eyes of the hooved creatures sparked with green fire and something weird was happening to the windows in the fairy-tale carriage. They shimmered with quicksilver light.

Alarmed, Hannah tried to grab Virgil off the driver's seat the next time he went past but she missed.

He chortled and sailed off out of reach on his pretty carriage.

"Elias!" Hannah shouted.

"Found it."

The carousel finally began to slow. The music receded. The glass eyes of the figures and the windows of the carriages dimmed. Hannah's senses calmed.

The platform came to a halt. Hannah scooped a deliriously excited Virgil off the carriage. Elias emerged from the booth. He looked as thrilled as Virgil.

"You should see the control system on this thing," Elias said. He stepped off the platform. "Amazing crystal technology. Incredible to think it's First Generation. That means it's two hundred years old. The engineer who built the carousel was a tech wizard. Way ahead of his time."

"Thank goodness you were able to stop it," Hannah said. "I was afraid Virgil was going to get flung off by centrifugal force. And I'm sure there was something weird going on with the glass eyes of the figures and the windows in those little carriages. From now on, don't touch anything, understand?"

"Okay, okay."

But she could see the hot curiosity in his

97

eyes. He was studying the other attractions the way a gambler studied a deck of cards.

"You used talent to activate the controls on that carousel, didn't you?" she said.

"Yep, it's what I do. Got a talent for working crystals. What can I tell you? It's in the blood. With a little practice I'm sure I can control the speed on that thing and the weapons on the platform."

"Weapons? They look more like clockwork toys and miniatures."

"Trust me, they're weapons," Elias said. "Be sure to note that fact in your inventory."

"I'll do that. Meanwhile, try to remember that we're not here so that you can run a lot of dangerous experiments. We're looking for a fortune-teller, remember?"

"Right." Elias looked around. "It was over there by the House of Mirrors."

They started through the maze of attractions and concession stands. Elias glanced at the sign over a tunnel that branched off the main room.

"WELCOME TO SCARGILL COVE, TOWN OF MYSTERY," he read. He glanced at Hannah. "What's the significance of that attraction?"

"Don't you know any of your Arcane history?"

"I'm a Coppersmith, remember? I'm also

98

an engineer. History is not my best subject."

"Scargill Cove was a little town in the Old World. It was where the headquarters of Jones and Jones was located during the twenty-first century, Old World Date, I think."

"Okay, I do know about Jones and Jones. So, was Aloysius Jones the only one who knew the location of this carnival?"

"No. The dreamlight talent who locked the gates knew it, of course. And a handful of people at the very top of the Society were aware of it. But over time the records got lost."

Elias glanced back rather longingly at the carousel. "Any idea of the history behind that merry-go-round?"

"I think the figures on that carousel are re-creations of Mrs. Bridewell's curiosities. She made clockwork toys back in the nineteenth century on Earth. She had a rare psychic talent for working glass. You will notice that all of the figures and sculptures are fitted with some weird dark glass."

"Huh. You're right. The eyes of the animals and the windows in the little carriages — they're all made of hot glass. Amazing. Glass has always been dangerous when it's combined with paranormal energy. The effects are highly unpredictable because it has the properties of both a solid and a liquid crystal. Who was this Mrs. Bridewell? Must have been some kind of Old World weapons dealer."

"Yes, I think so."

"Those psi-coded dreamlight gates make for serious barricades inside the tunnels," Elias said. "And it appears that the only entrance that leads directly to the surface has been blocked with hot psi for nearly two hundred years. I can understand why this place has been undisturbed for so long."

Hannah looked around. "There is another possibility. Maybe over the years a few people were able to unlock the gates and discovered this place but were either accidentally killed by one of the dangerous objects in here or got disoriented by the dreamlight and never made it out of the Underworld."

"Like the Ghost City," Elias said. "But that sort of thing just helps keep legends alive."

They walked past the House of Mirrors. Hannah glanced through the dark entrance, caught a glimpse of creepy glass light, and quickly looked away.

"Arcane is going to have to bring in a lot of experts to handle the artifacts in this place," she said.

"Yes," Elias agreed.

Hannah saw the fortune-teller booth and forgot about the House of Mirrors.

"There it is," she said. She hurried toward the booth. "I just hope my necklace is safe."

There was a life-sized figure inside the glass booth, a man dressed in a tall pointed hat and flowing robes decorated with stars and ancient alchemical symbols. He had a mane of shoulder-length white hair, a white beard, and sapphire crystal eyes. There was a huge pile of paper fortunes in front of the figure.

The colorful sign above the booth read, SYLVESTER JONES TELLS YOU YOUR FORTUNE.

"Like I said, I don't know much about history," Elias said. "At least, not Arcane history. But that name rings a bell."

"It should," Hannah said. "Sylvester Jones was the founder of the Arcane Society back on Earth." She paused to look around. "Do you see Virgil?"

"No," Elias said. But his attention was focused on the fortune-teller booth. "Those sapphire crystals look hot."

"*Virgil*," Hannah called.

A muffled chortle sounded from the vicinity of a row of arcade booths.

"He'll be fine," Elias said. "Let's get your

necklace."

She hesitated briefly and then told herself that Virgil was at home in the Underworld. He frequently went down into the Rainforest to hunt at night. He could take care of himself.

"I remember removing the back panel last night so that you could hide your necklace under the fortunes," Elias said. "But I never got a chance to activate the machine. Let's see what happens when I rez up old Sylvester."

"Considering what happened when you experimented with the carousel, I'm not so sure that's a great idea —"

But Elias had already pressed a red button.

There was a faint whir of machinery inside the booth. Hannah watched, wary but fascinated, as the Sylvester Jones figure came to life. The crystal eyes blinked a few times and brightened with energy. A deep mechanical voice boomed from a hidden speaker.

"Place your hand on the palm print," the robotic figure intoned. "You will receive your fortune."

Elias flattened one hand on the image of a palm. He snatched it back almost immediately.

"Shit." He shook his hand as though it had been burned.

"What was it?" Hannah asked.

"Damned if I know. Some kind of energy. Not strong, but definitely hot."

"Are you okay?"

"Yeah, I'm fine."

The concealed machinery whirred again. A piece of paper appeared from a slot. Elias picked it up somewhat cautiously and looked at it.

"Well?" Hannah asked. "What does it say?"

"It says *Beware of strangers selling waterfront property.*"

"Well, that's not helpful," Hannah said. "It's just a generic fortune like the one I got about finding true love soon."

"Right. Generic."

He sounded irritated again.

"My necklace," Hannah prompted.

"Give me a minute."

He took a small leather case out of the pocket of his jacket. Popping open the case, he removed a little tool and went to work on the back of the fortune-teller's booth.

"Got it," he said a moment later.

He removed the back panel of the booth and set it down on the ground. He stirred the pile of paper fortunes. When he pulled out his hand Hannah saw that he was holding her crystal necklace.

Relief splashed through her. "Thank goodness. I remember thinking that if those guys who were chasing us made it through the dreamlight gate, the necklace would be safe inside the booth."

"If Sylvester Jones can't protect a secret, who can?" Elias said. He closed the panel at the back of the booth. "Now all we have to do is rescue my team and then figure out who was chasing us last night."

"That's a serious to-do list." She fastened the necklace around her throat. And took a deep breath. "Well, at least we know why we got married. You were afraid the guys on the motorcycles were after me because they didn't want me rescuing your team. You thought that if we were married, the kidnappers would think twice about trying to grab me. You wanted to protect me by throwing the power of the Coppersmith Mining empire around me."

"Yeah, something like that." He zipped up the black tool case. "The Coppersmiths take care of their own."

Now he sounded disgruntled. She cleared her throat. "It was very nice of you."

He looked at her, eyes sharpening with a little energy. "Nice?"

She flushed. "I just want you to know I appreciate the gesture."

He gave her an inscrutable look. "All I can say is that it seemed like a good idea at the time."

"Right." She squared her shoulders. "Well, it's a complication for both of us but nothing that can't be remedied. Just a bit of paperwork to file."

"Which we won't have time to file until we get my team out of the ruins and find out who chased us into the Shadow Zone last night."

"No," she agreed.

He startled her with a quick, wicked grin. "Looks like we're going on an interesting honeymoon."

CHAPTER 7

He knew he had made a mistake the moment the words were out of his mouth. Hannah's jaw tightened and everything about her seemed to withdraw to some secret place where he could not follow.

She turned away and made a show of searching the bizarre carnival.

"Virgil?" she called. "Where are you? Time to leave."

This time there was no answering chortle. Hannah started toward the Scargill Cove scene. "Virgil? This is no time for games."

Unable to think of anything else to do, Elias went after her.

"Sorry," he said. "The crack about the honeymoon was just a bad attempt to lighten the situation."

"No problem," she said briskly. *"Virgil?"*

Muffled thuds and banging sounded from one of the arcade booths.

"That's not good," Hannah said.

Elias listened to the noises. "Over there."

He led the way past another attraction. The entrance was sealed with a psi-gate. The sign read LUCINDA BROMLEY'S PSYCHIC GARDEN.

"Do you know who Lucinda Bromley was?" he asked.

"She married Caleb Jones. Back in the nineteenth century, the two of them cofounded Jones and Jones."

"You know, this place makes me realize that my family needs to hire someone to get the Coppersmith archives organized. Right now they're just sitting in a big vault on the island."

"What island?"

"Copper Beach. Family compound."

"Oh, I see."

Once again he wished he'd kept his mouth shut. There was no need to remind her of her status as an orphan. On Harmony, family was everything. The First Generation founders had used every tool available — legal and cultural — to shore up the institutions of marriage and the family. The experts among them had concluded that those two institutions were the cornerstones of a strong society and the best hope for ensuring the survival of the stranded colonists.

The system worked well for the most part,

but no social system was perfect. Babies still got orphaned and people still wound up alone in the world.

The thuds and bangs got louder.

Elias followed Hannah past an ominous-looking attraction labeled HEADQUARTERS OF NIGHTSHADE. BEWARE THE DRUG.

Once again his curiosity was aroused. He was about to ask Hannah to explain the Nightshade reference but he stopped short when he saw that she had stopped in front of a glass-walled arcade booth.

The interior of the booth was filled with action figures, toys, and stuffed animals. There was a miniature crane-like apparatus equipped with a claw device that could be activated from outside the booth. The sign read PICK A PIECE OF ARCANE HISTORY.

In addition to the toys, there was also an outraged dust bunny inside the booth. Virgil was literally bouncing off the walls in a furious attempt to extricate himself and one of the action figures. All four of his eyes were open and there was a great deal of growling.

"Good grief," Hannah said. She came to a halt and stared at the arcade game. "How did he get inside?"

"Probably squeezed in through the prize chute," Elias said. "The problem is that it's not big enough for Virgil to get himself and the toy out at the same time."

Virgil continued to lunge around inside the booth, scattering toys and stuffed animals.

"He's not going to leave his prize behind," Hannah said.

"I like a guy who has his priorities straight," Elias said.

He went around to the back of the machine and took out his tool case again. He selected a tool that looked like it would fit the old-fashioned fastenings on the access panel.

When he opened the back door of the booth, a cascade of glittery toys tumbled out. Virgil chortled in triumph and leaped down to the floor. He dragged his chosen prize by one of the figure's legs.

Hannah reached down to pick him up and plop him on her shoulder.

"Let me see which prize you picked," she said.

She put up her hand. Fully fluffed once more, hunting eyes closed, Virgil graciously let her take the action figure. Elias watched her examine the doll. It was a woman wearing sturdy trousers and a shirt covered in an odd green, black, and brown pattern. A miniature utility belt was strapped around her waist. The belt held a tiny flashlight and an object that might have been a camera or some sort of communications gear. Her head was covered in a helmet of gray curls.

"Looks like someone's grandmother," he said.

"Assuming the grandmother wears heavy boots and Old World military camouflage." Hannah looked up, smiling. "It's Arizona Snow."

"Never heard of her."

"I'll fill you in on the way to the Ghost City. But first I need to go home, change my clothes, and pack some gear. Your poor team has been trapped long enough."

"Sounds like a plan. Sort of."

She cleared her throat. "I do have one personal question I'd like to ask."

"Just one?"

"Last night we went out to dinner together."

"So?" he asked, wary now.

"I just wondered if you always carry a miniature tool kit when you take a woman out to dinner."

"Always. I'm an engineer."

CHAPTER 8

The text message was more bad news.

> Complications encountered. Target was not acquired. Another attempt will be made when opportunity arises. Terms of the arrangement still stand. Work is guaranteed.

The fools had failed. How was that even possible? It was supposed to be a simple job. Grab the woman and drop Coppersmith into the Underworld without his amber. The Coppersmith family might spend a fortune hunting for one of their own but the police wouldn't waste much time searching for Hannah West. She wasn't important. She had no family to make a fuss when she went missing.

So close. So damn close.

The Collector raged back and forth across the room. After all the years of searching; after the success of his carefully baited trap;

after all the careful planning, the thick-headed idiots he'd hired had screwed up.

The Collector went past the table and glanced at the headline on the morning edition of the *Curtain.* He had gone out early to purchase a paper copy hoping that the online edition was a mistake. But there was no mistake. Coppersmith had married the woman.

That presented a new problem. True, the marriage was only a cheap MC but it was a legal marriage until it was dissolved. Elias Coppersmith might as well have announced to the world that Hannah West was now under the protection of the Coppersmith Mining empire.

There was only one reason why he would have done such a thing: He knew about the Lost Museum. He had seduced the silly woman with a cheap short-term Marriage of Convenience. And the little fool had fallen for it. She probably counted herself incredibly lucky. Given her lack of family and her shaky para-psych profile, an MC was all she could ever hope for when it came to marriage. An offer of an MC with a Coppersmith had probably dazzled her.

It wouldn't last long, of course — just long enough for Coppersmith to convince her to sign the papers transferring her claim to him. Once that happened the marriage would be terminated.

Unless she was too smart to be conned out of her claim.

The Collector went to the window and looked out over the bright lights of the Strip. He considered what he knew of Hannah West. She was a nobody from the DZ and her para-psych profile made her a freak. But he had to admit that she had been rather clever thus far. Perhaps she was the one manipulating Coppersmith, not vice versa.

The Collector picked up the nearest object, a drinking glass, and hurled it against the wall. He watched the glittering shards cascade down to the carpet.

He could not bring himself to abandon the project, not as long as there was even a slim chance of success.

CHAPTER 9

Hannah's phone rang just as she got out of the taxi. It was not the first call she had received since returning to the surface. She had dumped the first two, both of which had come from Grady Barnett.

She reached into her clutch, intending to terminate Grady's third call. Then she noticed the sleek steel blue Cadence parked at the curb.

"Well, what do you know?" she said, taking out her phone. "Your car did survive the night."

Elias finished paying the cabdriver and turned toward her. Virgil was on his shoulder clutching the Arizona Snow doll by one little booted foot.

"You thought the car would have been stolen overnight?" Elias asked.

"Or stripped. It's not that we don't have a pretty good neighborhood watch set up here in the DZ — we do. But it's designed to keep the local residents safe. Visitors are usually okay if they stick to the parking lots of the clubs and casinos because there's plenty of private security. But leaving a fancy car like yours on a side street overnight is a risky move. It must have been a big temptation to some of our less scrupulous entrepreneurs."

"My car can take care of itself."

"Really?" The phone in her hand rang again. She glanced at the screen, expecting to see Grady's number. A jolt of alarm spiked through her when she saw the identity of the caller. "Uh-oh."

"Something wrong?" Elias asked.

"It's my aunt Clara," Hannah said. "Pretty early in the day for her. She's a night person."

Elias glanced at the newspaper stand on the corner. It featured the latest copy of the *Curtain.* The headline about their marriage was in very large font.

"What could possibly go wrong?" he asked.

She gave him a withering look. "Don't worry. Even if she happened to see a copy, Clara knows you can't believe everything you read in the *Curtain.*"

"Everyone says that. But they read it anyway."

Hannah ignored him and took the call.

"Good morning," she said, trying to infuse her tone with an upbeat note. "How are you and Aunt Bernice doing today?"

"How are we doing?" Clara repeated, her dark, smoky voice much sharper than usual. "I'll tell you how we're doing. We would both have fallen out of our rocking chairs, if we had rocking chairs. The headlines in the *Curtain* say you married Elias Coppersmith last night. It says his family controls a huge chunk of the hot-rock mining rights in the Underworld. It says he's rich. It also says he's a scion. What the heck is a scion? Sounds like some kind of refrigerator or a car."

Clara Stockbridge was normally a monument of unflappability. When she had arrived in Illusion Town several decades ago, her name had been Clara Stockton. She'd had the height, the great bones, and the figure to get a job as a showgirl. She also had the intelligence, creativity, and savvy understanding of an audience, which had allowed her and her lover, Bernice Bridge, to create the masterful Ladies of High Magic show. The act had endured for nearly thirty years before Clara and Bernice had gracefully closed it down.

Somewhere along the way Clara and

116

Bernice had married and combined their last names into Stockbridge. They had insisted that the baby girl they had found on their doorstep call each of them "aunt" not "mother" because, as Bernice said, Hannah had a mother. Marla Sanders was dead but Clara and Bernice had been her friends. They were absolutely certain that Marla had loved her infant daughter with all her heart and therefore deserved to keep the title of mother.

"I can explain, Aunt Clara," Hannah said. "It's a little complicated."

"This is a yes-or-no question," Clara said. "Is the story true?"

"Sort of."

"Sort of. What kind of answer is that? Honey, are you okay?"

"I'm fine, Aunt Clara."

"What is going on?"

Hannah took a deep breath and plunged into the tale.

"Elias Coppersmith came to see me yesterday to get my help opening a dreamlight gate down at the Ghost City project. I agreed but before we could leave town a gang of bikers tried to grab one of us. We're not positive but we think they might have been after me. Elias thinks it may be a case of corporate espionage. They may have been

117

trying to keep me from rescuing the Coppersmith team."

"*What?*"

"Elias thought I would be safer if I was his wife. It's just an MC, Aunt Clara. Nothing to get excited about."

"You were attacked? By a motorcycle gang? Where are you?"

"Home, safe and sound. The gang showed up when we left the Green Ruin Café last night."

"But that's right here in the DZ. We've never had a problem with motorcycle gangs in this zone."

"Yes, I know, Aunt Clara."

"The Club wouldn't allow the competition," Clara observed somewhat absently.

It was a fact, Hannah thought. Illusion Town had the usual democratic trappings — an elected mayor and a city council. It also had an effective police force. But everyone knew that the real powers-behind-the-scenes were the members of the Illusion Club. It was a very exclusive organization. The membership list was short. The Club was made up of the owners of the largest casino empires in the city.

"I know," Hannah said. "I was amazed that the bikers would take the risk. Obviously, they're not from around here."

118

"Obviously," Clara said.

Elias held out his hand.

"Let me talk to your aunt," he said.

Hannah clamped the phone against her chest. "I'm not sure that's such a good idea."

"I heard that," Clara said, her voice somewhat muffled by Hannah's bosom. "Put that MC husband of yours on the phone."

Reluctantly, Hannah handed the phone to Elias.

"Meet Mrs. Clara Stockbridge," she said. "My aunt."

Elias took the phone.

"Good morning, ma'am," he said. "No, I realize it's not a good morning for everyone. Sorry, force of habit. I'm Elias Coppersmith."

He gave a quick, detailed account of events and wound up with:

"No, I don't know what's going on yet, but until I do, I think Hannah will be safer with Coppersmith Security around her, Mrs. Stockbridge. Also, as my wife she'll have an additional level of protection . . . Yes, ma'am. I understand. We're leaving for the jobsite just as soon as Hannah picks up her Underworld gear. Meanwhile, I'll have our security people coordinate with the Illusion Town police to start an investigation up here on the surface . . . Yes, ma'am, I agree, the Club won't like having some biker gang think it can roar through town and frighten the locals. Bad for business."

There was a lengthy pause.

Elias gave Hannah a speculative look as he listened to whatever Clara was saying on the other end of the connection.

"No, ma'am, I didn't know that. I'll keep it in mind," he said. "Yes, I'll take good care of her. Sorry about the headlines . . . What? No, I'm not sure what a scion is, either. I agree it doesn't have a good ring to it . . . Right. It won't happen again, Mrs. Stockbridge."

Elias ended the connection and handed the phone back to Hannah.

"Your aunt says she wants to meet me as soon as we get back to the surface," he said. "Also I'm not to call her 'ma'am.' "

"Yeah, well, we'll worry about that after the job is over."

"She's concerned about you."

"I know." Hannah exhaled slowly. "I love her, too. What did she say when you told her about the kidnapping attempt?"

"That got her to focus on the problem at hand," Elias said, "which is keeping you safe."

"I can take care of myself," Hannah said, feeling rather grim. "Like your car."

"I'm sure you can," Elias said soothingly. "But your aunt understood that you would be safer with me until we can sort things out. If the biker gang was hired to keep you from going down below to open the dream-light gate, the sooner we get that gate open, the better off we'll be."

"Amazing. Congratulations, by the way. Not many people can outtalk Aunt Clara."

Hannah rezzed the lock on the front door of her shop.

"Your aunt said something else, too."

There was a note in Elias's voice that made her pause and look back at him.

"What?" she asked.

"She said that she understood our MC was a security move, not a romantic one. Nevertheless, the arrangement would put you and me in close proximity for a time. She said I should not expect to be able to take advantage of the situation."

"Oh, geez."

"She said you had issues with intimacy because of the nature of your talent and that if I did try to take advantage, I would regret it."

"This is so embarrassing."

"I don't think she was threatening me,"

Elias said judiciously. "Not exactly. I think she just doesn't want to see you get hurt."

"Trust me, Aunt Clara was threatening you."

"Could you give me a hint, at least?"

"About the nature of the threat?" Hannah asked.

"Will your aunt call in some favors and have me disappear into the tunnels if she thinks I took advantage of you?"

In spite of her embarrassment, Hannah laughed.

"No," she said. "I'm not saying Aunt Clara couldn't call in a favor or two if she needed it, but it wouldn't be necessary in my case."

"How bad are the intimacy issues?"

"Ever had an out-of-body experience?"

"No, can't say that I have."

"Stick with me and you might get one. I'm told they are very exciting and not in a good way."

Her talent was also pretty much the last thing she wanted to talk about at the moment. She started to push open the door but paused when Elias's phone rang.

He stopped on the front step and took the call.

"Hi, Mom. Let me guess: you read the *Curtain*. What? Yes, it's true. Can't wait for you to meet her but got a job to do first . . .

122

You're right. The Ghost City is a strange destination for a honeymoon. This is about rescuing that team at the second portal. If anyone can open that gate, it's Hannah. I promise I'll call as soon as we're out of the Underworld. Right. Tell Dad not to worry. What? I can't hear you very well. Bad connection. Got to run."

He cut the connection and looked at Hannah.

"Turns out my mother reads the *Curtain*," he said.

"No kidding. This MC of ours is clearly a problem for a lot of people. But at least it's a totally fixable problem. We just need to file . . . *Crap*."

She stared, stunned by the scene inside her shop. Her collection of artifacts and antiques and interesting hot rocks looked as if it had been struck by a tornado. Glass cabinets had been smashed, the contents strewn across the floor.

The intruder's dreamlight prints were everywhere. They seethed on the floorboards and burned on everything he had touched.

She heard Virgil growl and she was vaguely aware that Elias was hauling her aside so that he could get through the doorway first. She noticed that he had the device he had called a silencer in his hand and she sensed his heightened energy field but she could not seem to wrap her head around the vandalism.

She said the only thing that seemed to sound logical.

"So much for the high-end locks I had installed," she whispered.

CHAPTER 10

"Your locks are decent," Elias said. "But obviously not good enough. Next time I'll make sure you get state-of-the-art tech from the Coppersmith labs. Stay here, I'll take a look around upstairs."

"Okay," she said.

The intruder had climbed the stairs to her private space. She could see his hot prints. He hadn't just invaded her shop, he had invaded her home.

She was oddly numb from shock and it must have shown in her voice because Elias gave her a quick, concerned look. He didn't waste any time consoling her, however. She waited just inside the doorway while he took the stairs two at a time.

He returned a short time later.

"All clear upstairs," he said. "This wasn't vandalism. They were looking for something."

She folded her arms very tightly across

her midsection, hugging herself.

"Not they," she whispered. "Him. There was only one person here."

Elias studied her intently. "You can tell that much?"

"He was in a very emotional state — frantic and angry, I think. He left his damned dreamlight prints everywhere."

"And you can see them."

She nodded.

"Did he come in through the front door or the back door?"

"Back door. No prints on the front steps. I can see that he didn't find the trapdoor in the floor. It leads down into the basement."

"Could you identify those prints again if you saw them?"

"Oh, yeah."

"That kind of evidence probably wouldn't stand up in court, but if we knew his identity we might be able to find hard evidence that would convince a jury."

She just nodded again. She couldn't think of anything to say.

Predictably, Elias took charge.

"We need to get out of here and fast. Change your clothes, collect your field gear, and we'll head for the Underworld. The sooner we get that team out of the ruins, the sooner we can get a handle on this situation."

She started toward the stairs. "Assuming this break-in is connected to opening your dreamlight gate."

He reached out and stopped her by gently catching her chin on the edge of his hand.

"Doesn't matter if it's connected or not," he said. "We'll figure it out."

"Okay."

She hurried up the stairs, reminding herself that the two of them had been through worse during the night. They had been attacked by a motorcycle gang. They had been psi-burned. They had gotten *married.*

But this intrusion into her home was more devastating, more personal. The cozy, private little world she had created for herself had been invaded. Virgil muttered anxiously in her ear and offered her his Arizona Snow action figure. Automatically, she took the doll. It was oddly comforting.

"Arizona Snow wouldn't have fallen apart in a situation like this, Virgil. I won't either."

Her private rooms were in the same condition as the shop. After a single, horrified glance at the chaos in the kitchen and living room, she went into her bedroom. Clothes had been pulled out of the closet and tossed on the floor. Her books had been swept out of the bookcase.

But it was the sight of the black boot prints on her almost new, pristine white quilt that sent a jolt of raw fury through her. Hot dreamlight simmered in the prints. The bastard had stood right there on her bed.

"Why?" she whispered.

Then she realized that the intruder had yanked the photograph of her aunts and herself off the wall above the headboard. Probably looking to see if she had hidden anything behind it, she thought.

She tightened her grip on the Arizona Snow figure. She could have sworn she felt a little energy whisper in the doll. For some reason it was just the bracing tonic she needed.

"When I get my hands on the creep who did this, he is going to be very, very sorry," she said.

"Yes," Elias said from the doorway. "He will be sorry."

She turned quickly to look at him. His eyes burned with promise.

By the time she got downstairs dressed in field gear — jeans, a black pullover, black utility vest, and low boots — she was no longer numb with shock. She was seething with a barely suppressed rage.

Elias glanced at the pack she had slung over one shoulder and then he looked at the sleeping bag she gripped under her arm.

"You won't need that," he said. "Copper-smith supplies all the basics at the jobsite."

"I have to have my own sleeping bag," she said.

He didn't question the statement, just nodded. "Okay. Ready?"

"Almost," she said. "I want to check my vault before we leave. There's no indication that the intruder found it but I want to be sure."

Elias glanced at his watch, his jaw tensing but he nodded.

"All right," he said. "But let's make it quick. I want to get you out of town."

She set her pack and her sleeping bag on the floor. Opening the concealed trapdoor, she led the way down the steps to the basement. There she opened the fake wall paneling to reveal the narrow, jagged entrance to the glowing green tunnels.

"My vault isn't far inside," she said.

He followed her through a short maze of glowing green tunnels until they reached her secret hiding place. One glance inside the chamber assured her that her most valuable treasures remained untouched.

Elias surveyed the neatly arranged artifacts and relics. "Huh."

"I know," she said. "It looks more like a secondhand shop."

She was well aware that the collection in the vault was not very impressive. A number of mostly amateurish paintings, sculptures, and other bad works of art were arranged on one side of the room. A set of shelves in the center held a motley assortment of items that ranged from old books and antique lamps to ragged comforters and quilts.

On the far side of the room stood a couple of sagging bedsteads, one of which was topped with a worn mattress. There were other items of bedroom furniture as well — a wooden chest of drawers and a wardrobe.

Her collection of mirrors took up one long side of the chamber.

Elias walked slowly through the chamber. She could feel energy shift in the atmosphere and knew that he had opened his senses.

"None of this stuff would tempt the average thief," he said. He touched a yellowed lamp shade. "So I'm guessing these things have a very personal meaning to you."

"They've all got one thing in common," she said. "Every item down here was once possessed or — in the case of the artwork — created by someone with a version of my kind of talent."

"Dream walkers."

"Yes. A few of the items are new. Some date back to the First Generation. Evidently, it's a talent that existed, at least in a latent way, in some of the colonists."

Elias moved to stand in front of one of the paintings. Like the other works of art, there was nothing particularly distinguished about the artist's style or talent. But there was a disturbing intensity about the surreal scene — a strange urban landscape illuminated in bizarre shades of blue, gray, and ultraviolet.

Elias moved on to another picture. It, too, was surreal but the setting was one of the old Alien ruins.

Hannah folded her arms.

"The energy infused into those pictures and the rest of the art in this room makes me think that they were all done by people who were trying to capture their dream-walking experience," she said.

Elias met her eyes. "This is your own personal research collection, isn't it?"

He understood, she thought. For some reason that lifted her spirits.

She touched her necklace beneath her

pullover. "I'm hoping that sooner or later I'll come across an object or a piece of art that will give me another clue to my ancestors."

"Have you found anything besides the necklace so far?"

"No, but the new genealogist I hired, Dr. Wilcox, thinks that if he gets a complete para-psych profile it will point him in the right direction. It's just a matter of time, he says."

Elias gave the chamber a thoughtful look. Then he turned back to her.

"You're sure you didn't tell Wilcox or Barnett about your necklace."

"No, absolutely not. Didn't want to take the risk."

Elias nodded. "Good thinking. What about the Midnight Carnival? Did you mention it to either of them?"

"No one except you and my aunts knows about the necklace and the carnival. I haven't told anyone else that I filed a claim on a certain sector of the Underworld, either. Once I do a deal with Arcane for the carnival, though, I will tell Wilcox about the necklace. I'm sure he'll think it's important."

"A claim is public information once it's filed," Elias said.

"Yes, but the description boils down to a set of coordinates that define a sector. There's nothing on the forms that describes what I found there. Besides, who would even think to look for a claim filed by me? Thousands of claims, large and small, get filed every year. The vast majority are worthless. Very few private prospectors get rich in the Underworld. The big companies like Coppersmith control the really hot sectors."

"Good point. Speaking of a hot Coppersmith project, we should be on our way." Elias took one last look around the chamber and then he walked toward her. "Ready to leave?"

"Yes."

"You're sure?"

She narrowed her eyes. Whatever he saw in her expression must have satisfied him.

"Right," he said. "Let's go."

They made their way back through the basement of her shop and up the stairs to the showroom floor. Elias took another look around as they moved through the space.

"I meant it, you know," he said. "After we rescue the team I will make sure we find the guy who broke into this place. Coppersmith Security is very, very good at that sort of thing."

"All right," she said. "Thanks. If you catch the guy I will consider that full payment for this job."

"No, you'll get paid as agreed," Elias said. "A contract is a contract."

She gave him a sidelong glance. "I'm not looking for any favors from you and your company, Elias."

"Finding the guy who broke into your home won't be a favor. Think of it as a wedding gift."

CHAPTER 11

The buzzer on the rear door of the shop
sounded just as Hannah and Elias were
preparing to go out the front door.

Buzz . . . buzz . . . buzz-buzz-buzz.

Virgil chortled. Hannah came to a halt.

"Just a second," she said. "That's Runner's code. I need to answer it."

She dropped her pack and her sleeping
bag at the front door and made her way
through the chaos of the sales floor. She
went into the back room.

Whoever had tossed the place had obviously hit a wall in that room. It was so
crammed with boxes, crates, and cartons
stuffed with antiques and collectibles that
even the most determined burglar would
have been forced to abandon any attempt
to search it. Judging by the pattern of the
hot psi-prints on the floor the intruder had,
indeed, opened a few boxes and then given
up. The vast majority of the cartons and

crates were still sealed shut.

She opened the back door and saw Runner. He was nineteen-going-on-forty with a narrow, sharp-featured face. His real name was Benjamin Swift but on the streets he was Runner. He was a hunter-talent with the usual preternatural night vision and speed. In a more perfect world he would have been invited to join the elite Federal Bureau of Psi Investigation, a big-city police department, or a private security firm.

But Runner had wound up on the streets at an early age. His formative years had been spent running errands for various and assorted shady characters in the Dark Zone. As a result he was stuck with a past that was way too iffy for the FBPI or any other high-end law enforcement agency.

In addition to having a hunter-talent's paranormal assets, he also had a head for business. The result was his recently established business — DZ Delivery Service. He had employed four other streetwise young males who all proudly wore the DZ Delivery Service uniforms — black leather jackets with the name of the business emblazoned on the back in fiery graphics. Below that was the company motto: *We Know the Zone.* DZ Delivery Service's sleek black scooters were now a common sight in the maze of crooked lanes and twisty streets of the Dark Zone. "Hey, Finder," Runner said in his trademark I-don't-give-a-damn drawl.

"Hey, Runner." Hannah smiled at him. "Little early for you. Everything okay?"

"Heard you and some guy got into trouble with an out-of-zone bike gang last night. Me and the guys looked for you. Couldn't find you, so we figured you'd gone down below." Runner reached out to pat Virgil. "Next thing I know, the *Curtain* says you married some kind of scone."

"I think that's supposed to be scion," Hannah said.

"What?"

"Never mind," Hannah said. "This is Elias Coppersmith. Elias, meet Runner. He's my brother."

Elias raised an inquiring brow. "Your brother?"

"Yes," she said. She said it very firmly. There was no blood connection between Runner and herself but that didn't change the fact that she considered him a brother. "He runs the finest delivery service in the DZ."

"Pretty much the only delivery service in the DZ," Runner said. A gleam of pride heated his eyes. "We're the only crew that can deliver anywhere in the zone. Like it says on the back of our uniforms, *We Know the Zone.* The regular delivery services get lost once they turn off Ruin Street."

"Pleased to meet you," Elias said.

He extended his hand.

Runner looked confused for a few seconds. Then he figured it out and shook Elias's hand. It was a careful, awkward handshake. Hannah knew that Runner hadn't had much experience shaking hands with men from Elias's world.

"You're the husband, huh?" Runner said, squinting a little at Elias.

"Yes," Elias said.

"That nice, new Cadence out front belong to you?"

"Uh-huh."

"Saw a couple of local chop-shop guys checking it out early this morning, but when one of them tried the door handle, he jumped back real quick. The dudes gave up and went away."

"The car can take care of itself. As Hannah said, we did have some trouble with a biker gang last night. Lost 'em in the tunnels."

"Yeah, smart move," Runner said. "What's up with the marriage?"

"A security measure," Hannah said quickly. "Elias hired me to open a dream-

138

light gate at the new Ghost City project. There's a team trapped in one of the ruins. We're heading to the jobsite now."

Runner's brow furrowed. "So why'd you get married?"

Hannah sighed. "Like I said. Security. Someone broke in here last night and tore the place apart."

For the first time Runner looked startled. "One of the bikers? He managed to find your place?"

"That's what it looks like," Hannah said.

"Hard to believe. Most folks from out of the zone would have a tough time finding your shop. GPS and the mapping systems are no good around here."

"I know," Hannah said.

"Shit. Think it was someone local?" Runner asked softly.

"No," Hannah said. "I don't. But I suppose we can't rule out that possibility, not entirely."

"We don't have time to deal with the problem now," Elias said. "But we'll find the guy when we get back. Hannah says she'll know his prints if she sees him again. Meanwhile, I'd appreciate it if you kept an eye on her place."

"No problem," Runner said. "I'll put the crew on a round-the-clock schedule. With five of us taking turns we can watch this place all day and all night. He probably won't come back, though."

"You never know," Elias said. "But if he shows up, don't try to stop him. If he's involved with the gang, he'll be dangerous. The bikers hit us with some serious ghost fire last night. I think they may be ex-Guild men."

"Don't worry about my crew." Runner sliced the air with one hand, dismissing any hint that he and his team couldn't handle the intruder. "Just take good care of my sister."

Elias smiled. "The thing about being a scone connected to a family that runs a mining empire is that I have access to all kinds of high-end security."

"Okay." Runner looked at Hannah. "See you when you get back to the surface."

"Tell any potential clients that I'm closed for business for a while but that I'll be back soon," she said.

"You got it."

Runner gave Virgil one last pat and then loped off down the alley.

Elias looked at Hannah. "Potential clients?"

"In addition to finding things online for my regular clients, I run a little side business. I give a friends-and-family discount to folks here in the DZ. Most of them couldn't afford my regular fees and commissions."

She locked the back door and led the way to the front of the shop. She hoisted her day pack and her sleeping bag and went out of the front door. Elias followed her.

She paused on the shop step to rez the lock.

"For all the good it did last night," she grumbled.

She went down the steps with Elias. They headed toward the sleek Cadence parked at the curb.

Elias had just gotten the passenger-side door open for her when she heard the high-pitched whine of a small, underpowered, fuel-efficient, environmentally correct engine.

The little vehicle braked to a sharp halt in front of the shop. Hannah turned to watch the driver extricate himself from the vehicle.

"Hannah, wait. I've been trying to get hold of you," Grady Barnett called. "I've been very worried. What is going on?"

"Just what I needed to make this day perfect," Hannah said.

CHAPTER 12

Elias gave the new arrival an assessing look. "You know this guy?"

"Oh, yes, I know him. Grady Barnett. That would be Professor Grady Barnett to you. He runs a para-psych research lab at the edge of the DZ. He's the expert I hired to prepare the para-psych profile that I was going to send to the genealogist."

Virgil hunkered down on Hannah's shoulder. He didn't growl but he watched Grady with deep suspicion.

"Virgil and Grady have a history," Hannah whispered to Elias. "They don't like each other very much."

"I trust Virgil's instincts," Elias said.

"So do I," Hannah said. "Now."

Grady was in his mid-thirties. He had curly brown hair, shrewd gray eyes, a very square jaw, and the slightly rumpled, just-emerged-from-my-study appearance cultivated in academic circles. But on Grady, the corduroy jacket with the leather elbow patches, jeans, and pullover top looked good.

"What is going on?" Grady came to a halt on the sidewalk. He gave Elias a quick survey and then he turned to Hannah. "I hear you're in an MC with one of the Coppersmith Mining heirs. I couldn't believe it. Figured there had to be some mistake."

"Oh, wow." Hannah widened her eyes. "You read the *Curtain,* too? This day is just full of surprises."

Grady ignored that. "Is it true? Are you in a Marriage of Convenience?"

"Yes, indeed. There's no mistake." She waved a hand rather vaguely in Elias's direction. "Meet my . . . uh, husband. Elias Coppersmith. Elias, this is Grady Barnett."

"Barnett," Elias said. He inclined his head in a brief acknowledgment of the introduction. "You'll have to excuse us. We're in a rush." He gave Grady a deceptively polite smile. "Honeymoon, you know."

"Coppersmith." Grady's expression was transformed as if by magic into a warm smile. He put out his hand. "I'm Dr. Grady Barnett of the Barnett Research Institute. Hannah's para-psych doctor."

"That is not true," Hannah said sharply.

"I hired you to do a profile, that's all. I didn't ask for medical advice."

But Grady was not listening. He was too busy trying to charm Elias. He finally noticed that Elias was not shaking his hand and hastily lowered it.

"This is a pleasure," he continued. "I'm aware of some of the research that has come out of your company's labs. Interesting work going on there."

"We certainly think so or we wouldn't be paying for it," Elias said.

Grady chuckled politely but his expression cooled. He glanced at Hannah's pack. "What kind of honeymoon is it going to be? You look like you're dressed for the Underworld."

"We thought it would be fun to go camping in the Rainforest," Hannah said. "You've got to admit, it makes for a unique honeymoon destination."

Grady's mouth tightened. "There's something that doesn't ring true here."

You had to hand it to Grady, Hannah thought. He might be a worm but he was not a stupid worm.

"Good-bye, Grady," Hannah said.

She slipped into the front seat of the car. Virgil hopped from her shoulder onto the back of her seat.

Grady leaned down to continue talking to Hannah. Virgil growled. Grady eyed him warily but he did not give up.

"Will you please tell me what is going on?" he said in his best clinician accent. "I'm worried about you, Hannah. This isn't like you. We both know that marriage is not for you. You've got serious intimacy issues."

"Here's the interesting thing, Grady." She gave him a blazing smile. "Elias isn't afraid of my talent or my issues."

Grady reddened. "You're fragile due to the nature of your talent. Your dream-walking ability makes you very sensitive."

"You think I'm some kind of freak. Don't deny it. I heard you talking to your research assistant about me. That was shortly before I walked in on the two of you going at it in the supply closet."

"Now, Hannah, I've told you that you misunderstood that situation."

"Which part did I misunderstand? The part where you told the lovely Kelsey Lewis that I gave you the creeps when I did the sleep test in your lab? Or the part where she was on her knees giving you a blow job in the supply closet?"

Grady's face went from red to a mottled shade of purple.

"It's not my fault that your talent makes it

impossible for you to have a strong, intimate relationship with a man," he snapped.

Cold energy shivered in the atmosphere. Out of the corner of her eye, Hannah saw the stone in Elias's ring spark with a little paranormal fire.

"That's enough," he said. "Do you really think I'm going to let you get away with insulting my wife?"

He did not raise his voice but there was an edge to it that made Grady flinch as though he had been struck. He straightened and glared at Elias.

"This is a confidential matter between Hannah and me," Grady said stiffly. "A medical matter, I might add. She is a patient of mine. I have an obligation to act in her best interests."

"I am not your patient," Hannah yelped, infuriated. "I fired you."

Virgil growled again and showed some teeth. Grady took a hasty step back.

"It doesn't matter who you are, Barnett," Elias said, his voice lethally soft. "I'm her husband, remember?"

He closed the passenger-side door, trapping Hannah inside. Hannah suspected that he was trying to put an end to the confrontation. But she was really, really pissed off now.

She immediately lowered the window.

"Quit telling people you're my doctor, Barnett," she said.

"I don't know what's going on here but as a qualified para-psych practitioner, I am very concerned," he said forcefully. "I'm sure this marriage is a sham. Coppersmith is trying to use you in some manner. We've discussed your issues, Hannah. You're too fragile for the physical side of marriage."

"Oh, shut up," Hannah said. "One more thing. When I get back I want my file — all of it, including those notes you made in your stupid notebook."

"I told you, the file is incomplete, Hannah," Grady said. "It's impossible to analyze at this point."

"I don't care. I paid for it. I want it. If you don't give it to me, I'll hire a lawyer."

"You heard the lady," Elias said.

He rounded the front of the Cadence, got behind the wheel, and rezzed the powerful engine.

Hannah flashed Grady her most dazzling smile.

"Sorry. Can't stay to chat, *Dr.* Barnett," she said sweetly. "Time to leave for our honeymoon."

"Hannah, listen to me," Grady said urgently. "Where, exactly, are you going?"

"That's confidential," she said. "I'm sure you understand."

Elias gave a crack of laughter and pulled away from the curb.

Hannah fastened her seat belt and sat back in her seat. It occurred to her that Elias drove the way he did everything else. Every move was controlled, efficient, and competent.

Controlled, efficient, and competent.

Just the opposite of her own highly emotional state lately. She thought she'd been doing quite well, given all she'd been through in the past several hours. But discovering that her shop and apartment had been invaded had triggered a wave of rage and frustration that had made her pulse pound. Grady showing up on her doorstep and informing her in front of Elias that she was fragile was the last straw, she thought. She clenched her hands on her thighs.

"I'm not, you know," she said.

"I know," he said.

She glanced at him and relaxed a little. He understood, she thought.

"Barnett started telling me I was fragile when I did the sleep test in his lab. I insisted he bring in a new cot. I knew I couldn't sleep on a used mattress."

148

"Because of the dreamlight prints laid down by other people?"

"Yes. Other people's dreamlight can be very . . . disturbing. Just to be sure I would be able to sleep at all, I brought my sleeping bag to put on the cot. I didn't trust the bedding that Grady's assistant insisted was new. Anyhow, it was all sort of embarrassing and Grady took my *eccentricities,* as he called them, as an indication of my parapsych fragility."

"How did the sleep analysis go?"

"Not very well. I only spent one night in the lab. Whatever Grady saw on the monitors that night really freaked him out. He tried to hide it but I went dream-walking while he was in the room. I could tell he was nervous. Of course, part of his anxiety may have been caused by Virgil."

"I could tell Virgil wasn't fond of him."

"I insisted on bringing Virgil into the lab with me that night. Grady viewed that as yet another sign of anxiety and fragility, of course. Anyhow, Virgil stood guard, I guess you could say. Every time Grady came into the room to check the monitors, Virgil watched him with all four eyes. Grady was very uneasy, to say the least. He acted as if he was afraid Virgil might go for his throat at any second."

"Everyone knows that when it comes to dust bunnies, by the time you see the teeth, it's too late."

"Yep."

Hannah reached up to pat Virgil a couple of times. He was fully fluffed once more and obviously enjoying the ride. Arizona Snow was securely clutched in one paw.

Elias was quiet for a moment.

"You mentioned that you *saw* Barnett's reaction to Virgil in the sleep lab," he said eventually. "Weren't you asleep?"

Her weirdness was the last thing she wanted to talk about, she decided.

"I was dreaming," she said. "For me, dreaming can be complicated. Turn left at the next corner. It will lead us to a shortcut through the DZ. It's a much faster route to the highway. We've wasted enough time as it is. Your poor team must be wondering if they're going to be locked inside those ruins indefinitely."

She held her breath but Elias did not ask any more questions about her dreaming experience.

"We'll get the crew out." He turned into the narrow lane. "The DZ really is a maze. No wonder Runner and his crew found a niche market just waiting to be exploited."

"The only people who really know their

way around are the locals who have lived here most of their lives. None of the cabdrivers from the other zones will take passengers into the DZ. You have to switch to a local cab on Ruin Street the way we did this morning."

She gave a few more directions. Some of her tension started to ease.

"Sorry about the scene back there on the street in front of my place," she said after a while.

"What scene? I come from a mining family, remember? Dad believed in raising his kids in the business. The result is that I grew up in quartz and hot-crystal camps scattered throughout the Underworld. Where I come from you don't get to call a scene a scene until someone pulls out a knife or starts throwing broken beer bottles."

CHAPTER 13

For some reason she suddenly felt a lot better. "I'm not fragile but Grady was right about one thing — I do have a few eccentricities that other people often find troubling."

"Such as?"

She clasped her hands in her lap. "I sleep alone for a reason," she said quietly.

"The dream-walking thing?"

"When I dream-walk, my aura gets very hot. It has a disturbing effect on anyone who happens to be sleeping nearby. It interferes with the other person's aura. My out-of-body experience can induce something similar in anyone who is in close proximity. But unlike me, most people aren't accustomed to such intense lucid dreaming. They wake up in the middle of a nightmare. Sometimes they think they've just died and that they've become a ghost. The sensation doesn't last long but while it does, people tend to panic."

"You did a little dream-walking this morning just before you woke up, didn't you?"

"Yes."

"I felt the shift of energy in the atmosphere. Didn't bother me."

She glanced at his ring, which had gone dark. "Probably because you're a strong talent yourself. But also because you were awake."

"Or maybe because it just didn't bother me. You said you went to Grady to get a para-psych profile for that genealogist you're working with?"

"Yes. I'm trying to trace my family tree."

"No luck at all?" Elias said.

"I hit a dead end when I tried to research my ancestors on my own. Couldn't get past my mom, who evidently had the talent. Couldn't find out anything about her parents, either. There were no leads on my father's side. So, over the years, I've hired several genealogists. None of them were helpful. Found Paxton Wilcox a couple of months ago. He's working at the leading edge of the field because he's using the latest para-genetics techniques."

"That's how you wound up at Grady Barnett's lab."

"Unfortunately. What can I say? Barnett

153

was the least expensive para-psych expert I could find. He gave me a discount because he was very intrigued by my particular version of dreamlight talent."

"Get what you pay for, I guess," Elias said.

"Gee, thanks for that insight."

"The bottom line here is that you still don't have a complete para-psych profile."

"No. I fired Grady and walked out of the lab before he could finish testing me."

"Interesting."

She frowned. "What?"

"You paid for a profile that you never received and the next thing you know you're being chased by a bunch of guys on motorcycles."

She was stunned by the implication. "You think what happened last night might be linked to Grady?"

"Damned if I know. Any chance those psi-prints inside your shop are his?"

"No," she said. "I'm absolutely certain."

"I guess that would have been too easy."

"Yeah. Grady is obsessed but it's with his research work. He wants to make his mark in the field of para-psych profiling. His goal is to publish very important, groundbreaking studies and get invited onto rez-screen talk shows. Turn right up there at the next corner."

Elias checked the rearview mirror and then returned his attention to his driving.

"We've got company," he said.

He rezzed the accelerator so quickly that Virgil was thrown backward off his perch. Hannah heard him chortling in the small rear compartment. A few seconds later he bounced up to resume his position. He waved the Arizona Snow doll, encouraging Elias to go faster.

Hannah turned around in her seat and peered through the rear window. She caught a glimpse of two helmeted figures on motorcycles.

"Turn left," she said. "They'll never find us in Bone Street."

Elias whipped the Cadence around a corner and shot down a narrow lane lined with empty, boarded-up warehouses.

"Looks like someone else knows about Bone Street," he said very softly.

He braked to a stop so suddenly that Virgil was thrown forward onto Hannah's lap. She clutched him and then caught her breath when she saw the two motorcycles that had pulled out onto Bone Street a block in front of their position.

"So much for hiding out on Bone Street," Elias said. "They know exactly where we are. We'll take cover in that warehouse. That will level the playing field somewhat. *Go.*"

He opened the driver's-side door, got out, and circled around the rear of the car. By the time he reached the passenger side, Hannah was out of the vehicle. Virgil clung to her shoulder, all four eyes and a lot of teeth showing. He gripped Arizona Snow as if the action figure were a weapon.

The old warehouse door was unlocked. Elias pushed it open and assisted Hannah through the doorway with a firm shove. He followed and swiftly turned to close the door.

"These guys don't seem to want to take no for an answer," he said.

Hannah watched through a crack in one of the boards that covered the windows. Four motorcycles halted in the lane. The big Raleigh-Stark engines continued to thunder.

"Your car," Hannah whispered.

Elias watched the lane through the same crack in the wooden panel.

"I keep telling you, my car can take care of itself," he said. He aimed the silencer through the crack. "And us, as well."

Hannah heard someone shouting over the roar of the idling motorcycles.

"They're both gone."

"Shit. Boss isn't gonna like it if we lose them

156

again —"

The rider never finished the sentence.

Hannah felt energy heighten in the shadowy space. The ring on Elias's hand sparked with energy. He rezzed the remote.

The Cadence seemed to glow as if lit from within by paranormal energy. Hannah realized she was watching it with her other senses. An instant later she felt the whisper of a paranormal shock wave. She knew it had come from the car.

High-tech crystal energy, she thought.

Outside, someone shouted a warning but the yell was cut off abruptly. A sudden silence descended on the narrow lane. The motorcycles no longer thundered. The four attackers were sprawled in the street. They did not move.

Virgil immediately lost interest in the proceedings. He was once again fully fluffed. He waved Arizona Snow in triumph.

Hannah watched the very still men in the street. "Are they — ?"

"Alive." Elias glanced at the device in his hand. "I think. Still working out a few bugs in the crystal-ware. I didn't want to risk using it with us inside the car, not at that power level. Too much chance of blowback. Might have taken us out, as well."

She swallowed hard. "I see. Wow. Okay.

Who needs a bodyguard when you've got an engineer handy?"

Elias startled her with a crack of laughter. She realized he was riding a post-burn high.

"Come on, let's get out of here," he said. "Fast. If the intention was to kidnap one or both of us, there will be a pickup crew following close behind. They may have more serious weaponry."

He got the warehouse door open again and moved outside. Hannah followed him.

The scene in the street looked like the aftermath of a bad multivehicle crash. All four motorcyclists were on the ground, unconscious. Two of the big bikes had toppled over.

Elias set about a quick search of the closest motorcycle rider. He confiscated some tech and a mag-rez pistol. Then he examined the back of the man's leather vest. Hannah could see elaborate lettering done in acid green script.

"What does it say?" she asked.

"Soldiers of Fortune," Elias said. "Looks like that's the name of the gang. But it could be a cover."

He checked the rider's heavily tattooed arm. Not satisfied, he peeled back the leather vest and looked at both bare shoulders.

He moved to another rider and repeated the process.

"What are you looking for?" Hannah asked.

"A tattoo that looks like a small tornado. That would indicate these guys are connected to an outfit called Vortex. It caused us some trouble at the Rainshadow jobsite a while back. These bikers have had a lot of ink work done, but I don't see a tornado."

"Is that good news or bad news?"

"Not sure yet, but this is starting to have the feel of a pirate operation. This bunch has all the hallmarks of hired muscle — contract workers. The Vortex people we encountered were full-time staff, so to speak. Professionals. And their gear was a lot more sophisticated, more upmarket."

Hannah shuddered. "Looks like your first hunch was correct. This is probably a case of corporate espionage. Someone paid this bunch to grab me so that I couldn't open the dreamlight gate at the Coppersmith jobsite."

"That's how it looks." Elias took out his phone and snapped off several photos of the scene and the faces of the bikers. "With luck there will be something here that will give Security a few leads."

Hannah got into the Cadence with Virgil.

Elias dragged one of the unconscious men out of the way and got behind the wheel.

"What's the fastest route out of here?" he asked.

"Depends. Are we going to go to the police or the portal jobsite?"

"The portal jobsite. We can't risk losing any more time. Also, if this is about keeping us from rescuing the team, the quickest way to end it is to get the job done."

"In that case, hang a right into that alley."

Elias rezzed the finely tuned engine and deftly guided the Cadence down a convoluted alley.

"I'll contact Coppersmith Security," he said. "They can coordinate with the Illusion Town police. I just hope we'll get cooperation from the locals."

"You will," she said. "Like Aunt Clara said, the members of the Illusion Club won't take kindly to an out-of-town gang thinking it can ride roughshod through the streets of our fair city."

"Good to know you've got the kind of city government that believes in keeping the streets safe."

CHAPTER 14

The dreamlight gate wasn't a roaring blaze of hot psi. It was a cold, senses-distorting, mind-numbing wall of paranormal night-mares. The barrier blocked the entire mouth of the great cavern.

"Alien dreamlight," Hannah said quietly. "Oddly enough, it's a lot like human dream-light. Weird to think that we have that in common with the ancients, isn't it?"

Elias looked at her. She was thrilled with the challenge of de-rezzing the dreamlight gate, he realized. There was a little heat in her eyes. Virgil appeared to be sharing her excitement. He was hunkered down on her shoulder like a furry gargoyle, his Arizona Snow figure clutched in one possessive paw.

"The ruins and the portal to the Ghost City are on the other side of that gate," Elias said. "We haven't been able to find another way in."

They had made good time on the highway

to the ruin site in the desert that was now serving as the aboveground headquarters of the Ghost City project. The descent into the catacombs had gone fairly smoothly, but once past the Rainforest gate, they had been faced with the two-hour trek through the paranormal-infused jungle to reach the portal cave.

By the time they had arrived at the camp, an ominous twilight was descending on the eerie, underground jungle. Once full night fell, travel would be nearly impossible. There were too many risks. It wasn't the wildlife that you had to worry about, Elias thought. Most of the problems were paranormal in nature — storms and rivers of energy that grew stronger and far more dangerous after dark.

The rule in the Rainforest was that if you got caught out in the open at night, you stayed put until dawn. Like it or not, he and Hannah would be spending the night at the portal jobsite.

The team's tents and equipment had been set up in the large clearing at the entrance to the vast cave system that housed the portal. The members of the Coppersmith team who had not been trapped inside the cave were watching from a safe distance.

Initially everyone had appeared greatly

relieved when Elias and Hannah had arrived. But the team's anxiety and outright skepticism was now a palpable force. A lot of people didn't think the gate could be derezzed.

"You know," Hannah said, "it looks like the Aliens were trying to send a message with this security gate. Clearly, they didn't want just anyone entering that cave."

"We assume the intention was to keep their people out of the Ghost City," Elias said. "They couldn't have known humans would show up a few thousand years later."

She smiled. "And they couldn't have known that finding ways to go through forbidden gates is pretty much a working definition of human."

"It's certainly the working definition of hot-rock mining," Elias said.

He watched Hannah examine the gate. She was intrigued but not particularly nervous. She could not take her eyes off the shimmering wall of energy. Her talent might be rare but it was the powerful and strong talents who were always compelled and fascinated by any and all forms of paranormal power.

Not unlike how he was compelled and fascinated by Hannah. His gut tightened. She looked sleek and a little dangerous in her black jeans, black pullover, black vest, and black boots. Her hair was caught up in a neat, tight bun.

She seemed unaware of the vibe between them. Either that or she was just very good at concealing her feelings. An orphan stuck with a high-end talent that made intimacy difficult and rendered long-term relationships problematic probably got a lot of practice hiding her emotions.

Hank Richman, the director of Security at the portal, came up to stand next to Elias.

"That damned gate slammed shut without warning," he said. "Hell, we didn't even realize there was a psi-gate at the entrance. We used a couple of talents to check for one but they didn't pick up anything. Nothing pinged on the para-rad detectors but that's not surprising. Down here in the Underworld we're stuck using only the most basic tech. None of the advanced stuff works in the heavy paranormal atmosphere."

"I know," Hannah said. "If it makes you feel any better, I don't think your high-tech sensors would have picked up this gate even if it had been located aboveground. It's very serious dreamlight from the deep end of the spectrum. Only another strong dreamlight talent would have detected the vibes."

Hank nodded. "I've got nine people on

the other side of that gate. None of them are inclined to panic. They wouldn't be on an advance team if they were. But that cave has got a lot of weird energy going on inside."

"Don't worry," Hannah said. "I'll get them out. This is dreamlight — my kind of dreamlight. I can disrupt the currents. That should open the gate. But things are going to get hot for a while. Tell your people to stand farther back. There might be a riptide effect. I don't want anyone caught in it."

Hank motioned to the small group of uneasy spectators.

"Give the lady some space," he said. "She says there might be a riptide effect."

No one argued. Everyone understood the dangers of a rip. The crew fell back several paces into the surrounding jungle. It dawned on Elias that the Rainforest had gone unnaturally quiet. No birds called in the heavy canopy overhead. There was no rustling in the undergrowth. Evidently the local fauna had opted to find safer sectors.

Hannah looked at him. "Aren't you going to move back, too?"

"I thought we made a pretty good team last night." He walked to stand beside her. "I might be able to give you a little extra juice if you need it."

She looked hesitant and then she held out her hand. "Hang on tight. We're about to take a walk on the wild side. If things get too rough I can give you some protection with my aura."

He gripped her hand very tightly.

He knew the instant Hannah went into her own talent. It hit him in a rush of sensation, stirring all his senses. He heard Virgil growl. The dust bunny was sleeked out, all four eyes focused on the gate.

For a couple of beats nothing seemed to be happening. And then he felt Hannah acquire a focus on some of the hot quicksilver currents in the gate. He knew she was concentrating on certain core wavelengths, looking for a way to disrupt them. It was standard operating procedure for dealing with Alien energy.

He already knew that Hannah was powerful. What he was learning now was that she could handle wild Alien energy with the elegant finesse of a brilliantly skilled musician.

At first the roiling currents of the gate responded to the delicate interference with sporadic power surges. As Hannah's intrusion grew more focused, the wall of nightmare energy responded like a great beast of prey trying to fend off an attacker. It lashed and coiled and fought the assault.

But gradually the core of the monster began to weaken. The sparking, flashing currents shimmered and thinned first at the center. The thinning radiated slowly outward. The gate became translucent and then transparent.

Now it was possible to see figures on the other side. Elias counted quickly. Relief shot through him when he realized that all nine of the crew members were alive.

Hannah made an attempt to free her hand but he tightened his grip. She abandoned the effort, clasped his fingers more firmly than ever, and started moving toward the gate.

He realized she needed to be closer to the epicenter of the violent storm of nightmares.

They were so close to the weakened barrier now that the raw energy was lifting the hair on his arms and the back of his neck. It was like being caught in an invisible wind. He could sense the primal horrors waiting to spring at his conscious mind and drown it in the ultimate nightmare — one that would not end.

The gate crackled with one last furious burst of energy.

And then it winked out of existence.

There was a moment of stunned silence

167

from the small crowd of onlookers.

And then the riptide struck.

There was a great surge of energy. Elias could feel it trying to drag him under into unconsciousness. He knew Hannah was not immune in spite of her talent.

They held hands and faced the storm together, fighting the wave of night. Somewhere in the darkness Virgil growled in fury. Elias sensed that somehow the dust bunny was adding his own energy to the battle via the psychic bond he shared with Hannah. The Arizona Snow figure glowed with raw crystal power for a few tense seconds.

A moment later it was over.

The crowd inside the cave rushed toward the newly opened gate. But the leader put up a hand, signaling them to stop. Reluctantly, they halted. Elias recognized Derek Hanford.

"Mr. Coppersmith?" Derek called. "Is that you?"

"It's me, Derek. Bring your team out."

Derek grinned and waved the rest of the crew out of the gate. They did not need a second invitation. Eight of them hurried out into the clearing. Derek followed. He was a Coppersmith leader to the core, Elias thought. In an emergency, the first priority was the welfare of the team. The guy in

168

charge doesn't leave until everyone else is safe.

Elias released Hannah's hand and clapped Derek on the shoulder. "Good job, Hanford. You kept everyone together. I'll make sure Dad knows how well you handled this situation."

"Thanks," Derek said. "Had to be sure it was you. Couldn't trust our eyes inside that damn cave. People started hallucinating. Every time we got near the gate it tried to suck us into a nightmare. Almost lost Parker. He got burned but we pulled him back in time. He'll be okay."

The rescued team members and their colleagues clustered around Elias, thanking him. He shook his head.

"It wasn't me," he said. He turned to introduce them to Hannah. "Meet the lady who opened the gate."

Hannah was standing off by herself. *She feels like the outsider here,* Elias thought.

"This is Hannah," he said, aware of a rush of pride and certainty. "My wife."

There was a chorus of whistles and shouts of congratulations. Elias was pretty sure he heard Hannah mumble something about the marriage being just an MC but no one was listening. Everyone was in the grip of euphoric relief. No one was paying attention to details.

Hank Richman grinned. "Got a lot to celebrate tonight, boss. Lucky for the two of you, there's a spare tent. We'll make sure to set it up a little ways from the main campsite so you'll have some privacy. After all, you're still on your honeymoon."

CHAPTER 15

"Well, this is awkward," Hannah said, careful to keep her voice very low.

They were alone in the small, two-person tent. An amber lamp burned on a stand between the twin cots.

Night had descended as it always did in the Rainforest, hard and fast. But the campsite was illuminated with softly glowing amber lanterns set up at the entrance to each tent and around the perimeter.

In addition to the amber lamps a silvery paranormal energy radiated from the interior of the portal cave. The combination ensured that the deep night of the jungle was kept at bay.

Virgil had spent the earlier part of the evening dining heartily on camp food and basking in the attention of a number of new fans. But when people headed for their tents, he had disappeared. Hannah suspected that he was showing off his Arizona

Snow action figure to some wild dust bunny pals. The result was that he was not available to play chaperone.

Not that she and Elias needed a chaperone, she reminded herself. They were roommates tonight, not honeymooners.

But it was going to be a very long night because she was afraid to go to sleep.

Elias sat on his cot, removing his boots. At her comment, he paused to survey the intimate interior of the tent. Then he shrugged and went back to his task.

"It won't be a problem," he said.

He kept his voice low, too. The tent they were sharing had been pitched a discreet distance from the main encampment and the normal jungle noises had returned now that the dreamlight gate had been opened. Nevertheless, there was still a chance they might be overheard by one of the security guards making the rounds or someone who got up to use the facilities.

"I think I can promise you that it will be a problem if I fall asleep and start dreamwalking," she said. She huddled on the edge of her cot, gripping the edge on either side of her thighs. She eyed Elias's cot less than two feet away. "There's not much room in here. My vibes are bound to interfere with your dreamlight once you fall asleep."

Elias yanked off his other boot. "We don't know that. We've never run the experiment."

"You and I have never run the experiment, but I am not without some real-world experience," she said evenly. "I'm telling you, it's going to be really awkward if you start screaming at three in the morning."

Elias flashed her an unnervingly wicked grin. "Depends on the reason I'm screaming."

She groaned. "You're not going to take this seriously, are you?"

His amusement vanished in a heartbeat. "Here's the thing, Hannah. Neither of us has any choice about where we sleep tonight. I'm sure as hell not going to let you spend the night alone."

"Because you want everyone to believe we're really married?"

"We *are* really married."

He looked irritated. She reminded herself that he'd had a long, hard day, too.

"You know what I mean," she said.

She took off her own boots and went to work unrolling her sleeping bag on her cot.

Elias watched her. "Yes, I know what you mean. But we're going to spend the night together as a precaution."

"A precaution against what? We're safe with your people now. A Coppersmith

173

Security team is patrolling the perimeter as we speak. You said this jobsite has round-the-clock security."

"Right."

"What is the problem?"

For a few seconds Elias sat quietly on the edge of the cot, forearms resting on his knees, hands loosely clasped. She got the impression that he was trying to decide how much he wanted to say to her. Comprehension slammed through her.

"I get it," she said softly. "You're wondering if what happened here — the gate closing — was an accident, aren't you?"

"I don't know," he said quietly. "You're the expert. What do you think?"

She considered the question for a moment. "Only a dreamlight talent as strong as I am could have deliberately rezzed it. Got anyone like that here on your team?"

"No. At least I don't think so. But it's possible that someone faked their resume to conceal a heavy talent. That wouldn't be the biggest surprise in the world. Really powerful talents do it all the time."

"Because a lot of employers are afraid to hire very powerful talents," Hannah said. "Look, for what it's worth, I think the triggered-by-accident scenario is more likely. You said yourself there's a lot of

174

unknown radiation inside that cavern. But if it gives you any peace of mind, I can promise you that the gate won't be closing again. I obliterated the frequencies. That's why the riptide was so powerful."

He smiled a little. "Thanks. That does give me some peace of mind. But that still leaves us with the problem of those bikers. Until I figure out what's going on, I don't want you to be alone. I'm responsible for your safety."

His stern, stubborn expression warned her that there was no point trying to persuade him that he did not have to play bodyguard tonight. He felt responsible for her safety and he was the kind of man who took his responsibilities seriously.

"Okay," she said. "I understand." She climbed into her sleeping bag without taking off any more clothes. "I'll try to stay awake."

He looked grimly amused. "I wondered why you were drinking coffee after dinner."

"The thing is, I'm not sure the caffeine will be enough to keep me awake. I burned a lot of energy taking down that gate. My senses are exhausted. But maybe, if I do fall asleep, I won't dream. It's not like I do it every night."

"What does cause you to dream-walk?"

"I can do it on command. It's a form of

lucid dreaming. I use it to find things when I go looking for an artifact or something that has been lost. But it also happens when my intuition is trying to tell me something." She waved a hand. "On those occasions I don't have much control over the process. But the problem here at the jobsite has been resolved and, like I said, I'm pretty wrecked. So maybe I won't dream tonight."

His mouth kicked up a little at the corner. "Does that mean there's not much chance that I'll end up screaming at three in the morning?"

She glared at him. "Not funny."

"Sorry. Just a little honeymoon humor."

"This is not a honeymoon." She groaned. "And no fair setting me up with a bad joke. Go to sleep."

"Okay. You do the same. We both need the rest."

Elias removed his flamer from his utility belt and put it on the floor beside his cot, within easy reach. He turned down the amber lamp, plunging the interior of the tent into dense shadows. The Rainforest was a bioengineered wonder but it was under-ground. There was no moon and no stars. The Aliens had created an artificial source of sunlight during the daylight hours but evidently they hadn't deemed it necessary

to provide nighttime illumination. Nevertheless, the proximity of the softly glowing cave
and the amber lanterns ensured that some
light filtered through the thin walls of the
tent, enveloping the interior in deep shadows.

Hannah listened to Elias climb into the
Coppersmith-issue sleeping bag that one of
the staff had given him. There was some
rustling and then things became very quiet.

After a while she stirred and folded her
hands behind her head.

"Are you awake?" she whispered.

"I am now."

"How will you go about figuring out who
sent those bikers to grab me?" she asked.
"Assuming it was me they were after and
not you."

"The first question you ask in a situation
like this is, why? When I know the answer,
I'll know where to go from there."

She smiled a little. "That's my first question, too."

"What do you mean?"

"When I go dream-walking, the first question I have to remember to ask is, why am I
searching for the object? Knowing why a
client wants it helps guide me."

"What happens if you don't like the answer?"

"I turn down the job and make some polite excuse."

"Are you always looking for something when you dream-walk?" Elias asked.

"Always. I go in asking questions but I rarely get straightforward answers."

"That's the nature of intuition. You'll get a flash of insight but you don't always know where it's going to take you." Elias paused. "And you don't always like the answers you get."

"True," she said. "Do you like being director of research for the Coppersmith R-and-D labs?"

"Yes. But I think that gig will be coming to an end, soon."

"Why?"

"Because it's become obvious that the Ghost City project is too big and too important to be managed as part of the regular R-and-D system. Dad has decided to spin off the venture. It will be set up as a separate division with its own corporate hierarchy and its own dedicated labs."

"Your father is going to put you in charge of the special labs for this project, isn't he?"

"It's not like he's got a lot of choice. My brother, Rafe, doesn't want the job. He opened up his own private investigation business a few months ago right after he got

178

married. Consults for the FBPI and Jones and Jones."

"What about your sister?"

"Leanna is the real scion in the clan, assuming we've actually got one. She received all the executive talents in the Coppersmith gene pool. Everyone assumes she'll be taking Dad's place as the CEO of the company one of these days."

"What about you?"

"Me? I'm the family geek. I was born for R and D."

"That makes you a geek?" Hannah asked.

"I have it on good authority that I make a really boring cocktail-party guest."

"Whose authority?"

"Various and assorted dates."

"If you don't do cocktail party chatter very well, you should probably consider other venues for your dates," Hannah said.

"Hey, thanks for the suggestion. Why didn't I think of that? I could try taking a date out for an evening of fun and games — running from a horde of would-be kidnappers on motorcycles, for example. Then we could visit a creepy carnival featuring a lot of weird Arcane artifacts. Wrap things up with a romantic Marriage of Convenience at a tacky MC wedding mill and spend our wedding night at a low-rent motel in the

Shadow Zone. The next morning we would wake up with no memory of what happened."

She smiled into the shadows. "All in all, it sounds more interesting than a cocktail party."

"Think so?"

She turned on her side. "Good night, Elias."

"Good night, Hannah."

She thought about the flamer he had put on the floor of the tent next to his cot.

To date, as far as the experts had been able to determine, the only creatures in the Rainforest that occasionally proved dangerous to humans were other humans.

CHAPTER 16

The dream-walking started the way it always did. Her doppelgänger got up from the cot and paused to look down at herself. The dreamer was curled on her side, snuggled into her special silk-lined sleeping bag. She appeared to be sound asleep. But she knew she was dream-walking.

She'd been lucid dreaming since her teens but she still got a little jolting thrill of panic and wonder each time she found herself going into the out-of-body experience. After all these years the one thing she knew for certain about her dream-walking was that it always had a purpose. It was her intuition speaking to her. It was up to her to figure out what her doppelgänger was trying to tell her.

Her doppelgänger looked down at Elias. He was sleeping on his side, still clad in a T-shirt and his field trousers. As she watched, he stirred.

Her dreaming self knew that he was starting

to sense the vibes of her strong dreamlight currents.

"I need to wake up before I disturb his aura," the dreamer said in the language of dreams.

"There's something important happening," the doppelgänger said. "Something that could change everything."

As her doppelgänger watched, Elias opened his eyes. He seemed a little bemused at first, but not alarmed. After a few beats he opened the sleeping bag, sat up slowly, and swung his legs over the edge of the cot. He looked at the dreamer. He was curious now; intrigued. He did not look like a man who thought he was trapped in a nightmare.

"He's not afraid," the doppelgänger said.

"Is that all you have to say to me?" the dreamer asked.

"What other man has been able to sleep so close to you and not wake up in a panic when you went dream-walking?"

"Okay, so he's strong. But let's not push the envelope here. I'm going to wake up now."

Hannah awoke on a hot rush of adrenaline. A shudder went through her as she crossed the never-never land between the dreamscape and the waking state. In the next breath she had her bearings again. She was no longer dream-walking.

She opened her eyes and saw Elias sitting

quietly on the side of his cot. He watched her with a little heat in his eyes.

"Was that it?" he asked matter-of-factly. "Were you dream-walking?"

"Yes," she said. She unzipped her sleeping bag and sat up slowly. "Are you . . . all right?"

"I'm fine. Your vibes woke me up, but no big deal."

She wasn't sure where to go with that. No other man had ever described the experience as *no big deal.*

"What was it like for you?" she finally asked.

He was silent for a moment. She held her breath, afraid of the answer.

"Different," he said at last.

"Bad?" she asked, more uneasy than ever. "I tried to tell you —"

"No," he said. "Not bad. Just unusual." He seemed to be searching for the right word. "Intimate."

"Intimate?"

He nodded, satisfied with the word. "I think that's the best way to describe it."

It was her turn to be confused. "Creepy intimate or weird intimate?"

"More like sexy intimate."

She felt the heat rise in her face and was grateful for the shadows.

"No one has ever described it that way," she said. "When I spent the night in Grady's lab he told me the instruments registered severe disruption of my dreamlight patterns during the dream-walking episode. He said he had seen more stable patterns in dreamlight talents who were locked up in parapsych wards. He said it was a wonder I was still . . . sane. Between you and me, I'm pretty sure he has a few doubts."

"I've known some crazy talents. You're not one of them. Obviously, Barnett's instruments were not sophisticated enough to measure your aura patterns accurately."

"How can you be sure of that?"

"Hannah, I'm an engineer with a talent for working with paranormal crystal energy. In addition, I am descended from a family with a gene pool that is anything but normal. I can tell you with absolute certainty that there is still a hell of a lot we don't know about para-biophysics and the human aura. What's more, our instruments for measuring those things are still extremely primitive."

"But you think my dreamlight energy feels . . . normal?" she asked.

"Your aura is no more normal than mine. But it's strong and it's stable."

"Grady said —"

"Do we have to talk about Barnett tonight?"

She caught her breath. "Excellent question. No, we don't have to talk about him."

"You're not exactly normal. Neither am I. Coppersmiths don't have a problem with not being normal. You could say it's a family tradition."

"You don't know how much that means to me," she said. "Thank you."

"It's not a compliment, damn it. It's just a fact."

She smiled. "It's the best gift you could have given me tonight."

"Yeah, well, I wouldn't call it a gift."

"Depends on your point of view, I suppose. You see, so many people have told me that my para-psych profile is creepy weird that, deep down, part of me believes it. The fact that I've got certain intimacy issues has just reinforced the negative stuff."

"Understandable."

"Well, enough about me. Let's talk about you."

"Okay," Elias said. But he sounded wary.

"When I was dream-walking a few minutes ago, my dopp was trying to tell me something important about you."

"Your dopp?"

"Doppelgänger."

185

"That's what you call your dream-walking self?"

"Yes. When I go into the lucid dream trance it's like there's two of me. The metaphysical me and the . . . other . . . me, the physical me."

"What was your doppelgänger telling you?"

"That's just it. I don't know. All I'm sure of is that it was important. I suppose sooner or later I'll figure it out."

"It's been a rough couple of days. You need sleep."

"We both need sleep," she said.

But she made no move to crawl back inside the sleeping bag. Elias did not move, either. He just watched her, his eyes burning with a smoldering kind of heat.

She did not want to sleep, she thought. Not just yet. A sparkly delight, a rare excitement, was unfurling deep inside her, heating her blood and stirring her senses — all of her senses.

The hot, giddy sensation was probably the result of lack of sleep combined with the primal paranormal energy of the surrounding Rainforest, she thought. Not to mention the subtle influence of the paranormal vibes whispering out of the portal cave.

"Would you mind very much if I kissed

186

you before I go back to sleep?" she said.

There was a short, tension-infused silence. Her heart sank. She had misread the vibe in the atmosphere between them. Okay, maybe he didn't think she was borderline crazy, but that didn't necessarily mean he wanted to go to bed with her.

She was trying to come up with a diplomatic way out of what had to be the worst moment of her always awkward social life when Elias moved. He reached across the short, shadowy space between them and stroked the side of her cheek with his fingertips. His hand was a little rough but in an exciting way, and very strong. It was the hand of a man who worked with tools and raw quartz. It was the hand of a man who had spent time in the Rainforest and mining camps — the hand of a man who knew how to handle power, his own as well as the kind locked in hot gemstones and charged amber.

That just made the tender gesture all the more beguiling.

"I would like it very much if you kissed me," he said.

He wrapped his palm around the back of her neck.

She shivered.

Gently he tugged her toward him.

Excitement splashed through her. He wanted her. And she wanted him.

She literally threw herself across the short distance that separated the cots, going straight into his arms.

Elias groaned, the sound low and rough, as though it emanated from some deep, secret place inside him. He fell back onto his cot, taking her with him. She sprawled on top of his hard, muscled chest, intensely aware of the heat of his body.

He captured her face between his palms and kissed her, fiercely urgent and seemingly desperate.

She could feel the power and the strength of him through the layers of clothing. His erection strained against the fabric of his trousers. She reached down and covered him with her hand. He sucked in his breath as if he were in pain. But in the next moment he found the sensitive skin of her throat with his mouth and it was her turn to catch her breath.

She gasped and pressed herself more tightly against the whole length of his body. His hands slid to her waist and then up under the hem of her black pullover. She felt him pause.

"You wear a bra to bed?" he asked, his voice a hoarse whisper in her ear.

"Not usually," she said, chagrined. So much for the cool, always-in-control image. "Tonight is different."

"You can say that again."

With a few determined moves he stripped off the pullover and then the practical, very unsexy bra she always wore when she went into the Underworld.

When she was nude from the waist up he somehow managed to reverse their positions on the narrow camp bed so that she wound up on her back. His breathing was growing harsh now. The knowledge that he was so deeply aroused kicked her excitement level higher.

He crowded close along the length of her and went to work unfastening her jeans. He managed to haul them down over her hips. When he got them all the way to her ankles, she kicked them off.

He removed her panties inch by inch. By the time they went sailing over the side of the cot she was soaking wet between her thighs. A great urgency was building within her.

He stroked her intimately and groaned again when he found her hot and damp.

Reluctantly, he freed himself to roll to his feet beside the cot. He peeled off his trousers and briefs. When he lowered himself back onto the cot, she made a place for him between her legs, welcoming him.

He mantled her with the hard, masculine weight of his body. Again he reached down between them and stroked her in a shatteringly intimate way that left her breathless and consumed with a dizzying sense of discovery.

She clenched her fingers in his hair and raised her knees.

"Now," she whispered into his ear. "Now."

She felt him pushing into her, slowly but with unrelenting force. The skin of his back was damp with sweat. He was fighting to control himself.

He filled her with a slow, deep thrust. The sensation was almost unbearable. She had never come so close to the precipice.

Belatedly, she realized that she was about to lose control. She never lost control. She did not dare to lose control.

The old panic rose like a tide within her. She froze.

Elias went very still and raised his head. When he spoke, his voice was a harsh, grating whisper.

"Hannah? Are you . . . all right?"

"Yes. No." She clutched him close even as she knew she should let him go. "It's just that I'm afraid that if we . . . finish this . . .

it might affect your aura."

He rested his damp forehead against hers. "My aura can damn well take care of itself."

She couldn't help herself. She laughed. It was a soft, shaky laugh, but it was real.

"Like your car?" she said.

"Something like that."

She thought about how they had held hands and walked through the dreamlight gate that guarded the Midnight Carnival, and then she remembered how he had gripped her hand while she took down the portal cave barrier. She had trusted him to know his strengths and limitations on those two occasions. She would trust him now.

"Okay," she said. "Okay."

She wrapped her legs around him. He groaned and started to move within her, going deeper and harder and faster.

Once again the sweet, frantic tension built rapidly within her. She was caught up in a rushing river of energy that tangled her senses and stole her breath. And Elias was there with her. She stopped trying to resist the inevitable.

He moved within her one last time, and this time she tightened herself around him, refusing to let him withdraw again.

They plunged over the falls together.

He covered her mouth with his own,

silencing her shriek of pleasure and surprise. The kiss also muffled his deep, aching growl of release.

The energy of their clashing auras was a thrill ride unlike any other rush Hannah had ever known.

And then, for a heartbeat or two, she was certain that the currents of her aura were actually resonating with the waves emanating from Elias's energy field.

It was the most profoundly intimate experience she had ever known.

So this is what it's like, she thought as she tumbled into the pool below the waterfall.

CHAPTER 17

The dream-walking started again . . .

"What now?" the dreamer asked, annoyed by the interruption to what had been an otherwise luxuriously peaceful, dream-free sleep. It was the first time she had gone to sleep in a man's arms without suffering unfortunate repercussions.

But her doppelgänger refused to pay attention. She rose from the camp bed and looked down at the dreamer.

"Get up," the doppelgänger said in the silent language of dreams.

The dreamer tried to resist.

"It's too quiet," the doppelgänger said.

This was not an observation. It was a warning. The dreamer knew better than to ignore the urgent message her intuition was sending.

Reluctantly, the dreamer stirred. The doppelgänger returned to the cot. The metaphysical and the physical merged once more.

The shock brought Hannah fully awake,

her heart pounding. Instinctively she tried to sit up but something heavy pinned her to the cot. In a wild panic now, she fought the weight.

"Easy," Elias said. He spoke directly into her ear. "Hush."

The weight was abruptly removed from her chest. She realized in a somewhat blurry fashion that it had been Elias's arm wrapped around her that had briefly trapped her. She took some deep breaths, trying to calm the rush of adrenaline and psi.

But there was another kind of weight in the atmosphere. It pressed on her, urging her to sink back into sleep. She struggled to resist it, automatically rezzing her talent.

The oppressive sensation receded.

Her first thought was that Elias had been wrong. His aura couldn't handle her dream-light currents, after all. At least he hadn't awakened screaming. But then, this was Elias. It would take a lot to make him wake up in a raw panic.

"Sorry," she mumbled, mortified. "I'm not used to sleeping with anyone."

"Quiet." He touched his fingers to her lips. "Feel the silence?"

She started to ask him what he meant. But the doppelgänger's words came back to her. *It's too quiet.*

194

It was as if the entire camp had been smothered in a senses-muffling fog. She had to use a lot of energy to resist the tug of a deep sleep.

"Yes," she said. "I can feel it."

Satisfied that she had received the message, Elias released her and sat up on the edge of the cot. She watched him pull on his trousers and boots with quick, efficient moves. He scooped up the flamer and went to the entrance of the tent. His broad shoulders were silhouetted against the soft glow of the amber lantern that burned at the entrance.

The stone in his ring glowed with a dark, paranormal fire. She knew then that he was using his talent to fend off the pressing weight of an unnatural sleep.

"Get dressed," Elias ordered softly.

But she was already on her feet. She struggled into her panties and jeans, ignoring the bra. She yanked the pullover down over her head and shoved her feet into the ankle boots.

Elias unfastened the flap that sealed the entrance of the tent. Four eyes, two of them a predatory yellow-gold, stared into the interior.

Virgil blinked and scurried through the opening. Hannah caught him and plopped

195

him on her shoulder. He was sleeked out, ready for the hunt. There was no welcoming chortle and no growl. Like all natural-born predators he was at his most dangerous when he went silent. She noticed that he still had his Arizona Snow doll.

Elias was moving quietly, too. He made almost no sound when he eased out of the tent. He paused a moment and then motioned for Hannah to follow him.

When she stepped through the opening she realized that the heavy silence weighed like a shroud on the entire campsite. The amber lanterns still glowed, illuminating the scene, but nothing moved.

"There's no security," Elias said, keeping his voice low. "Whoever did this probably took the guards down first."

She wanted to ask him why he was so certain that the frightening silence had been induced by a human. There was, after all, a great deal of unknown energy drifting through the Rainforest. But this didn't seem like the right time to get into a technical discussion of the problem.

He led the way through the orderly rows of tents. No one stirred. When he reached the perimeter he stopped and crouched beside what appeared at first glance to be a lump of laundry. It took Hannah a couple of seconds to realize that it was a man dressed in the uniform of a security guard. She caught her breath, her pulse skidding wildly.

Elias touched the guard's throat and then tried shaking the man's shoulder. There was no response.

"He's alive," Elias said quietly. "Just fast asleep. I don't think I can wake him."

Hannah went closer and jacked up her talent. The dreamlight in the guard's aura was strong but dark.

"He's in a very deep sleep, more like a trance," she said.

Elias looked around at the unnaturally still scene. "Someone put everyone under."

"I'm not claiming a vast amount of experience in this sort of thing, but I do know a fair amount about dreamlight," she said. "I think it's safe to say that a single talent could not have mustered the kind of energy it would take to put so many people into such a deep trance."

"I agree. I'm not aware of any human-made para-tech that could do this, either. Even if some lab has come up with a device powerful enough to put a lot of people under simultaneously, it wouldn't function well in the Underworld. We can barely get amber lanterns and flamers to work down here."

Hannah looked at him. "That leaves Alien tech, doesn't it?"

"That's the most logical conclusion. Looks like someone found a really interesting artifact and figured out how to use it."

"So why aren't we sound asleep?"

"Got a hunch it was your talent that saved you," Elias said. "Your ability to handle dreamlight probably gives you some natural immunity to whatever did this."

"What about you?"

He held up his hand, displaying the dark fire in his ring. "This is my own private alarm system."

"But why would someone do this to a camp full of people?"

"I don't know for sure yet, but my working hypothesis is that whoever is behind this is the same bastard who tried to trap nine people inside the ruins."

"Pirates?"

"Probably — with the help of someone on the inside."

"You're sure of that?"

"It's the only explanation that makes sense. I'm going to try to wake Hank Richman."

"If he's locked in a trance like this guard,

I might be able to bring him out of it."

"And the others?"

"I think so, but it will take time and a lot of energy."

"Richman, first; he's the head of security," Elias said.

He led the way to one of the private tents at the edge of the clearing. The waterproof plastic flap that served as a door was closed but unsealed. Elias pushed it aside and aimed a flashlight into the interior.

"Richman is gone," he said. "What the hell happened here?"

"Want me to take a look? If I get a fix on his psi-prints inside the tent, I can probably follow them to see where he went."

"You can make out psi-prints in this environment?"

She knew he was referring to the heavy atmosphere of the Rainforest.

"If he went into the jungle I won't be able to track him," she said. "It's an ocean of paranormal energy. But if he's still here in the clearing, I should be able to see his prints, particularly if he was in the grip of some strong emotion — fear or anxiety or alarm."

"Take a look."

Hannah cautiously rezzed her senses and focused on the interior of the tent. Hot, disturbed energy swirled on everything that the occupant had touched — the floor, the bed, the pack in the corner.

She got a fix and looked down at the glowing prints on the bare ground outside the tent.

"Richman was really jacked," she said. "I think I can follow his trail, at least through the camp."

"All right." Elias started to let the flap fall back over the entrance but he paused to give the interior another survey. "I don't see the flamer or his jungle knife. He took both with him."

"It's hard to determine specific emotions in psi-prints," Hannah said. "But I'm pretty sure that Richman was scared and excited."

"Richman is a hunter-talent. Maybe he was able to sense the disturbance of the trance energy, just as we did, and used his talent to resist it. Probably got up to see what was wrong."

"Maybe."

She concentrated on Richman's prints. It wasn't easy because there were a lot of hot tracks on the ground. In the last twenty-four hours, Richman and several other members of the team had spent a great deal of time anxiously milling around the clearing, waiting for the rescue of their trapped colleagues. In the process they had laid down a lot of tracks.

But tonight Richman's fresh prints burned with something very close to panic.

She was so intent on reading the dreamlight that she did not notice where she was until Elias caught her gently by the arm.

"That's far enough," he said. "Take a look."

She caught her breath when she saw that they were standing in front of the de-rezzed dreamlight gate. Richman had gone through it and into the cave.

"He's in there," she said. "And there's no sign that he came back out."

Elias studied the glowing entrance of the cavern. "You're sure he's still inside?"

"Positive. Why would he go in there?"

"Good question."

"He may be in trouble," Hannah said. She glanced at Elias. In the paranormal radiance of the cave energy his profile looked hard and grim. "You want to go inside and look for him, don't you?"

"Yes. But I don't want to leave you alone, not until we figure out what happened out here."

She suppressed the flicker of dread that iced her insides. She hated doing missing-persons work. In her experience things never ended well. Either the missing person in question did not want to be found or the person commissioning the search did not like what awaited at the conclusion of the search.

But Elias needed her help. And like it or not, she was good at this kind of search.

"I'll go with you," she said. "You're going to need my help finding him once you're inside."

Elias hesitated. "Any indication that he followed someone else into the cave?"

She stopped focusing on Richman's prints and studied the layers of dreamlight tracks at the entrance of the cavern.

"I don't think so. There were nine people trapped in here for several hours and they were all very anxious, so there are a lot of hot prints scattered around. But the only fresh tracks I can make out heading directly into the cavern are Richman's."

Elias gave the silent camp one last considering look. Then he turned back.

"All right," he said. "But stick close. There's a lot we don't know about the energy inside this cave or the Ghost City on the other side of the portal."

"Don't worry. I don't plan to wander off on my own and get lost."

They walked through the open gate, following the path of psi-prints. Virgil was still sleeked out and uncharacteristically quiet.

Once inside the vast cavern, the paranormal illumination seemed much more intense. The rocky walls glowed with a pale, grayish light. The floor seethed with energy, too, making it harder, but not impossible, to follow Richman's prints.

"He walked through the cavern," she said. "Straight to that tunnel on the right."

"That leads to the portal ruins," Elias said. "What the hell is he doing here tonight?"

They walked deeper into the cavern, following the hot prints through a glowing tunnel. It seemed to Hannah that there was something ominous about the energy inside the cavern. It stirred her senses, but not in a good way. Unlike the Rainforest and the green-quartz catacombs, it didn't give her a pleasant buzz. It was as if, with each step they took, they were being warned off.

Automatically she reached up to touch Virgil. He muttered in her ear. It was clear he was still on high alert. Like Elias, she thought.

"What is this place?" she asked softly.

"At this point, all we know for certain is that it serves as an entrance to the Ghost City," Elias said. "My brother discovered another portal a while back but it is red-hot because of a major psi-firestorm in the ruins. Rafe can get through it and a handful of very strong talents can navigate the storm. But there was no way we could take a working crew inside."

"How did you find this entrance?"

"Rafe got me through the storm to the first portal. I was able to gather a fair amount of data. Armed with that information, the lab techs and I were able to come up with a way of detecting the unique energy of a portal. After that, we did things the old-fashioned way: we went prospecting."

"And you discovered this portal."

"Rafe happens to have a talent for prospecting," Elias said.

"But now he's a private investigator?"

"Turns out he'd rather hunt bad guys and find answers for people who need answers."

She smiled. "I get that. But you like the engineering side of the mining business."

"Like they say, it's in the blood. But finding another portal was just the beginning. After that we had to go back to the drawing board to come up with a way to navigate the energy inside the Ghost City. Amber doesn't work well in there."

"You discovered something that does work?"

"Yes. There's a certain kind of quartz that can be tuned to the energy in the city. But the quartz is rare. At the moment we've only got five prototype keys. The core mission of this current exploration team is to test those key stones and calibrate the frequencies."

"Got any theories about the Ghost City?"

"None that hold water. Some of the experts on the team have suggested that it was an Alien burial ground."

Hannah shivered. "I can see how they might have come to that conclusion."

"If you think it's weird here in the cavern, you should see what's on the other side of the portal."

"Do you think it's possible that you're going to be conducting mining operations in a big Alien graveyard?"

Elias hesitated. "Who knows? We haven't had a chance to go very far into the city. Like I said, we're still in the testing and calibration stages with the prototype keys."

"And now your director of Security has decided to go to the portal alone."

"That raises a hell of a lot of questions," Elias said. "You know, it occurs to me that whatever put the rest of the team into a deep sleep might have had a different effect

205

on Richman."

"What do you mean?" Hannah asked.

"Think he might be sleepwalking or in some kind of hypnotic trance?"

She studied the burning prints on the tunnel floor. "I can't say for sure, but I don't think that's the case. There's a lot of stress and tension in his prints. People who are in the grip of a trance don't usually generate this kind of energy. Neither do sleepwalkers. They appear unnaturally calm. I think Richman is wide awake and he's in a hurry."

"There's the entrance to the portal chamber," Elias said.

Hannah looked at the glowing opening in the cavern wall. The energy radiating from the inner chamber was much more intense than the currents emitted by the cavern walls. Instead of a murky gray light, the portal room glowed with a dazzling quicksilver energy. It was as if hundreds of small lightning bolts were snapping and crackling inside the chamber.

Richman's prints went through the opening.

"He's inside," Hannah said. "No sign that he came out, at least not through this entrance."

"There is no other way out except through the portal," Elias said. "He'd need one of the keys. He has no reason to go into the Ghost City, and even if he did, he wouldn't be fool enough to try it without backup. Wait here."

When he started forward, Virgil rumbled.

"Elias, stop," Hannah said urgently.

Elias paused and glanced back at Virgil. "Something you're trying to tell me, pal?"

Virgil muttered.

"That's not his warning growl," Hannah said. "But I don't think we're going to like whatever is inside that chamber."

Elias readied the flamer and unsheathed his knife.

"Richman," he called. "This is Coppersmith. Can you hear me?"

There was no response.

Elias moved to the chamber doorway. He flattened his back against the wall and looked around the corner.

"Damn," he said. "He's in there, all right. And he's down."

He went swiftly through the doorway. Hannah followed him. The bright energy was disorienting. It was like walking into the middle of a lightning storm. The flashing sparks of energy made it almost impossible to focus with her normal vision. She had to rez a little talent to take in the scene.

The first thing she saw was the circular,

colonnaded ruin that dominated the center of the chamber. The columns were capped with a dome-shaped roof. Instead of the familiar green stone, the structure was made of a strange silvery quartz.

A pool of dazzling energy shimmered in the floor of the ruin. A flight of steps led down into the pool and disappeared beneath the surface.

The second thing she saw was Hank Richman's body. It was crumpled on the floor of the ruin not far from the edge of the brilliant pool. A river of blood ran across the quartz floor and spilled over the edge.

There was a knife on the floor near one of Richman's hands. It was stained with blood.

Elias crouched beside the body and felt for a pulse. He shook his head and got to his feet.

"We're too late," he said.

Hannah hugged herself and turned away from the sight of the body.

"This is why I hate doing missing-persons work," she whispered. "It always ends badly."

Elias did not seem to hear her. She realized he was busy sorting through facts and plausible scenarios.

"There must have been another person in this chamber tonight," he said. "That person

208

murdered Richman. It's the only possible explanation."

"But we didn't pass anyone on the way in here," Hannah pointed out. She looked around the sparking, flashing chamber. "Are you sure there's no other exit?"

"Positive. But that doesn't change the facts on the ground. There must have been someone else in here. Hank hasn't been dead very long. The blood is still fresh. See any recent prints besides his?"

Hannah refocused her talent on the floor of the portal chamber. Hot psi-prints burned.

"Yes," she said. She took a breath. "The killer entered this chamber and left it the same way. He used the portal pool."

"Call me psychic but I had a feeling you were going to say that."

A whisper of familiar energy feathered Hannah's senses. It wasn't portal energy. It was another kind; energy that she recognized.

She turned slowly, searching for the source. It wasn't easy searching the chamber because the dazzling light made it difficult to focus. But she found what she was looking for behind one of the silver quartz columns.

The relic was small, only a few inches

across and shaped in a gentle curve. But the instant she touched it she knew that it had not been created for a human hand. It was made of a transparent crystal that was nearly invisible in the sparking, flashing room.

"What did you find?" Elias asked.

"It's a relic," she said. "Alien. I don't know who murdered Hank Richman but I think I know what triggered the dreamlight gate. And I'm pretty sure why the entire camp went into a trance tonight."

CHAPTER 18

Two of the five portal keys were missing from the equipment locker.

The whispers began to circulate around the jobsite as soon as the initial shock of the murder wore off and people learned of the missing keys.

The gossip gained strength, feeding on the incendiary fuel provided by fear and speculation. Elias knew that Hannah was aware of the low-voiced murmurs and the suspicious glances angled in her direction.

"Your people think that I'm responsible for using that relic to put the camp into a trance last night," she said quietly. "They figure I'm involved in the theft of the keys because I was the only stranger in their midst; the unknown quantity. They're convinced I murdered Hank Richman."

He wanted to reassure her but there was no point lying. The rumors were spreading like wildfire.

They were standing at the entrance of their tent, drinking coffee and pretending to ignore the veiled glances. Virgil was sticking close to Hannah, hovering protectively on her shoulder. Elias figured the dust bunny could sense the vibe in the atmosphere.

The entire camp had been in the process of awakening from the trance by the time he and Hannah and Virgil emerged from the ruins with the relic and Hank Richman's body.

Aboveground, moving a body at a crime scene before a proper investigation had been conducted was a crime in itself. But the rules were different in the Underworld. Getting the body to a lab on the surface as quickly as possible was the primary goal. The natural paranormal forces belowground destroyed biological evidence very rapidly.

A three-person team charged with the task of transporting Richman's corpse to the surface had left an hour ago. They had taken the trance-inducing artifact with them. It was headed for the nearest Coppersmith vault.

The theft of the two navigation keys had been discovered when Elias had ordered an inventory of the equipment vault. The log showed no record of the keys having been checked out.

Hank Richman had been in charge of the log.

Officially, Richman's subordinate, Sylvia Thorpe, was now in charge of camp security and the murder investigation but everyone knew that when a Coppersmith was on site, he or she was ultimately the boss.

"The hell with the gossip," Elias said. "I'm your alibi."

But he knew that the vow — because that's what it was, as far as he was concerned: a promise to protect her — wouldn't be enough to reassure her. True, in the last forty-eight hours the two of them had faced danger together and shared the hottest sex he'd ever experienced, but the bottom line was that they had only met face-to-face a couple of days ago.

Sure, they had been communicating online for a couple of months before their first encounter in Visions, but he doubted that Hannah considered what they had a real relationship. No smart, savvy woman would trust a man after such a short period of time, regardless of what they had been through.

"No offense," Hannah said, "but I don't think the fact that we slept in the same tent is going to be enough to convince your people that I'm innocent. Some are specu-

213

lating that I used the artifact to put you into a trance along with the others, lured Richman into the ruins, murdered him, and then returned to rouse you and pretend to help you discover the body."

"That's not what happened."

She folded her arms very tightly and gave him a thin, brittle smile. "See, here's the thing everyone knows about a trance — the victim can't recall what happened while he was in dreamland."

He drank some coffee while he searched for a logical rebuttal to the argument. He came up empty.

"We need to find the killer," he said.

"Whoever it was escaped through the portal, remember?"

Elias paused his mug halfway to his mouth. "Huh."

Hannah's brows snapped together. "What?"

"Hank found that trance weapon somewhere, most likely in the illegal Alien-tech market."

"I won't be able to help you trace it to the original owner, if that's what you're thinking. I don't deal in that market."

"I do," he said.

That caught her off-guard.

"Really?" she asked, fascinated.

"Illegal Alien tech, especially the weaponized version, is a major problem for businesses in the Underworld. Pirates are always trying to get their hands on anything that will increase their firepower. Same goes for that Vortex operation I mentioned. Alien tech is almost always based on quartz energy and I'm the company expert on hot rocks. So, yes, I keep tabs on the illegal market."

"I see. Okay, that makes sense."

"But I won't be able to start an investigation until I get back to the surface."

He stopped talking because Sylvia Thorpe was coming toward them. She was in her thirties, a tall, athletically built woman with a preternatural talent for observing details and seeing patterns. If she had not joined the Coppersmith Security team, she would most likely have ended up on a big-city police force or become a Federal Bureau of Psi Investigation special agent. She gave Hannah a reserved, but polite nod and then turned to Elias.

"My team finished searching the jobsite, sir," she said. "No sign of the two missing keys."

"Well, it's not like we expected to find them," Elias said. "But we had to go through the formalities. Did you find anything else

215

of interest?"

"The time lock on the vault indicates that Richman opened it at two twenty-three this morning. Presumably that's when he removed the keys. Looks like everyone else was in that damned trance at that time." Sylvia cast a sidelong look at Hannah. "Except for the two of you, of course."

"We were both asleep," Hannah said evenly. "It was the currents of the trance energy that woke us up."

"Right," Sylvia said. She kept her attention on Elias. "According to your report, sir, you and Ms. West followed Richman into the ruins. As far as we can tell, you were only a few minutes behind him."

"Took us a while to figure out that he was gone," Elias said. He realized he was having to work to rein in his temper. "By the time we caught up with him he was dead. The killer escaped through the portal. We assume he took both keys with him."

Sylvia's jaw tightened. "Hank stole the keys, didn't he?"

"That's how it looks, Sylvia. I think he's also responsible for closing the dreamlight gate."

"Why would he do that?" Sylvia asked.

"I don't think it was intentional," Elias said. "It's more likely that it really was an accident. After all, he was carrying a very powerful dreamlight relic around the job-site. He probably didn't know much about it, just that it could induce a trance. At some point he must have gotten too close to the gate."

"And accidentally triggered it?" Sylvia asked.

"That's what it looks like. I'm sure it was as much of a shock to him as it was to the rest of the team. I'm sorry. I know you admired him. Hell, we all did. He was very good at his job. That's why he was in charge of security down here."

"I know. It's just that it's hard to wrap my head around the possibility that he was the thief."

"Assuming our theory of the crime is right, he met the killer inside the portal chamber," Elias said. "That raises another very interesting question."

Sylvia's expression sharpened. "You're thinking that the killer must have had a key of his own. That's the only way he could have navigated the Ghost City to get to the portal where he met Hank."

"I think so," Elias said.

Sylvia spread one hand in a short, frus-trated arc. "But if the killer had his own key, why take the risk of stealing two from

Coppersmith?"

"I can think of one possible reason," Elias said.

Hannah and Sylvia both looked at him.

"Maybe the killer's key is flawed or failing," Elias said. "We know it didn't come out of our lab because we've still got three of the five keys. That means it was produced in someone else's lab. It's inferior technology so someone wants to upgrade to a better model."

"In other words, this is a nasty piece of corporate espionage," Sylvia said. "That might explain a lot. Hank struck a deal with the devil and got murdered by a partner."

"There's something else to consider here," Elias said. "The killer has found another portal into and out of the Ghost City. We know he didn't use ours."

"No telling how many portals there are into the city," Sylvia said. "Coppersmith has already found two. There could be a dozen more for all we know."

"For now we have to assume that's the case," Elias said.

Sylvia exhaled deeply. "Well, one thing's certain. If we're right about the killer escaping through the portal, we don't stand a chance of tracking him inside the Ghost City. Our best bet is trying to locate his operation aboveground."

Hannah contemplated the glowing cavern. "No guarantees, but I might be able to track the killer inside the Ghost City."

Sylvia looked startled. Then she grimaced. "No one can track through the Ghost City."

Hannah shrugged. "You may be right. But we won't know for sure until I take a look."

Elias opened his mouth, intending to tell her that he wouldn't let her take the chance. But her stubborn, determined expression made him hesitate. She wanted to clear her name, he thought. Finding the killer was the only way she could do that.

As Rafe so often said, the longer it took to start the hunt, the colder the trail got. The odds were best if the search for the killer began immediately.

"Hannah and I will go in together," he said.

"Alone?" Sylvia shook her head. "You should take backup."

"Who, Sylvia? Richman is dead and you're in charge of security here at the camp. None of the other guards have gone through the portal. As for the rest of the team, they're all experts in their fields but they have zero security training. If we take other people with us, I'll spend most of my time keeping an eye on them. Hannah can handle strong energy. She and I have worked together before. We make a good team."

"If the killer came through another portal," Sylvia said, "it will be well guarded."

"As well guarded as ours is?" Elias asked dryly. "We've had experience with two portals to date. One thing is clear, no one can tolerate the energy inside a portal pool chamber for more than a few minutes. Any guards stationed at the other portal will be outside the chamber, watching the entrance. The last thing they'll expect is trouble coming through the portal."

Sylvia looked toward the cavern. "Because it would mean that someone tracked the killer through the Ghost City. You're right. It probably won't occur to them that would be possible."

Hannah spoke up. "It might not be possible. But I won't know until I see what things are like on the other side of the portal."

Sylvia turned back to Elias. "You'll need to use one of the keys."

"I know," Elias said, trying to be patient. It seemed to him that he could hear a clock ticking somewhere. They were losing valuable time.

"The keys haven't been thoroughly tested," Sylvia reminded him. "That was the primary objective of this initial exploratory venture, remember? We're still in the early-testing phase."

"I understand, Sylvia," he said.

She groaned. "I really, really want to know who murdered Richman and stole the key."

"So do I," Elias said.

"I do, too," Hannah said.

Sylvia gave her a searching look. "You haven't experienced the energy inside the Ghost City. It's incredibly disorienting. What makes you think you can track someone's prints in such a psi-heavy atmosphere?"

"Like I said, I won't know until I try," Hannah said. "But I'm good."

"Yes," Elias said, aware of a flash of pride. "When it comes to reading dreamlight, my wife is the best."

CHAPTER 19

"It's a little like underwater cave diving," Elias said. "Except you don't need a flashlight and you can breathe the atmosphere. But you go in on a line and you never, ever let go of that line until you're on the other side. Understood?"

"Understood," Hannah said.

"You don't have to physically hold the line — it's locked on to the vest you're wearing. But we've had a couple of people panic and try to unhook themselves. One went so far as to strip off his vest. We barely got him out in time."

"I'll try not to panic," Hannah said.

Her excruciatingly polite tone made Elias smile briefly.

"I know," he said. "Don't know why I'm bothering with the lecture."

They were standing inside the ancient portal ruin, looking down into the pool of glowing liquid crystal. It was like looking into a white-hot mirror except that there were no reflections. Even though she was standing above it she could not see anything beneath the surface.

The silvery lightning bolts of dazzling psi were very intense this close to the portal. Once again she had the feeling that the Aliens who had constructed the portal had built in a series of psychic warnings. It was as if there was a very large sign over the portal that read: *You really don't want to do this.*

She had Virgil tucked under one arm. He was fully fluffed. His Arizona Snow doll was clutched in one paw. He was evidently unconcerned by the heavy waves of energy rolling off the surface of the pool.

Elias was crouched nearby, checking and double-checking the contents of the two packs they were going to carry. The key to the portal hung around his neck on a metal chain. It didn't look very impressive, just a chunk of murky gray quartz, but every so often Hannah caught flashes of power seething deep inside the stone.

Sylvia Thorpe and two of the guards hovered near the entrance of the chamber. They were clearly uncomfortable with the energy in the room. It was also obvious that they were not optimistic about the outcome of the tracking mission.

Bunch of downers, Hannah thought. None of them had any faith in her ability to find the killer. She thought about telling them that she was the Finder — she could find just about anything. But she knew they wouldn't be impressed. After all, most of the team was still convinced she was involved in Richman's murder and the theft of the two keys.

No one trusted her except Elias.

The sooner she and Virgil finished this investigation, the better, she thought. This wasn't her world. She belonged in the Dark Zone where she had friends and family she could trust.

Satisfied with the contents of the packs, Elias got to his feet and held one of them out to her.

"This doesn't come off, either," he said.

"Like the vest." She touched the leather vest she was wearing. "I understand. But why would I be tempted to take off my pack?"

"Because it gets very weird inside the Ghost City. The energy sometimes makes people want to do stupid things."

She didn't try to remind him that she'd had a lot of experience in the Underworld and that she wasn't likely to do anything stupid. That would just make her sound inexperienced. People who spent time in a psi-heavy environment knew that every twist and turn in the catacombs or the Rainforest was fraught with the unknown.

"What's inside the pack?" she asked.

"Just the usual field gear. Energy bars, water, an emergency medical kit, a couple of extra cartridges for your flamer and some spare tuned amber."

"Which won't do us any good inside the Ghost City."

"No. Nav amber doesn't work inside but if we find the portal the killer accessed and get an opportunity to go through it, we can use our amber to get a fix on the coordinates. That will help us track the pirates."

"Got it," she said.

She slipped the pack on, trying not to let the others see her uncertainty. She was good at putting on a mask of cool confidence. But the truth was she had no idea if her plan would work. All she knew for sure was that she had to try. It was the only way to clear her name.

She was a very small player in the world of hot antiquities, but within that world, reputation was everything. The rumors already circulating around the Coppersmith encampment could ruin her if they were not squelched fast.

She plopped Virgil on her shoulder so that both of her hands were free.

"Ready," she said.

Elias tugged on the line one last time, testing the hookups, and nodded at Sylvia.

"All set," he said.

She nodded once. "Good luck, boss."

Elias looked at Hannah. "Follow me. It will feel like we're going into a pool of warm water at first, but it's actually just a unique kind of psi-gate. Once you're under the surface you'll find yourself in a storm zone. You'll get hit with a lot of dark energy that will try to scare you into turning around and going back the way you came. Use your talent to push through it. When we get through the energy storm you'll see the doorway to the Ghost City."

"Sounds like a plan."

Elias started down the flight of quartz steps into the mirror-surfaced pool. The liquid crystal did not splash or create ripples and small waves; instead it began to churn in a vortexlike manner. Hannah felt the energy level in the chamber start to flare. Sylvia and the guards retreated farther into the relative shelter of the cavern tunnel.

Elias walked down through the quicksilver

storm and disappeared into the fathomless depths.

Hannah felt the line between them grow taut. She took a breath and went quickly down the steps. The strange liquid crystal lapped at her boots. Her feet disappeared beneath the surface. Now the small pool of energy was up to her knees . . . her waist . . . her neck.

Now that she was actually in the pool she realized it did not feel at all like water; it was more like walking through the eye of a storm — intense, disturbing, and oddly thrilling.

One more step took her under the liquid crystal barrier. Virgil's fur stood on end. So did her hair. Instinctively, she closed her eyes and held her breath but Elias was right; once she was beneath the swirling surface of the mirror-like energy pool she could breathe normally.

Virgil chortled with excitement and waved Arizona Snow.

"Piece of cake. Right, pal?" she whispered.

Below the surface of the pool was a storm of hot, bright energy. Elias was a dark shadow moving ahead of her. She realized there was a narrow beam of energy radiating from the gray quartz he wore around his neck. His ring was hot, too.

She kicked up her senses and followed him deeper into the silently howling gale.

The violent energy swirled around them in a senses-blinding whiteout. The harrowing images came from all directions, some mere ghosts in the dazzling fog, others unnervingly realistic. Monsters from the primordial past, crazed killers, wildly burning ghosts — the storm sent all of them and more.

And every spectral vision carried the same message: *Go back.*

But years of handling her talent had given her the tools she needed to keep the visions at bay.

The journey through the portal seemed to be endless. But abruptly she found herself following Elias up another flight of gray quartz steps.

They surfaced through a liquid crystal pool similar to the first and climbed out in an identical colonnaded rotunda made of the same hot gray quartz as the cavern pool.

But this rotunda was inside a featureless structure fashioned of the same gray quartz. There were no windows but there was a single, arched opening. Through the opening Hannah could see a heavy gray fog.

Virgil chortled and shook himself as though shedding water from his fur.

"Welcome to the Ghost City," Elias said. He gave Hannah a critical survey. "How are you doing?"

"I'm fine," she said, going for her patented I've-got-this vibe.

"Yeah." Elias smiled, looking coolly satisfied. "I can see that. In which case, it's time to get to work. Can you detect the killer's prints in here?"

Her senses were still rattled from the trip through the portal but she pulled herself together and focused on the gray quartz floor.

She saw the hot tracks immediately. The killer had been in the grip of strong emotions when he emerged from the crystal pool. The combination of having committed a bloody murder and navigating the disorienting portal had rezzed his senses.

"Got 'em," she said. "Looks like he was nervous — scared, maybe — anxious to get to safety." She motioned toward the door. "He went through that opening."

"Straight into the heart of the Ghost City." Elias contemplated the endlessly shifting fog on the other side of the arched opening. "Whoever he is, he's strong."

"Yeah, well, so are we."

Elias gave her an oddly cheerful smile. "We are, aren't we?"

"Plus we've got Virgil and Arizona Snow."

"We're a hell of a team. All right, the key is our lodestone. It's tuned to this portal so we can find our way back. One piece of advice — try not to think about the fog when you walk through it. For some reason it's easier that way."

"All right."

She followed him through the arched opening and out into a fog-drenched landscape. The strange, seething mist threatened to overwhelm her senses. Panic whispered through her. How was she going to track the killer through such a miasma?

She remembered Elias's advice, cranked up her senses, and concentrated on finding the killer's prints.

The great weight receded somewhat. She was finally able to make out her surroundings.

They were standing in a narrow, fog-infused lane. A strange array of structures loomed in the mist. The buildings were unmistakably Alien in design — the proportions struck the human eye as slightly wrong. But unlike most of the ruins Hannah had seen both aboveground and in the Underworld, everything in the Ghost City appeared to be crafted of the same smoky gray quartz. And all of it glowed with an icy energy that raised the hair on the back of her neck.

"Just like the old fairy tale," she whispered. *The City of Ice and Fog.*"

The city was enveloped in an eerie silence. Nothing moved. No creatures stirred in the ruins. The strange mist that swirled in the streets had a muffling effect.

"This isn't normal fog, is it?" she said.

"No. It's infused with paranormal currents. We haven't had a chance to analyze it."

"I have to admit, I'm curious. What *was* this place?"

"Good question," Elias said.

"I'm not sure we want to know the answer," Hannah said.

"Always better to know the truth."

"A counselor once told me that wasn't always the case, at least not when it came to asking questions about the past."

"Obviously you didn't take that advice," Elias said. "You went out and hired a professional genealogist to dig up your past."

She almost smiled. "This is true. Several of them over the years, actually. I've spent a lot of money on genealogists."

"I wouldn't have taken the advice, either," Elias said. "Like I said, knowing is always better than not knowing."

She reached up to touch Virgil, expecting a reassuring chortle in response. Instead he rumbled in her ear and hunkered down on her shoulder. She turned her head to look at him and was startled to see that all four of his eyes were open.

You knew you were in trouble when a dust bunny got serious, Hannah thought.

Belatedly, she remembered she had a job to do. She pulled hard on her talent, pushing back against the endless waves of fog, and looked at the gray quartz street. A familiar set of hot psi-prints glowed in the strange mist.

"He went down this street and turned to the right," she said. "He was in a hurry. Running, I think."

"Let's go," Elias said.

They walked the street side by side, their flamers at the ready. The trail led through a narrow canyon formed by the looming quartz structures. Every so often they passed a doorway sealed with some mirror-like energy.

It was hard work pressing forward, demanding physical as well as mental energy because the seething energy in the atmosphere was unrelenting. It just kept coming in seemingly endless waves. At this rate they would be exhausted by the time they reached the pirate's portal. On the plus side, the pirate would probably be tired, too.

"What's behind the doors?" she asked at one point, more for the sake of hearing Elias's voice than for anything else.

"Only tried a couple so far," Elias said. "Nearly got psi-fried both times. We're working on a better strategy."

"Meanwhile, don't open any doors, right?"

"Right."

"What if the pirate opened one?"

"We'll face that question if it arises."

The trail led deeper and deeper into the fogbound city. Every few steps, Elias called a halt to check the key stone. Hannah wondered if he was afraid it would fail because of the heavy psi they were encountering. The keys were prototypes, after all.

The prints wound around a narrow curve in the street and came to an abrupt halt at a doorway sealed with quicksilver energy. It looked exactly like all the other doors they had passed but Virgil growled a warning and sleeked out completely.

Hannah stopped abruptly. "What?" Elias asked.

"The killer went through that door. Virgil is concerned. And when he gets concerned —"

"We all get concerned. Move back. I'll try the door. Whatever you do, stay out of the way. If I have to retreat, I'll be doing it really fast."

"Right."

He paused to slip the chain holding the key stone over his head. He put it around her neck.

"If anything happens to me, use the key stone to get back to the Coppersmith portal. It's set to the coordinates. Just get a fix on the vibe and follow it. If something goes wrong do not try to come after me. Got that? Go back to the portal and get help. Do not follow me through that door unless I tell you it's safe."

She opened her mouth to tell him that she didn't intend to abandon him if the situation went to hell. They were a team. She had a flamer and she had her talent. She was better backup than anyone they had left behind at the jobsite. And she was a lot closer.

But she did not bother to give the lecture because she knew he didn't want to hear it.

"Understood," she said instead. Which was the truth. Pretty much.

Elias started toward the door.

A sudden, shocking stillness gripped the street. A moment ago the Ghost City had been seething with unrelenting waves of energy but now the currents had receded.

Virgil growled a fierce warning.

"Elias," she said, "wait. We may have a bigger problem than finding the pirate. Something is wrong. Feel the change in the atmosphere?"

Elias surveyed the narrow passageway in which they were standing. She knew he was running hot, trying to identify the source of the strange stillness.

"Wave dynamics," he said. "This is what happens before a tsunami hits land. There is a drawback of the water from the shore. The deeper the drawback, the bigger the wave that's coming at you."

Virgil was very agitated now. Hannah could feel him urging her to move.

"Something is coming all right," she said. "We're going to be trapped out here in the open if we don't move."

The atmosphere was shifting again. She could sense a roaring wave of dark psi gathering energy. Somehow she knew that when it struck, nothing human could stand against such a violent force. She looked at Elias and realized that he, too, sensed impending doom.

"There's no time to retreat," Elias said. "We're going through the door."

He grabbed her hand. She saw his ring flash with energy, felt Virgil's little claws dig into her shirt. Arizona Snow glowed.

Elias went through the door first, moving fast, flamer out in front. He hauled Hannah and Virgil in his wake.

The quicksilver gate shimmered faintly, resisting at first, and then it gave way. Hannah stumbled but managed to stay on her feet. Virgil snarled but he was still more or less securely perched on her shoulder.

They stumbled to a halt inside the chamber.

Elias released her immediately.

"Down," Elias ordered. "Stay there."

She did as ordered, sprawling awkwardly on the stone floor. Virgil adroitly leaped off her shoulder.

Elias swung around in a swift, tight arc, sweeping the chamber with the flamer. No one leaped out of the shadows. That was a good thing, Hannah told herself. A very good thing.

She twisted to look back through the doorway and watched in horror as a great tide of intense darkness engulfed the lane. She knew with every fiber of her being that the roaring wave of psi would have crushed all three of them.

The quicksilver door became a solid,

mirror-bright gate once again, sealing them inside the chamber.

CHAPTER 20

Elias slowly lowered the barrel of the flamer. The room was empty except for the three of them. There was no way to know how long that situation would last, but for now they could catch their breaths.

He took a closer look at the gray quartz room. It was circular. The ceiling was approximately two stories high. There were no windows.

There was, however, an arched opening in the wall. He could see the beginning of a corridor that curved away out of sight.

All of it glowed with the murky gray light of the quartz.

Virgil was grumbling and he still had all four eyes open but he was fully fluffed. He scuttled across the floor to Hannah. She sat up, bracing herself on her arms, and looked at the doll he clutched in one paw.

"Oh, good," she said. "Arizona Snow survived in one piece. No surprise, I guess.

She was one tough lady."

Virgil chortled happily. Hannah looked at Elias.

"What was that stuff?" she asked.

"Psi wave of some kind," he said. "But not like any I've ever experienced or read about."

"A tsunami of psi." Hannah scrambled to her feet. "Do you think it will recede like a regular ocean wave now that it has spent its energy?"

"Good question. The only way to find out is to open that door and that is definitely not a good idea at this time."

She shuddered. "You're right. It's still flooding the street. I can feel it."

"No way to know how long that hot energy will hang around. We need to find another way out. Can you see the killer's prints?"

He felt her raise her senses again and knew she was regaining her focus.

"Yes," she said. She looked at the arched opening. "They go down that corridor."

"Figured you were going to say that."

"The plan was to find the pirate's portal, wasn't it?"

"Plan A," he said, "was to locate the portal, get the coordinates, and then go back the way we came. But we have a new problem."

She groaned. "Oh, really? What could possibly go wrong?"

"The key you're wearing is starting to lose power."

"What?" Shocked, she looked down at the gray key stone. It was no longer illuminated. "Crap. What happened to it?"

"The onset of that psi wave must have shattered the quartz. I told you, all five keys are still in the development phase. There are a few bugs left to work out."

She swallowed hard. "How much longer will it last?"

"I don't know. Let me have it."

"Have we got a Plan B?" she asked as she handed it to him. "Because even if the tsunami disappears, I've got a feeling that it will have buried our psi-prints and those of the pirate as well. We probably won't be able to follow him back to the Coppersmith portal."

"There's always a Plan B," Elias said. He kicked up his talent a little, seeking the frequency of the fading key stone. "The good news is that there's a little juice left in this thing. I think I can push some energy through it using my ring."

She managed a shaky little smile. "Good to know. And don't forget we've got Virgil.

Among other things, he's a terrific alarm system."

Virgil chortled and vaulted up onto his favorite perch on her shoulder.

Elias looked at Hannah for a couple of beats. Her smile and the gritty determination in her eyes did something to his insides in the vicinity of his heart. He knew some strong women, he thought — the men in his family were attracted to the type — but Hannah West was in a class by herself.

"So," she prompted. "Plan B?"

"Right," he said. "Plan B. We get out through the pirate's portal before the key stone fails altogether, and we hope like hell the pirate is gone. It makes sense that he'd head back to the surface now that he got what he came for."

"Assuming pirates operate on the same logic that engineers use."

"Assuming that," he agreed. "Check the charge on your flamer and let me know if Virgil goes into combat mode. From now on try not to make any noise. Sound doesn't carry well in this atmosphere but there's no sense taking any more chances than absolutely necessary."

She nodded and started toward the entrance to the ghostly corridor. He fell into step beside her, covering her so that she could concentrate on the psi-prints. He kept one eye on Virgil. The dust bunny appeared alert but not frantic as he had been just before the tsunami hit. Maybe he, too, understood that this was the only way out.

The spectral radiance cast by the gray crystal walls, ceiling, and floor of the corridor played tricks on the human eye. Ominous paranormal shadows appeared and disappeared in the translucent walls. Strange silhouettes materialized and vanished between one step and the next. Elias kept his senses fully rezzed and his finger on the flamer button. He knew that Hannah was doing the same.

They reached the end of the corridor and stopped at the arched entrance. In the chamber beyond the doorway was a familiar-looking gray quartz rotunda, complete with a quicksilver portal pool.

As he had anticipated, there were no pirates guarding this side of the portal.

Hannah motioned toward the pool, indicating the psi-prints halted at the top of the steps.

"We can talk now," Elias said. "Sound doesn't pass through the portal. If someone comes through from the other side, we'll get a warning. The portal energy will start to change."

"So, whoever is on the other side will get a warning if we try to go through?"

"Sure, if they happen to be in the portal chamber on that side but we've got two advantages. The first is that they won't be expecting us. I doubt very much if the killer allowed for the possibility that someone might be able to track him through the city."

"What's the second advantage?"

"This." He held up his hand, showing her the hot crystal in his ring. "It seems to be working fine in this environment."

"That sounds nice, but how is that going to be helpful in our current situation?"

"I have no idea. But as we engineers like to say, the more power you've got, the better."

He walked to the edge of the pool and looked down. "I'll go first. Stay close."

Another shuddering wave of tsunami energy reverberated down the corridor. Virgil growled. Hannah reached up to touch him.

"Don't worry," she said. "Virgil and I are not going to hang around this place any longer than absolutely necessary."

He nodded once, jacked up his senses and went swiftly down the steps. The energy field of the portal engulfed him in its weird, dreamlike atmosphere. He felt the line that linked him to Hannah grow taut and then loosen. She was right behind him.

The key stone was fading but he was able to get a little more energy out of it by easing psi through his ring. Nevertheless, the key was almost dead by the time they stepped through the portal into another quartz rotunda.

He did a quick sweep of the chamber. Empty.

Hannah emerged from the pool, flamer in hand. Virgil clung to her shoulder, all four eyes wide.

"It's all right," Elias said. "We're alone in here." He looked around. "Another cave system. Fresh air is coming from that direction." He motioned with the flamer. "Probably still in the Rainforest. Wait here while I look around outside."

"Take Virgil," Hannah urged. "Like I said, he's a great alarm system."

Virgil chortled when he was transferred to Elias's shoulder.

Elias followed the scent of fresh rain and vibrant growing things down a tunnel and emerged into a small cavern. At the entrance he could see part of a clearing. Beyond that was the rich, paranormal green foliage of the underground jungle.

He paused at the mouth of the cave,

listening with all of his senses.

He could hear the normal sounds of the Rainforest but no human voices.

He went out into the clearing. A quick survey turned up the one sure indication that humans had recently been present — energy bar wrappers, empty water bottles, and other assorted litter. The Aliens had left behind some amazing, almost indestructible ruins, he thought. But humans always seemed to leave a lot of garbage around.

He was about to go back into the portal chamber to let Hannah know the area was safe, but he stopped when he caught sight of a booted foot sticking out of the undergrowth.

He changed course to take a look. The booted foot was attached to the body of a man dressed in Rainforest gear. He was sprawled facedown. The back of his jacket was saturated with rapidly drying blood.

The second body was a few feet away. The throat had been cut.

Small insects were already starting to feast on the remains.

One person's garbage was another creature's take-out dinner, Elias thought.

CHAPTER 21

Hannah stood a short distance away and watched Elias search the bodies and gather up the dead men's gear.

"It looks like there were three of them," he said. "Someone concluded that a one-way split of the profits was preferable to a three-way split."

"He figured the jungle would dispose of the bodies and any crime-scene evidence," she said.

"It was a reasonable assumption. If we hadn't been close behind the killer, these two would have disappeared without a trace."

"Are we going to try to haul the bodies out of here?" she asked. "That's not going to be easy. We can't go back the way we came, so we'll be walking out through the Rainforest."

"We'll take some of their gear and leave the bodies behind," Elias said.

She watched him get to his feet. "Did you find anything that will help the cops identify the killer?"

"No Vortex tattoos. But there may be some leads. The killer was in a hurry. He took their wallets and locators but he didn't bother with the rest of the gear. Probably didn't want to be bothered hauling it out of the jungle. With luck, there will be something useful in their packs."

Hannah looked at the bodies. "What is going on here?"

"Can't be positive yet, but here's a scenario. Someone found another portal and figured out how to make a device that could be used to navigate the Ghost City. But for whatever reason he figured the devices engineered in the Coppersmith labs were superior. That individual set up Hank Richman and this pair. Last night Richman used the trance artifact to put the camp into a deep sleep. One of the pirates used the inferior navigational device to enter the Ghost City through this portal and meet Richman at the Coppersmith portal."

"Richman gave him the two Coppersmith lab key stones and then got murdered by the pirate."

"Got a hunch the plan was to steal all four of the remaining keys but for whatever reason, Richman got nervous. Or maybe he was holding out for a bigger share of the profits on the grounds that he was taking the biggest risk."

"So instead of delivering all of the proto-types, he only took two into the portal cave last night," Hannah suggested. "He wanted to cut a different deal."

"Maybe they argued. Maybe Richman threatened to expose the scheme if he didn't get what he wanted. Whatever the case, the pirate murdered him. The killer now has two keys, both of which are worth a fortune on the black market."

"So this is a classic case of no honor among thieves?"

"Whoever the fourth pirate is, I doubt that he ever planned to split the profits. Rich-man and these guys were playing out of their league. They never stood a chance."

A sudden rustling sound sparked a jolt of alarm through Hannah. She turned quickly, flamer at the ready, and saw a large grocery sack tipped on its side. It was gyrating wildly.

Virgil emerged from the sack dragging a bag of potato chips. He chortled excitedly and ripped into the bag.

"Oh, for heaven's sake, Virgil," she said. "That's probably evidence."

"Or at least a snack we could have eaten on the hike out of here," Elias said.

It was too late to save the chips but Hannah crossed the clearing to see if there was anything else of an edible nature inside the bag.

The bag was empty but there was a paper receipt fluttering at the bottom. She pulled it out.

"It says the chips and some energy bars and bottled water were purchased at the Lost Ruin Stop-and-Go, mile marker fifteen on Highway Twenty-nine two days ago." She looked up. "Looks like they also recharged a car engine there, as well. And here's the best part — someone used a credit card. Maybe you'll be able to trace the transaction."

Elias smiled a thin, cold smile. "Wouldn't be much of a tech guy if I couldn't."

CHAPTER 22

Grady Barnett heard the text message ping on his phone just as he was preparing to leave his office for the day. Excitement mingled with relief. It was about time Hannah returned his call.

He grabbed his phone out of his pocket and looked at the screen. Anticipation evaporated in a heartbeat. Not Hannah.

The text message was short:

The subject is back in town. Still married. Any progress on our project?

Grady stared at the screen for a long time trying to think of yet another diplomatic way to say *no progress.* He had left a dozen voice mails and text messages for Hannah but there had been no response. He had assumed that meant she was still on the Coppersmith job — he refused to believe she had actually gone on a real honeymoon with Elias Coppersmith.

It was obvious that Coppersmith had offered her the Marriage of Convenience as a way of giving the affair a semirespectable face. When people from Coppersmith's world got married for real they married their own kind — wealthy spouses who descended from equally wealthy, powerful, *respectable* families. They did not contract lifelong alliances with an orphan whose mother had been an Illusion City showgirl. But men like Coppersmith were notorious for using MCs as a way of seducing a potential bed partner.

He must have needed Hannah's talent very badly to go through the trouble of a Marriage of Convenience. The real surprise was that Hannah had fallen for the offer of a tacky MC, Grady thought. He had done enough research on her to know that, while she'd had a few discreet, short-lived relationships, she had never gone in for MCs. He'd suspected that, deep down, even knowing that a real marriage was not in the cards for a woman with her para-psych profile, she had secretly hoped that the man of her dreams would someday show up.

The truth was that any man who was willing to get involved in an affair with an off-the-charts dream walker would have to be pretty damn weird himself. The thought of a sexual relationship between two such freaky psychics would strike most people as bizarre. But he had to admit that, as a scientist, he was fascinated.

It would make for a terrific case study, the kind of paper that would attract a lot of attention in the right circles. That attention would translate into funding for more research. If Coppersmith and Hannah really were sleeping together, he would give a great deal to get them into the lab, hook them up to the monitors, and see what happened to their auras when they slept in the same bed and dreamed.

In addition to enhancing his status in the para-psych world, he could market the results of the tests to corporations and businesses that were insatiably hungry for data on potential new customers. The elite matchmaking agencies, including Arcane's, would pay big bucks for a deep analysis of the dreamlight patterns of exotic talents. People with powerful or extremely rare paranormal abilities were notoriously difficult to match. His data would allow the matchmaking firms to tweak their algorithms so that they could expand their pool of clients.

And then there were all the pharmaceutical companies that were forever trying to develop drugs for sleep and dream disorders. Those problems had always plagued the human race, and now that the descendants of the colonists were rapidly developing their latent psychic senses, the ancient sleep and dream issues were growing more complex — and, therefore, potentially more profitable.

He slumped back against his desk. He'd had a few dreams of his own when he started working with Hannah — dreams that involved appearing on talk shows and giving speeches at conventions of dreamlight researchers. Dreams of making a hell of a lot of money.

Those dreams had all walked out the door with Hannah the day she discovered him in the supply closet with Kelsey. Nevertheless, he'd been certain he could find a way to lure Hannah back into the lab. When every attempt had failed he'd begun to think that all was lost.

Then he had received the text message giving him one last chance. All he had to do was persuade Hannah to do what she did best — find lost and missing artifacts.

Be careful what you wish for, he thought.

He focused his attention on the text message for a long time and finally tapped out a reply.

Will arrange meeting with subject immediately.

The response came back instantly.

You assured me there would be no problem securing the subject's cooperation. If that is not possible, say so. I will make arrangements elsewhere.

Fuck that, Grady thought. He straightened his shoulders and tapped out a message.

Meeting with subject today.

CHAPTER 23

"Don't get me wrong," Hannah said. She dropped her pack and sleeping bag just inside the door of Visions and surveyed the ransacked interior. "It's always nice to get away for a while. Nothing like a little vacation to refresh a person, I always say. But when you get home it's back to real life."

And in her case that meant returning to a vandalized shop and apartment.

Elias slipped his pack off his shoulders and set it down next to Hannah's. He gave the chaos a grim-faced survey. "Looks like the magic fairy housekeepers didn't show up while we were out of town. Hard to get good help these days."

"You can say that again."

Virgil chortled and wriggled free from Hannah's grasp. He vaulted down to the floor and immediately began touring the wreckage with his Arizona Snow doll. He soon disappeared behind a jumble of green-quartz urns and bowls.

"I'll help you clean up," Elias said.

"Thanks," she said, "but this is my problem. I know you've got your hands full dealing with the fallout from the arrest."

"Coppersmith Security is working with the FBPI and the Guild to close the case. I'm no longer involved. They've got a car plate and a decent photo of the fourth man from the Lost Ruin Stop-and-Go. My contact says they've ID'd the guy as a career criminal. Just a matter of time before they pick him up. So, I'm free to help tidy up."

She smiled. "Hard to envision you as a housekeeper but I'm not going to turn down your offer. Thanks."

"You're welcome. Besides, Coppersmith owes you big-time."

She wasn't sure where to go with that remark. It had the effect of putting their relationship firmly back on a contractual footing. Just business.

The hike out of the jungle to the nearest Guild-controlled gate had taken over three hours. Trekking through the Rainforest was hard work. They had both been worn out from the experience in the Ghost City. Neither of them had enough spare energy to carry on a serious conversation. It had been a case of putting one foot in front of the other until they reached the gate into the tunnels.

Once inside the catacombs it had not taken long to get to the surface but Elias had spent the next couple of hours immersed in the details of coordinating the manhunt. An FBPI team led by the Guild had immediately gone down into the jungle to salvage what they could of the physical evidence at the pirates' portal.

Elias headed toward the stairs. "Let's start with your apartment."

Virgil appeared from behind the heap of urns. He had a crystal-beaded bracelet in one paw. He bustled through the clutter, hopped up onto the sales counter, and carefully deposited the bracelet in the glass bowl. He chortled at Hannah and vaulted back down to resume his search for his scattered treasures.

She smiled. "Got to give dust bunnies points for positive thinking. Nothing gets them down for long. Find dead bodies, chase a killer through some spooky ruins, nearly get psi-fried by a paranormal tsunami, hike out of the jungle, and come home to a burgled apartment. No sweat."

Elias paused on the stairs. "What's he doing?"

"Playing hide-and-seek. He's searching for

257

his personal collection of sparkly things."

Elias watched Virgil hop up onto the counter with another small glittering object.

"Life is simple for a dust bunny," he said. "It's a priorities thing, I guess. What didn't kill you in the past isn't worth obsessing about and there's not much point trying to anticipate what might try to kill you in the future."

Hannah wrinkled her nose. "Because whatever it is, it will probably come from the one direction you least expect it to come from."

"Exactly. And there endeth the philosophy lesson for today," Elias said. He started toward the stairs that led to her private rooms.

She paused at the foot of the stairs, one hand gripping the newel-post. "You must be exhausted."

He didn't stop, just kept climbing. "We're both exhausted. That's why we need to prioritize. We'll straighten out your personal space and then we'll send out for a pizza. Then we'll open a couple of beers or a bottle of wine or whatever you've got in the cupboard."

"Wine," she said. "White wine." She cleared her throat. "Very inexpensive white wine, I'm afraid."

"I'm not feeling real picky at the moment."

He reached the landing and disappeared down the hall.

She started to follow him up the stairs but paused when her phone rang. She took it out of her pocket and glanced at the all-too-familiar number. Grady Barnett. Again.

Upon returning to the surface she had discovered a string of voice mails and text messages from him. She had dutifully sampled a few just to make sure he didn't have anything new to tell her but they had all struck the same theme.

". . . It's very important that I speak to you as soon as possible . . ."

". . . Can't discuss this over the phone. Need to see you . . ."

". . . Where are you? Call me as soon as you get this message. This is business, damn it . . ."

She was about to end the call without answering but curiosity got the better of her. Business was business.

She took the call.

"What is it, Grady? Make it fast. I am currently prioritizing my life and you are not at the top of my to-do list."

"It's about time you answered. Where have you been?"

"On my honeymoon, remember?"

"Bullshit. You went on a job for Copper-smith, didn't you?"

"That's none of your business, Grady. Look, if you don't have anything really interesting to tell me, I'm going to end this call."

"All right, all right. Calm down. Yes, I do have something of interest for you. This is of serious interest to both of us."

"Doubtful. What do you want from me, Grady? I am not going back into your lab so that you can hook me up to your machines again. That's not negotiable. By the way, I do plan to drop by your office to pick up my file."

"I keep telling you it's incomplete. As a professional I don't feel right about releasing it."

Something about his quick answer pinged her intuition.

"You made a lot of hard copy notes," she said. "You were always jotting stuff down in your notebook. I saw you."

"Those are my confidential medical notes."

"They're *my* confidential notes. I paid for them. I want them."

"All right," he said smoothly. "You can pick them up whenever it's convenient. But

260

in exchange, the least you can do is listen to what I have to say. This isn't about research. I'm offering you a job."

She gripped the banister and watched Virgil recover another one of his scattered treasures, an amber earring.

"What's the job?" she asked, not bothering to conceal her suspicion.

"Nothing out of your usual line," he said quickly.

Maybe too quickly.

"You're trying to reassure me," she said. "That is not a good sign."

"I'm serious. This is about locating a lost artifact. Hey, you're the Finder, right? Look, I really cannot talk about this on the phone. I'm representing a serious collector. You know what they're like. Paranoid."

"Since when are you in the antiquities business?"

"He approached me because he found out that you were one of my patients."

"I wasn't a patient of yours. I paid for a para-psych analysis for genealogical purposes — not because I wanted you to play doctor. And how did this collector find out that I hired you?"

"It's not exactly a secret."

"Yes, it was a secret. I sure as heck didn't blab it all over the DZ. So who did?"

There was a brief pause on the other end of the connection. Then Grady heaved a weary sigh.

"Kelsey is acquainted with this individual. She happened to mention that I am currently working with a patient who has a very high-end talent for dreamlight. She told him that this particular patient is very, very good at finding lost antiquities."

"Wow. The lovely Kelsey has no respect for confidentiality, either, is that what you're telling me?"

"I assure you, she did not divulge your identity."

"I am, of course, thrilled to know she's got a few ethics."

"Look, this collector is willing to pay well for your services." Grady sounded like he was speaking through gritted teeth now. "He contacted me because he had no luck with any of the regular antiquities dealers. He's desperate."

"And you immediately thought of me."

"I'm acting as a go-between because I know you are very cautious when it comes to taking new clients," Grady said. "My professional intuition tells me this guy isn't dangerous but he is definitely eccentric. I thought you would be more comfortable if I brokered the deal, so to speak."

"Okay, now I get it. Just how much is this collector going to pay you for acting as a go-between?"

"Look, I'll admit this is a big deal for me. The collector has offered to fund some new state-of-the-art equipment for my lab if I can persuade you to help him locate this particular antiquity."

"So you get some new lab equipment? What do I get?"

"Name your price," Grady said. "I'll contact him and give him the number. If he agrees to pay it we'll both come out of this with a whole new retirement plan."

She thought about that while she listened to the muffled sounds of Elias moving around inside her apartment. It was oddly pleasant to have him here, in her home, trashed though it was. The situation wouldn't last forever but for now it was very nice.

However, business was business. With the Coppersmith job concluded, she had to consider the future.

"I'll think about it and get back to you, Grady," she said.

She started to end the call but he started talking very fast.

"Look, I'll level with you, this guy gave me forty-eight hours to find a dreamlight talent who could do this job. If I don't come through for him he's going to go elsewhere."

"You mean if you can't deliver me within forty-eight hours you lose your lab equipment."

On the other end of the connection Grady exhaled heavily. "Yeah, that's pretty much the bottom line here. Just tell me the flat-out truth. Are you interested in this three-way partnership or not?"

"Like I said, I'll think about it and get back to you. I promise to give you my decision within forty-eight hours. Bye, Grady. Got to go."

"Go where? I thought you just got back."

"We're home and very tired."

"You and Coppersmith — ?"

"Still married. Can you believe it? At the rate we're going we'll be celebrating our one-week anniversary before you know it."

"And the sleeping arrangements?" Grady asked cautiously.

"Are none of your damn business."

"I was only inquiring in a professional capacity." Grady sounded hurt.

"You want me to tell you what you can do with your so-called professional capacity?"

"Hannah, please. I'm trying to do both of us a favor —"

"Good-bye, Grady."

She ended the call and went up the stairs. She could tell that Elias was in her bedroom. No man had ever been inside that room. It was odd to realize that Elias was in there right now. He probably expected to sleep in her bed.

It was awkward being tied up in a marriage. Sure, it was only an MC, but it was still a marriage. Somehow the very fact that it was a tacky Marriage of Convenience only seemed to make the situation more troubling. Not that she wanted a Covenant Marriage, of course. She barely knew Elias, after all. It wasn't like they moved in the same social circles. In the Dark Zone you only had two social circles. One consisted of the people you trusted. The other was composed of the people you didn't trust.

But Elias now belonged in the first group, the very small crowd of people she trusted.

She reminded herself that he would probably want to terminate the MC as quickly as possible. There was really only one reason why it had come into existence in the first place. He had wanted to protect her with the power of his family's name. The marriage was a complete fiction, nothing more than a cover story. It had served its purpose.

At the top of the stairs she went down the short hall to the bedroom. Elias had already stripped the bed. He greeted her with a bundle of burglar-contaminated sheets in his arms.

"Not my business," he said, "but it sounded like you were chatting with that dreamlight researcher."

"Yeah, that was Grady." She sighed. "At least I now know why he's been so insistent about trying to get my attention. Turns out his assistant told a collector about my talent and the work I do. The collector knows I only work through referral so he's asked Grady to broker a contract."

"Does this collector know your identity?"

"No, I don't think so. He probably would have tried to contact me directly if he knew how to find me. I'm a small player in the paranormal antiquities world."

He smiled. "I found you."

"Yes, you did," she admitted.

"So Grady is trying to broker a deal between this wealthy collector and you."

"It wouldn't be the first time I've worked with a go-between," she said. "It's actually quite common in my business. A lot of us who trace lost and missing artifacts prefer to keep some distance between ourselves and the collectors. So long as I know the intermediary and trust his professionalism, it's a reasonably safe way to work."

"Do you trust Grady?"

"About as far as I can throw him. But I know him well enough to believe that in this case his motives are purely financial. I'm good with that. Business is business."

"What about his assistant?"

"The lovely Kelsey?" Hannah shook her head. "She has access to Grady's files so she knows how to find me. If she decides to sell the info to the collector there's not much I can do about it. But if that happens I definitely won't take the job."

Elias whistled softly. "And here I always thought the mining business was a little rough around the edges. My world's got nothing on yours when it comes to risk. You pretty much work without a net, don't you?"

"It's not that bad. I take precautions." She waved her hand to indicate the world outside the window. "And I've got friends and family here in the DZ."

"Right." He held up the bundled sheets. "Where's the laundry room?"

She pulled herself together. "I'm not going to wash those sheets. They're going straight outside into the alley along with the quilt and the pillows and blankets. The mattress cover goes, too."

He frowned at the mattress cover. "Looks like real silk."

"It is silk. Cost a small fortune. Luckily I always keep a spare around."

He raised his brows. "You're going to throw all of it out into the alley?"

"Trust me, those sheets and the rest of the bedding will be gone by morning. We've got what you might call an after-hours market here in the DZ. Someone will be thrilled to get that bedding. It's practically brand-new. I'll get a box to put it in."

Elias's eyes darkened with understanding. "It's a dreamlight talent thing, isn't it? You're afraid there might be enough residual energy in the psi-prints the intruder left behind to affect your sleep and maybe your dreams, right?"

"You can't wash out that kind of paranormal residue," she said. "Fortunately, silk makes a decent barrier. That's what saved the mattress. Otherwise I'd be looking at buying a new one. Do you have any idea how much mattresses cost?"

He thought about it. "No, can't say that I do."

Of course not, she thought. He was a Coppersmith. In his world there were people — staff — who took care of the mundane things in life.

"Never mind," she said. She started to turn away. "I'll get a box for the bedding.

I've got plenty in my back room."

"Don't," he said quietly.

She paused, looking back over her shoulder. "Don't get a box? I don't want to put that nice bedding on the pavement."

"I'm not talking about the damned bedding. I mean don't try to shut me out of your world just because things are a little different where I come from. That's what you were thinking, isn't it? My family has made a fortune over the years, therefore I don't have a clue about what life is like in your world. I don't even know how much a mattress costs because I've never had to shop for one. You're right. But it shouldn't be an issue, not for us."

She went very still. "Why isn't it an issue?"

"Because you and I have spent the past couple of days getting to know each other under some very rough circumstances. Got a hunch we know more about each other now than most couples do who meet through one of the high-end matchmaking agencies."

She caught her breath. "Do you really believe that?"

"What I believe is that I'd trust you to have my back anytime, anywhere. I trust you, full stop."

Whatever she had been expecting to hear, that was not it, she thought.

"Here, in my world, that is the most important thing in a relationship," she said.

"It's the most important thing in my world, too."

His eyes burned with a little heat. She opened her senses to the strong, steady currents of his aura. A curious shiver of certainty whispered.

"I trust you," she said.

He smiled. "So maybe the we-come-from-two-different-worlds thing shouldn't be a big problem for us."

It probably would be a big problem, she thought. But not just now.

She smiled. "Forget the crack about the price of mattresses."

"Deal."

She found a carton in the back room of the shop. Together they folded the almost-new sheets, pillowcases, and expensive quilt. She placed the bedding in the box. Elias carried it out into the alley.

By the time he returned, the apartment immediately felt less tainted.

She went back upstairs to get the old set of sheets and bedding out of the cupboard. She started to make the bed by herself but Elias came up the stairs without a word and helped her finish the task.

He tucked the sheets in with a precision that told her it was not the first time he had made a bed. She thought of the cool, competent way he did everything, from driving his car to packing his field gear.

She had not known him for long, she thought. But the time they had shared together had been shot through with stress and danger and, yes, passion.

He was right. You learned a lot about a person under such conditions.

When they finished making the bed Elias straightened and met her eyes across the short distance that separated them.

"Will you be able to sleep here tonight?" he asked.

The taint of the intruder's dreamlight was gone. She would probably have a few bad dreams because even though the bastard's energy had been removed, there was no getting around the knowledge that her home had been invaded.

"I think so," she said.

"You need some real sleep. I'll take the sofa."

It wasn't a question. He wasn't trying to guilt-trip her into inviting him into her bed. He was giving her space.

She smiled. "Your choice. But just so you

know, you're welcome to sleep here. With me."

He visibly relaxed. "Okay."

"I have to warn you, though, this might be a bad night for me."

"Even with the clean bedding?"

"Even with the fresh bedding."

He shrugged. "Might be a bad night for me, too. If my dreams disturb yours, just wake me up. I'll move to the sofa."

"It's more likely the opposite will happen," she warned.

He shook his head. "I can handle your dreams if you can handle mine." He took out his phone. "Right now I need a drink and that pizza."

"Sounds like a plan."

CHAPTER 24

The small stones struck the window just as
Hannah set the pizza carton on the table.
Ping, ping, ping. A pause, and then, *ping,
ping.*

"That's Runner's signal," she said.

Virgil had been engrossed with his self-
appointed task of supervising the prepara-
tions for serving the pizza. But the pings
distracted him.

He chortled, hopped down from his perch
on the back of a kitchen chair, and vaulted
up onto the windowsill.

"Looks like Runner knows you're back in
town," Elias said.

"Word travels fast in the DZ. Besides, his
crew has been keeping an eye on this place
while we were gone, remember?"

She crossed to the window. Elias had been
pouring a second glass of wine for each of
them. He set the bottle aside and went to
join her.

She opened the curtain and looked down into the alley. Night had fallen hours ago, but thanks to the nearby ruins, it was never entirely dark in the DZ. The alley behind the apartment was steeped in acid green shadows but it was easy to see Runner standing below the window. He was dressed in his signature black leather jacket and black trousers. A black cap was pulled down low over his eyes, partially concealing his profile but there was no mistaking his expensive running shoes and his lean, wiry build.

Hannah unlatched the window, hoisted it, and leaned out.

"Hi, Runner," she said, keeping her voice low.

"Heard you were back," he said. He tipped his head a little to look up at her. His attention switched to Elias. "Also heard the husband was still hanging around."

"Yeah, I'm still here," Elias said. He gripped the windowsill. "Out of curiosity, do you mind telling me how you heard that we were back?"

Runner's shoulders shifted in an elaborate shrug. "Word on the street, man. I just came to check it out. Make sure Hannah was okay."

"I'm fine," Hannah said. "I finished the

out-of-town job and I'm ready to reopen for business. Well, I will be as soon as I clean up the mess the intruder left behind."

Elias leaned forward a little and looked down at Runner. "Any luck identifying the guy who tossed Hannah's place?"

"I got nothing on him," Runner said. He sounded deeply disgusted by the failure. "Sorry, Hannah. I'll keep asking around."

"Maybe you've got more than you realize," Elias suggested.

Runner squinted up at him. "What's that supposed to mean?"

"If the intruder was from the neighborhood you would have a name by now, right?"

"Oh, yeah," Runner said. "In the DZ you can't keep a secret like that for long."

"So we know he's an outsider," Elias said. "How often do you get strangers this deep into the Dark Zone?"

"Not often. When we do get 'em, it's usually because they wandered in by accident. They don't hang around for long, at least not after dark. The energy around here tends to freak out a lot of people."

"This out-of-zone guy knew exactly where he was going, yet Hannah says she's never seen his prints in her shop until the night he tossed the place."

"Huh." Runner sounded intrigued. "Hadn't thought about that. But what does that tell you?"

"Not sure yet but we know something else, as well. This guy from out of the zone hit Hannah's place the one night she was gone all night. We didn't get back here until after dawn the next morning."

Startled, Hannah looked at Elias. "I never thought about that angle. How did he know I wasn't home that night? Do you think he's been watching me?"

"Nah." Runner sounded very sure of himself. "Someone in the DZ would have noticed a stranger hanging out in this neighborhood, keeping an eye on you."

"Good point," Hannah said.

Elias considered that briefly. "Maybe he paid someone local to watch her?"

Runner grunted. "Anything's possible, I guess. But people in the DZ are pretty tight. If someone did get paid for selling out a local, it would be big news around here. Haven't heard anything like that."

Hannah drummed her fingers on the windowsill. "There is another, simpler possibility."

Elias and Runner looked at her.

"What?" Runner asked.

"The photo of us leaving the Enchanted

Night Wedding Chapel was in the early edition of the *Curtain* yesterday morning," Hannah said. "That edition was already going into the newspaper vending machines by the time we left the Shadow Zone Motel. We saw a delivery van, remember? By the time we got back here we were both fielding phone calls from people who wanted to know if the story was true."

"That photo was taken around midnight," Elias said. "We know that because that's when we showed up on the doorstep of the wedding mill. But the so-called reporter probably filed the photo and the piece naming us within minutes. It would have appeared online almost immediately. No self-respecting editor at the *Curtain* would have sat on that story for long."

Runner shrugged. "I saw it around two that morning on my phone. I was making a delivery in Star Hook Lane."

"There you go," Hannah said. "No need to look for a rat among my neighbors. All we have to do is get a list of the *Curtain*'s online subscribers. The perp will probably be on it."

Elias and Runner looked at her as if she had lost her senses.

"Are you kiddin'?" Runner demanded. "Everyone reads the *Curtain*. Must be thousands of online subscribers."

"I know," Hannah said. "Just trying to lighten the mood with a little humor. I really need to get some sleep."

CHAPTER 25

The dream-walking started the way it always did . . .

The doppelgänger got up from the bed and looked down at the two sleeping people. At the foot of the bed, the dust bunny stirred and opened all four eyes. He looked at the dreamer — not at the doppelgänger. He appeared attentive, but not alarmed by the heavy currents of dark dreamlight that shifted in the atmosphere. He recognized the dreamer's vibe. He also sensed in the unfathomable way of animals that when the dreamer went walking on the astral plane, it was important.

The man had been lying on his back but now he stirred, turned, and settled onto his side. He wrapped one arm around the dreamer's waist, cradling her against his body. The crystal in his ring glowed with a little heat.

"Amazing," the doppelgänger said. "We're not giving him nightmares."

"Yet," the dreamer said. "Look, I'm trying to

279

sleep here. Been a tough couple of days in case you weren't paying attention. I'm not in the mood to do any dream-walking tonight."

"You love him, you know."

"Just a case of mutual attraction and circumstances."

"I don't think so."

"Is that why we're chatting here?"

"No." The doppelgänger crossed to the mirror. "You can deal with that problem some other time. Tonight there is something else you need to think about."

"What?"

The doppelgänger looked into the mirror, as though entranced by her own reflection but there was no image reflected in the glass. There never was.

The doppelgänger reached out toward the top drawer of the dressing table with hands that could feel nothing; nor could they grasp the knob on the drawer. But the gesture reminded the dreamer that she had put her clutch in that particular drawer.

"My purse?" the dreamer said. "Again? What now?"

"The fortune you got from Sylvester Jones, the fortune-teller at the Midnight Carnival," the doppelgänger said. "It's still in the purse you carried that first night."

"What about it?"

"It's important."

"Why? What are you trying to tell me?"

"Pay attention. It all started with the carnival."

The doppelgänger turned and drifted back to the bed, fading fast. The dreamer tried to hang on to the fragments of the dream, trying to discover clues. There were more questions to be asked.

But the doppelgänger had finished dreamwalking.

Hannah came awake on the familiar shock of reorientation. Jolted by the adrenaline rush she sat straight up in bed, pulse skittering. Elias's arm fell away.

Virgil fluttered across the bed. She gathered him close and took a few deep breaths while he made small, comforting noises.

After a moment her senses calmed. She suddenly remembered Elias. When she turned her head she saw that he was still lying beside her, his arms folded behind his head on the pillow. He watched her with understanding eyes.

"Bad dream?" he asked. "Or a dream-walking episode?"

He sounded matter-of-fact, as though he was fine with being rudely awakened by what must have been a storm of dreamlight.

Well, at least she hadn't sent him running

281

out of the bedroom screaming.

"Dream-walking," she said. She hugged Virgil a little tighter. "Geez, I hate reentry. Takes a few seconds to adjust."

"Understandable." He unfolded his arms and held one hand in front of his face so that he could contemplate his ring. "Interesting."

"Your ring getting a little hot? Maybe it's what protects you from the effects of my dreamlight."

"Huh." He continued to contemplate the crystal. The fire at the heart of the stone was rapidly disappearing. "I don't think so. There's something else going on here — maybe something involving our auras."

Alarm jolted through her. "Do you think my talent is starting to affect yours?"

That sort of thing was rare between powerful talents, but when it did occur it was considered the ultimate toxic relationship.

Elias looked at her, his eyes heating a little. "Maybe but in the nicest possible way."

Energy shifted in the atmosphere. She knew he had deliberately jacked up his talent, letting her feel the power in it.

Virgil, evidently growing bored with the complexities of human relationships, wriggled free of Hannah's arms, grabbed the

Arizona Snow doll, hopped off the bed, and scurried out the bedroom door.

Hannah ignored him. She could not look away from Elias. His eyes continued to burn and she knew he could see the heat in her own gaze. They were both running hot now.

"Aura interference is not a subject that most talents consider a joking matter," she said.

"Who's joking?" Elias said. "For the record, it doesn't feel like interference — it feels like your aura is sort of whispering to mine."

"Whispering? Really?"

"Can't think of any other way to describe it. Whatever is going on between us, I like it a lot. Are you okay with the connection?"

She wrapped her arms around her knees and opened herself to the touch of his aura. The strong currents of his energy field did, indeed, seem to be whispering to her. The silent communication — the sense of intimacy it created — stirred all of her senses. It was, she decided, the ultimate seduction.

I know this man as I have never known any other man, she thought. She reminded herself that what she was experiencing was probably only a temporary bond forged by circumstances and mutual attraction. But her doppelgänger had told her the truth.

283

She was falling in love with Elias. And there was nothing in sight to break that fall before it was too late.

"I'm okay with your aura," she said, her voice a little wobbly. "Fine, really."

He put his hand very deliberately on her shoulder. She could feel the warmth and strength in his fingers through the light fabric of her nightgown.

The physical contact acted like a spark of energy transmitted through perfectly tuned amber — the sense of connection was immediately intensified and enhanced by orders of magnitude. She doubted that any para-physics instrument ever devised could measure the breathtaking intimacy of the sensation.

"Just okay?" he asked softly. "Just fine?"

"No," she said, too transfixed by his touch to try to evade the question. "No, I like the feel of your aura a lot."

He stroked his fingertips over her shoulder and down her arm to her elbow. His touch was tender, intimate, and irresistible. The wonder of the moment stole her breath.

She stopped hugging her knees, and leaned over him. She lowered her mouth to his until there was only an inch of space between them.

"In fact," she said very deliberately, "I love

the feel of your aura."

"Good."

He didn't say anything else. Instead he gently wrapped one hand around the back of her head and brought her mouth to his.

The kiss turned fierce and desperate, setting fire to the energy that infused the atmosphere.

She tore her mouth free from Elias's and kissed his throat, his ear, the curve of his muscled shoulder, indulging her senses in his scent and the exciting feel of his warm skin. She knew she was storing up memories for an uncertain future, but she didn't care. At the very least, when she was an old woman she would have an interesting past to share with the aging showgirls, magicians, and card dealers in the Dark Zone.

Elias groaned and tightened his grip on her. She gloried in the knowledge that she could induce such an elemental response in him.

One of his hands slid slowly down her back and then lower still. His fingers closed around the curve of her hip, squeezing gently. He drew the hem of her nightgown up to her waist and touched her ever more intimately, touched her until she was wet and aching and consumed by the urgent need to join with him in the most elemental way of all.

His forehead and chest were damp with sweat and she knew it was because he was fighting to hold himself in check until she was ready. Another time she might be tempted to see how far she could push him. But not tonight. Tonight was for the past, present, and future.

She pushed herself up off of his chest and straddled him. He sank his fingers into her thighs and watched her with hot, half-closed eyes as she took him slowly, deeply.

The night burned.

CHAPTER 26

A long time later she felt a soft thump on the bed. Virgil was back. He bustled up the rumpled bed to greet her. His fur was cool with the chill of dawn and the wild Rainforest. She knew he had been hunting.

"About time you got back," she mumbled, still half asleep. She patted him affectionately. "Hope you had fun. I sure did."

"What?"

Elias's voice was low, freighted with sleep and somewhat muffled by the pillow. Nevertheless, the sound of it jolted her into full wakefulness. She sat up quickly and stared at the large man beside her. Fortunately, he was on his side, facing the nightstand. He could not see her startled expression.

Old habits die hard, she realized. After a lifetime of sleeping alone, waking up in bed with a man took a little getting used to.

"Nothing," she said. "Just chatting with Virgil. He's back."

"Good for Virgil."

She swung her legs over the side of the bed, got to her feet, and grabbed her robe off the hook.

"Didn't mean to wake you," she said. "It's still early. I'll just go start the coffee."

Good grief. She was blathering.

Virgil fluttered across the bed and hopped onto the nightstand so that he was face-to-face with Elias. He chortled a cheery greeting.

Elias gave him a pat. "Morning, pal. Hope the hunting went well."

Virgil chortled exuberantly. Then, evidently concluding he had fulfilled his social obligations to a houseguest, he jumped down from the nightstand, dashed across the bedroom, and disappeared out the door. Hannah knew he was headed for the kitchen.

Elias stretched, shoved the covers aside, and sat up on the side of the bed. He was wearing only his briefs and he seemed to take up a lot of space in the little bedroom.

She realized he was half aroused. Hurriedly she averted her gaze and concentrated hard on tying the sash of the robe.

"Are you okay?" Elias asked.

She tied the knot in the sash very, very tightly. "Yes, of course. Just dandy, thanks."

"You sure there's nothing wrong?"

"Absolutely. Like I said, just off to start the coffee. You can have the shower first if you like."

"You seem to be in a rush," he said. "Trying to find a diplomatic way to kick me out of your apartment?"

She stared at him, appalled. It dawned on her that she might have hurt his feelings.

"No, really," she said. "Seriously. I mean, I'm just not used to this kind of thing."

"What kind of thing?"

"This." She waved a hand in a rather vague gesture that included the bedroom and everything that had happened in it during the night. "A man. In bed. In the morning."

"Ah, so that's it." He smiled a rather smug, distinctly masculine smile. The crystal in his ring flashed with a little fire. He crossed the room and kissed her nose. "Look on the bright side. I know how to make a bed."

The affectionate little kiss on the nose eased the morning-after awkwardness. She relaxed and smiled.

"Sorry," she mumbled. "I'm still new at this sleeping-together thing."

"I know. If it makes you feel any better, so am I."

She raised her brows. "I find that a little hard to believe."

He threaded his fingers into her sleep-tumbled hair. "As a rule, I prefer to sleep alone."

She tried — and failed — to read his eyes. "Why?"

"If I don't spend the night, it feels like a date. But if I spend the night —" He broke off, shrugging.

"If you spend the night, it feels like a relationship."

"Exactly." He nodded once, evidently satisfied. "So that makes this a relationship. Now, if you don't mind, I'm going to take you up on that offer of a shower."

"Okay."

"We can talk about your dream at breakfast."

"My dream. Good heavens, I almost forgot about it."

He looked pleased. "You were probably distracted."

"Probably." She turned toward the dressing table. "The message I got was clear enough. I'm just not sure how to interpret it yet. That's always the problem, you know, interpretation."

"What was the message?"

Hannah crossed to the dressing table and

opened the top drawer. She took out the evening clutch and opened it. The paper fortune was still inside. She removed it, aware of a faint tingle of energy, and held it up so that Elias could see it.

"My doppelgänger walked over here to the dressing table, looked in the mirror, and then reminded me that the fortune from the Midnight Carnival was still in my purse. I got the impression that it was important."

"The fortune?"

"No, I don't think she was referring directly to the fortune. I think she was trying to tell me that the Midnight Carnival is the answer to all the questions we've been asking."

Elias contemplated the fortune for a long moment.

"Which questions?" he asked finally.

"That's the problem with dream-walking," Hannah said. "The literal message usually comes through loud and clear. But I don't always know the right questions to ask."

"I'm going to need that shower and some coffee before we start trying to interpret your new dream."

CHAPTER 27

"Last night, just before I fell asleep, I rezzed my talent and focused on a single question," Hannah said. "I really, really want to know who trashed my shop and apartment."

Elias had been concentrating on the mountain of fluffy scrambled eggs on his plate. He paused his fork briefly in midair, the engineer in him curious as usual.

"That's how you work when you set out to find something?" he said. "You ask a specific question?"

"I ask it just before I go to sleep. I don't have a great deal of control over the dream-walking process. I can't tell myself *not* to dream, for example. If I could, my personal life would probably be a lot different."

Elias looked around the small, cozy kitchen and beyond into the tiny living room. Everything about the apartment, from the single reading chair in front of the amber fireplace to the minimal number of dishes and glasses in the cupboards, had clearly been designed for a woman who lived alone. *Okay, make that a single woman who shared space with a dust bunny.*

It dawned on him that, as much as he treasured his privacy, he always knew that he had options. He had grown up in a warm, close-knit family. Sure, there were arguments, emotional scenes, and pressure from the older generation to get one's act together. But for the most part he got along well with his brother and sister and most of his cousins. He went home to Copper Beach Island several times a year for holidays and family celebrations of one kind or another. In addition, he had always known that he would someday have a wife and children of his own.

Sure, there was a downside to family life. As his mother liked to say, it wouldn't be a family if there were not a lot of drama and a few secrets. But there was also a sense of connection that went bone deep. The members of the Coppersmith clan were forever bound by a shared past and the knowledge that, when crunch time came, they always stood shoulder to shoulder against the threat from outside.

He could only imagine a life that was not founded on the bedrock of a strong family.

On the other side of the table, Hannah gave him an oddly reassuring smile.

"It's okay," she said gently. "I do have a family. It just doesn't look like your family."

"How did you know what I was thinking?" he asked.

"Call me psychic."

He smiled. "Okay, Madam Psychic, tell me about your dream-walking experience."

She drank some coffee and set the cup down with great precision. "Like I said, I can't *not* dream whenever I like but I do have the ability to dream to order, at least to a degree. The trick is to ask the right question just before I go to sleep and really focus on it with a little talent."

"Last night you asked who trashed your apartment?"

"Something like that. I asked who would want to trash my apartment."

"Ah, looking at motive first." He ate some of his eggs. "Good idea."

"It's not the first time I've asked the question but there has been so much going on lately and we've had so little sleep, I guess my doppelgänger has had to prioritize."

"But last night she told you the answer was the Midnight Carnival."

"What she said — and this is always the murky part — is that it started with the

Midnight Carnival."

A small shock of comprehension arced through him. He put down his fork and looked at the string of clear crystal beads that circled Hannah's throat.

"The Midnight Carnival is linked to your necklace, isn't it?" he said.

She reached up to touch the crystals with her fingertips. The small stones sparked briefly with a little color.

"It was just a broken necklace until I found the missing crystal. But when I found that at an online estate auction, I knew it was important. I got it very cheap because there was no competition. As soon as I had the stone set in place in the necklace, I knew I had the key I'd been looking for all these years."

"The key to one of the most valuable finds ever made in the Underworld," Elias said softly. "You're thinking that someone else is looking for the Midnight Carnival and that individual knows that you have the key. That's why he searched your apartment."

"I can't be positive, but the timing of events fits that scenario. I think that's what my doppelgänger was trying to tell me."

"Lay out the timeline for me, right from the beginning."

She pushed her plate aside and folded her

295

arms on the table. "I didn't set out to search for the Midnight Carnival. I didn't even know it existed. I was just trying to find the missing crystal. The necklace is all I have of my mother's. I wanted to repair it. I located the crystal a couple of weeks before you showed up at my door. I paid to have it hand-delivered by courier. When it arrived I immediately took it to a jeweler I know and trust. As soon as the stone was in place I realized that I had a psychic map of some kind."

"Did the jeweler understand what you had?"

"No, I'm sure he didn't," Hannah said. "He realized that the crystals were a little hot but that's not unusual in his line. Anyhow, that night I wore the necklace to bed, fired up my talent, and went into a dream-walking trance."

"You make it sound simple."

"Sometimes it is. I woke up with an intuitive understanding of how to use the map."

He drank some coffee and lowered the cup. "It's a psi-code map. You figured it out because your para-psych profile is similar to that of the person who created the map."

"Yes. After the first dream, I knew I needed to know more about the map itself. When I consulted Miss Le Fay she said she was sure that the map could only be fired up by someone with my para-genetic profile."

"Who is Miss Le Fay?" he asked. "Is that her real name, by the way?"

"I'm sure it's a stage name that she adopted years ago. Morgana Le Fay is a retired stage psychic. Used to be a big headliner at the Glass Palace. She still uses the name and in this town it's considered rude to ask about other names."

"And she told you that you probably had a genetic connection to whoever had crafted the dreamlight gate?"

"Exactly."

"Son of a ghost," he said very softly. "When you found the missing crystal you found the clue to your family history."

Excitement sparked in Hannah's eyes. "Miss Le Fay said that I almost certainly have to be a direct descendant of whoever encoded the map into the crystals in my necklace."

"All right, does Le Fay know that the necklace is the map to a hugely valuable discovery in the Underworld?"

"She knows it leads to something, of course, but I'm sure she assumes it's just some old First Generation family heirloom. A lot of families try to collect First Gen antiques and memorabilia that have a connection to their bloodline. She wished me luck finding what I was looking for and that was the end of it."

"Still, she is aware that you've acquired a psi-code map."

"Yes, but I've known her all my life. She's a friend of my aunts. I trust her. Besides, she realizes that I'm the only one who can decipher the map. If she wanted a piece of the action she would have tried to cut a deal — not steal the necklace."

"All right, who else knows about the necklace?"

"Are you kidding? I've worn it ever since my aunts gave it to me on my sixteenth birthday. People here in the DZ are used to seeing it on me."

"You wore it before you found the missing crystal?"

"Yes. I doubt if most people noticed the missing stone. Would you be aware of one missing bead on a woman's necklace?"

He thought about it. "I might, if I realized the stones in the necklace were hot."

"Well, you're a crystal engineer. You aren't most people."

"All right, sounds like we've got a town, or at least a neighborhood, full of suspects."

"I can guarantee you that whoever

stomped all over my bed was not a neighbor and definitely not a friend. I told you, I would have recognized the psi-prints."

"That still leaves a lot of people who live here and a few thousand more who come and go as tourists. I don't see how your dream gets us any closer to identifying the intruder."

"I think what my doppelgänger was trying to tell me is that we should take another look at the timeline and try sorting out events in a different pattern," Hannah said. "We've been assuming that the intruder was connected to the pirates. But what if that isn't the case?"

He thought about that. "You think we're dealing with two different problems?"

"Exactly. It's not like things didn't get very confusing for a while. We've been assuming that the pirates are linked to that motorcycle gang that tried to stop you from hiring me to open the gate at your jobsite. But what if the bikers are connected to the guy who broke into my place? What if my doppelgänger — my intuition — is right? Maybe the intruder is after the Midnight Carnival?"

"Then you'd have to explain the co-incidence of the timing. Why would someone choose the one night that you're not home to search your apartment?"

"Simple," she said. "Opportunity. There may also have been a sense of desperation. After all, we'd escaped the biker gang, disappeared into the tunnels, and gotten married. I signed a contract with your company. We were about to leave for the portal project jobsite. Whoever is after the Midnight Carnival might have been convinced that he was in danger of losing the one person who could lead him to the big find — me."

"There are a couple of other questions here," Elias said. "First, how did the intruder know that you had found the missing crystal in the first place and that you had used it to find the carnival?"

She bit her lip. "Okay, you've got me there. I kept it very, very quiet, believe me."

Elias tapped his finger against the side of the mug. "But you registered a claim about two weeks ago."

Hannah went very still. Her eyes widened. "I registered a claim on a small portion of a sector in the Underworld. There's nothing on the claim forms I filled out that describes what I found there or hoped to discover within that sector."

"But if the intruder knew that you had recently acquired a psi-code map and shortly thereafter filed a claim on a certain sector in the tunnels, it would be easy to

300

put two and two together. He would have had every right to assume you had found something valuable."

"But that would mean he's been watching me from afar for heaven knows how long," Hannah said. "And I still don't see how he could have known that I had found the final piece of the map."

"You're the one who told me that collectors can be very obsessive. What if this particular collector has been hunting for the legendary Midnight Carnival for a while now?"

"But how would he know that I had acquired the map and found the carnival?"

"Mind if I take a closer look at the necklace?"

She reached up, unclasped the necklace, and handed it to him. "What are you looking for?"

"I'll know if I find it."

He spread the necklace across the palm of his hand and rezzed a little talent. His ring heated a little, searching for frequencies. The inexpensive crystals were of varying colors, transparent and cut to reflect the light in an attractive way. He could tell that they were psi-locked.

"Which crystal is the one you recently bought online?" he asked. "The one you said completed the map?"

"The ultraviolet one in the center. You can see the color when you view it through your para-senses."

He caught the ultraviolet crystal between his thumb and his forefinger and kicked his talent up a little higher.

And there it was, a fine bit of tuning that had nothing to do with the psi-locked map.

"You said this came from the estate of a collector who had recently died?" he asked.

"That's right. I kept an eye out for it for years but it never showed up in the underground market because it was locked away in the collector's vault. He was an elderly man who had probably acquired it decades ago. I doubt that he had any idea that it was a piece of a map. The firm that handled the estate certainly didn't know anything about it. There was no mention of that in the information about the stone that was posted online at the auction site. As far as I can tell, no other collectors knew the significance of the crystal because I was the only bidder."

"How did you recognize it when it popped up in the estate auction?" he asked.

"Two reasons. The first was that it was ultraviolet. You'll notice the crystals form a paranormal rainbow. I always knew that the ultraviolet crystal was the one that was missing. The second reason I could identify it was because of the cut. The faceting of each of the stones in the necklace is identical. I've always had a pretty good idea of the size, shape, and color of the missing crystal. I kept an eye out for it in both the regular crystal markets and the underground markets. When it showed up I recognized it immediately."

"The ultraviolet crystal is hot," he said.

Hannah looked at the necklace. "Well, yes. All of the stones have some resonating power. Someone was able to tune the whole set so that it functioned as a map. Each crystal had to have some power."

"I'm not talking about the psi-code tuning," he said. "This crystal is sending out a second frequency. Whoever possessed this necklace before you is either a very skilled tuner or he paid a good technician to do the job."

"What are you talking about?"

"The ultraviolet crystal is set to transmit a strong, unique signal," he said. "Anyone who knows the frequency and has the right equipment could track this stone."

Hannah took a breath. "Someone traced the crystal to my shop?"

"That's what it looks like. If I'm right, the

303

ultraviolet crystal was the bait in an elaborate trap. Someone was looking for the Midnight Carnival. At some point he managed to obtain one of the psi-coded stones."

"The ultraviolet crystal."

"Right. But he needed the whole necklace and someone who could crack the psi-code and follow the map."

"All right, I'm following you, so far," Hannah said. "The person searching for the remaining crystals put the single ultraviolet on the market and waited to see who would take the bait."

"It was a risk. Some other collector might have grabbed it before you did." Elias stopped. "No, it wasn't a risk. You said you were the only bidder. But can you be sure of that?"

"No, not really. I just know that I got the crystal at a very cheap price. The firm running the auction told me I was the only bidder so I assumed that was the case. I had no reason to think otherwise."

"Have you worked with that particular auction site before?"

"Once or twice," she said. "They rarely handle the kind of things I am usually looking for."

"Do you trust it?"

"I have no reason not to trust it, but then,

all I care about is the quality of the antiquities being auctioned. That particular firm has never tried to cheat me. The few items I've picked up at that site have always been as advertised."

"People who run auction sites take a commission on the sales. I think that someone paid that firm well to run a very special auction for a single crystal that had no obvious value — except to the one person who recognized it."

Hannah exhaled slowly. "Me."

"Here's how I think it all went down," Elias said. "We have an obsessive collector who is looking for the Midnight Carnival. He's got a piece of the map, a single crystal, but he can't find the rest of the necklace. It occurs to him that another collector might have acquired it. He also knows that if that collector is aware of what he has, he will be watching for the ultraviolet crystal to come onto the underground market."

"He put it out there and waited to see who would pounce on it," Hannah said.

"When you jumped on it, he must have realized that you probably knew its real value. You were very likely the only bidder. That's why you got it so cheap. But it also indicated that you might know something about the rest of the necklace. He tuned a tracking frequency into the ultraviolet crystal, had it delivered to you anonymously, and then sat back to watch your every move."

"Oh, geez." Hannah slumped in her chair, thoroughly irritated with herself. "I led him straight to the carnival. He didn't even have to follow me. As soon as I filed my claim he had the approximate location."

"But he couldn't get through the dreamlight gate," Elias said. "He was probably trying to figure out how to overcome that obstacle when I showed up. Being a paranoid collector, he assumed that I was after the carnival, too."

"So he hired those bikers to try and grab me."

"I'm not sure if the bikers were hired to get rid of me or grab you. They were able to follow us into the tunnels — probably had your personal amber frequency — but they lost us when we ducked into the Midnight Carnival. The collector would have lost the signal from the ultraviolet crystal at the same time. All he could do was wait for you to show up aboveground again."

"And then, sometime around two that morning, he sees the story about our midnight marriage in the *Curtain*."

"The photo in the *Curtain* was sharp and

clear," Elias said. He tightened his fingers around the crystals. "He could see that you aren't wearing the necklace. He panics. Now he's wondering if you discovered the tracking frequency on the ultraviolet crystal and neutralized it. All he knows for sure is that you are no longer wearing the necklace."

"He's desperate. He breaks into my apartment, maybe hoping to find the necklace or at least figure out what is going on."

"You are his only hope for getting through the dreamlight gate. He wants to get you back under his control."

Hannah glared. "I was never under his control." She hesitated. "But you're right. He's a paranoid collector who has just lost his only lead to the Midnight Carnival. That probably explains the rage that I saw in his psi-prints."

"We're going to need a little help finding this guy and nailing those bikers," Elias said. "If this were any other city I'd contact Jones and Jones or the Federal Bureau of Psi Investigation. But this is Illusion Town — your town. Got any ideas?"

Hannah smiled. Her eyes heated, not with passion, he concluded, not this time. The excitement he sensed radiating from her was the thrill of the hunt. After all, she was the Finder.

"We start with a phone call to my aunts," she said. "And then we pay a call on Uncle Ollie."

CHAPTER 28

It was going on ten o'clock when Hannah and Elias walked through the door of Ollie's House of Pizza. Hannah had Virgil tucked under one arm. He clutched Arizona Snow in one paw.

Like most restaurants in Illusion Town, there was a slot machine at every table and a bar.

The night was still young and the crowd was light, mostly regulars who lived in the neighborhood. The out-of-zone tourists wouldn't show up until after midnight. They had to have time and a few drinks to work up their nerve to leave the safety of the bright lights and the high security in the Amber, Emerald, and Sapphire zones.

Virgil considered himself one of the regulars. He wriggled free of Hannah's grasp, bounced down to the floor, and scuttled across the floorboards to an empty stool. He scrambled up to the seat and from there vaulted onto the polished surface of the bar. There was another round of greetings.

Virgil, always ready to play to an adoring audience, went into full cute mode. He fluttered the length of the bar, proudly displaying his Arizona Snow doll and accepting affectionate pats en route.

When he reached the far end of the polished bar top, Jake, the bouncer-turned-bartender, put a dish of bar snacks in front of him. Virgil set Arizona Snow aside and went to work emptying the bowl of salty tidbits.

"Interesting doll, Virgil," Jake said. He patted Virgil and gave Elias an appraising look before nodding approvingly and turning to Hannah. "Interesting husband. Congratulations, Finder."

"About time you took the plunge, honey." Milly Lamont, a former chorus line dancer perched on a stool at the end, hoisted her martini glass. "But why do your friends and family have to learn this from the *Curtain*?"

A small, tightly muscled woman seated at one of the tables spoke up.

"Heard the name was Coppersmith," she said. "Would that be Coppersmith, as in Coppersmith Mining?"

Elias looked amused. "So I'm told."

The woman gave him a sultry smile. "I'm

Venus, by the way. I'm one of the artists in the Alien Visions show at the Glass Pavilion. I'll make sure you and Hannah get tickets. Wedding gift."

"Appreciate it," Elias said.

Someone proposed a toast. There was a round of cheers and best wishes.

Hannah felt the heat rise in her cheeks. Luckily, Ollie's House of Pizza, like most such business establishments in Illusion Town, existed in a state of eternal night carefully engineered by low lighting and heavily darkened windows. She was reasonably sure that no one could see her turning red.

"Thanks, everyone. But really, it's just an MC," she mumbled.

"So what?" Ned Higgins said. "It's a marriage. That calls for a celebration."

Ned was a retired croupier who supplemented his pension with small-time blackjack games conducted in various back rooms scattered around the Dark Zone. Jake was a very good card counter. He had a psychic talent for it. He was so good that he had been quietly but firmly informed that he was not welcome in any of the major casinos, at least not as a player.

Alexandra Collins, one of a team of aging waitresses who worked at Ollie's, crossed

311

the room to give Hannah a hug. She stepped back and studied Elias. Energy whispered in the atmosphere around her.

Hannah held her breath, waiting for Alexandra's verdict. Alexandra operated a small side business as a storefront psychic in the DZ. She had a talent for reading people.

For some reason Hannah was relieved when Alexandra gave Elias an approving smile.

"Welcome to the DZ," Alexandra said. "As long as you're married to Hannah, you're one of the family."

"Thanks," Elias said.

Hannah decided to take charge.

"Thanks for all the good wishes," she said. "Afraid we can't stay. Just dropped in to see Uncle Ollie."

"About time you showed up, honey. Let's have a look at this new husband of yours."

The big voice boomed from the large, barrel-chested man who emerged from a back room. He was in his seventies with a lot of shoulder-length silver hair, which Hannah suspected was not all his own, and an unnaturally tight face that was kept firmly in place by regular visits to a discreet cosmetic dermatologist. His dark eyes glinted with a little heat as he examined Elias.

Ollie had a last name but he hadn't used it for years. He was "Ollie" to almost everyone in the DZ and "Uncle Ollie" to Hannah. Once upon a time he had managed the Lost Colony casino, one of the scruffier establishments in the Emerald Zone. At the time it had been owned by Maxwell Smith. When Smith sold the business in order to move upmarket with the new, flashy Amber Palace, Ollie had retired from the fast lane. He claimed he had always wanted to run a small neighborhood restaurant.

"This is Elias Coppersmith," Hannah said. "And it's just an MC, Uncle Ollie. My life has gotten a little complicated lately."

"Yeah, marriage will do that to you," Ollie said. He offered his hand to Elias. "Welcome to the DZ, Elias. I met your dad a few decades back."

"Do I want to know the circumstances?" Elias asked.

Ollie chuckled. "He used to show up at the Lost Colony every few months. He'd win just enough to get my attention and then he'd leave. My security people checked him out and said he wasn't cheating so they figured he was some kind of talent, one we didn't know how to detect. I sent in a cooler to try to take the edge off his streak. Didn't work. My security team suggested we just

313

ask him to leave but I decided I'd like to talk to him first."

Elias smiled. "Dad told you he was using your casino to run some real-world lab tests on some quartz samples, right?"

"Yeah. Claimed his lab instruments weren't nearly as good as a casino for running some kinds of tests."

"Dad tends to be very lucky at cards."

Ollie snorted. "You can say that again. Your father would have made one hell of a professional poker player."

"He likes a friendly game, but generally speaking, when he risks big money it involves opening up a new hot-rocks territory."

"When I figured that out, we made a deal," Ollie said. "I told him he could continue to test his samples at the Lost Colony provided he let me invest in the territory the samples were coming from. Turned out to be the Sapphire Mine."

Elias grinned. "It was one of our most profitable territories. Still is, for that matter."

"Tell me about it. How do you think I financed this place? And now you're married to my niece. Whatever you need, you got it. Family is family, right?"

Elias smiled. "It is where I come from."

"Same here in the DZ," Ollie said. "So what can I give you two by way of a wedding gift?"

"What we need is a little extra protection, Uncle Ollie," Hannah said. "The cops can only do so much. Runner and his crew are good but there's only five of them and they don't carry a lot of firepower. The guys we're worried about are running around on big motorcycles and they're armed with mag-rez pistols."

Ollie squinted a little. "You're talking about that gang of out-of-zone bikers that tried to grab you the other night."

Hannah smiled. "Should have known you'd have heard about that by now."

"Can't keep stuff like that quiet in the DZ. I doubled the neighborhood watch on your street as soon as I heard about what had happened. You know, the Club isn't going to be at all happy about this."

"Funny you should mention that," Elias said. "Hannah's aunts arranged an appointment for us with Smith at the Amber Palace this evening."

"Excellent." Ollie chuckled. "Those bikers are gonna find out real quick who runs things here in Illusion Town."

CHAPTER 29

It was just after midnight and the atmosphere on the gaming floor of the Amber Palace was hot with energy. Elias knew that some of the charged heat seeped in from the nearby ruins but most of it was generated by the players. There was a reason why the excitement of gambling was often described as a fever.

Games of chance had always held a peculiar fascination for humans, and people who possessed even a minimal level of psychic talent were the most easily attracted.

"You'd think people would understand that being psychic doesn't mean that somehow the laws of probability have been repealed," Hannah said.

Elias watched a player roll a pair of red dice. "Having a little talent just gives people a false sense of confidence. Makes them think they can beat the house."

"In this town, the house always wins in

the long run," Hannah said.

Elias smiled. "Sure. Because in addition to having the math on their side, the casinos double down on the odds by hiring dealers who have some talent and a lot of really good crystal engineers to program the slots."

She slanted him a curious, sidelong glance. "Do you play?"

"Hell, yes. I'm in the mining business, remember? Of course I play. But in my world the stakes are usually higher. Coppersmith makes multimillion-dollar bets on new territories all the time."

"Ever lose?"

"Oh, yeah," he said. "That's what keeps the game interesting." He paused a beat. "But we don't lose often."

She gave him a knowing look. "Something tells me you and Mr. Smith will get along very well."

The invitation from Maxwell Smith, the owner of the Amber Palace, had come within minutes after Hannah had made the call to her aunts. It seemed that Mr. Smith, one of the powerful members of the Illusion Club, was only too happy to do a favor for his old friends, Clara and Bernice.

The interior of the Amber Palace glowed and glittered and sparkled. An adventurous tourist could find the raw world of hard-core gambling and sleazy nightclubs in the shadowy establishments in some of the other zones. But the Palace was one of the flashy towers in the brightly lit Amber Zone. Here, over-the-top flash successfully concealed the gritty, sweaty, perilous businesses that sustained Illusion Town.

The crowded gaming floor was thronged with men and women dressed for an evening of glitz and glamour. The dresses were cut very low, the heels were very high, and for the most part, the fit of the men's tuxedos had the slightly off look that indicated they had been rented for the night.

The dealers' tuxes, on the other hand, were all elegantly tailored. The gossamer costumes on the attractive men and women offering free drinks to the high rollers were designed to leave little to the imagination.

Elias glanced at Hannah walking at his side and got a rush of pride and old-fashioned male possessiveness. *His wife. At least for now.* She was far more discreetly dressed than the cocktail servers but everything about her riveted his senses. The little green slip of a dress and the dainty, sparkling high heels underscored her sleek curves. Her hair was swept up in a cute twist anchored by a clip he hoped to unfasten later in the privacy of her bedroom.

She wore minimal makeup compared to most of the women in the room, but in his opinion that just made her the most attractive female in sight. Her jewelry was limited to a pair of amber earrings and her necklace. In a city built on illusion she was breathtakingly real. The energy of her aura whispered secrets to him; secrets that beckoned and aroused him.

She carried her little evening clutch, secured with a chain around her wrist, in one hand. Virgil was tucked under her other arm. He had the Arizona Snow figure clutched in one paw.

"There's a private elevator that will take us to Mr. Smith's private quarters," Hannah said. "We'll check in with his personal security people first."

"I assume no one gets to Mr. Smith's private quarters without an armed escort," Elias said.

"You don't get to his level of power in this town without making a few enemies along the way," Hannah said.

They threaded a path through the crowd. The deeper they went into the casino, the more feverish the energy became. The stakes were higher in this section of the gaming floor.

Wide strips of amber-and-mirror panels

on the walls were arranged to reflect the glamorous scene as well as the paranormal currents that seethed and swirled in the atmosphere. A lot of good crystal engineering and architectural talent went into designing a successful casino. It was all built around the goal of separating people from their money.

The high, vaulted ceilings were painted with scenes of fantasy landscapes. The themes were taken from myths and legends familiar to every child on Harmony. Ethereal emerald castles, strange cities built of transparent crystal, and startling, surreal scenes of the Rainforest and the catacombs abounded.

There was no need to go back to Old World fairy tales for inspiration, Elias reflected. When the First Generation human colonists had arrived two hundred years ago, they had discovered ample material for new stories amid the ruins of the long-vanished Alien civilization. Humans were very good at storytelling.

The casino's security office was positioned near a private elevator lobby. When Elias and Hannah approached, a muscular man dressed in a tuxedo that was cut to conceal a shoulder holster looked up from his computer. Everything about him signaled ex–ghost hunter. Private security work was a common second career for retired hunters.

The guard gave Hannah a warm smile and reached out to pat Virgil.

"Miss West, we've been expecting you and your husband," he said. "And the little guy, too, of course."

"Hi, Fred." Hannah returned the smile. "How are Nancy and the kids?"

"Doing great, thanks. Kids are all in school this year and Nancy is working part-time in the Palace gift shop. She loves it. Got a real talent for selling fancy watches to the high rollers." Fred gave Elias an assessing look. "Congratulations on your marriage, by the way."

Hannah flushed a bright pink. Elias wondered if she was going to try to explain the hasty wedding. For some reason he got irritated every time she alluded to the temporary nature of their relationship.

"Thank you," Hannah said. She paused, looking somewhat bewildered about what she was supposed to say next. "This is him. My husband, Elias Coppersmith."

"Figured as much." Fred chuckled. "Welcome to the Amber Palace, Mr. Coppersmith, and congratulations."

"Thanks," Elias said.

He offered his hand. Fred shook it with

genuine enthusiasm.

"Mr. Smith is looking forward to meeting you," Fred said. "Carl will escort you and Miss West to the penthouse."

A bulked-up guard who also radiated a retired ghost hunter vibe emerged from another office.

"Hey, Miss West," he said. "Nice to see you. Heard you were married. Congratulations."

"Thanks, Carl," Hannah said.

Elias offered his hand again. "I'm the husband."

"Yes, sir, Mr. Coppersmith. I recognized you from your photo ID. I'm the one who conducted the background check on you."

"Is that so?" Elias glanced at Hannah and then turned back to Carl. "Did you run that check today after Mr. Smith invited us for drinks?"

"Nah. Mr. Smith ordered up a check as soon as he saw the news of your marriage in the *Curtain.* Hannah's a local, after all. We look after our own. Come with me, both of you. I'll take you upstairs."

He led them into a small foyer. The plush carpet was a deep red. The walls were mirrored and the elevator was trimmed in amber and gold. Carl punched in a code. The doors opened in near silence.

Hannah chatted with Carl on the short trip to the top floor. Elias realized he was starting to feel like extra baggage. He knew he wasn't the most scintillating conversationalist in the world but he wasn't a doorstop, either.

Damn. Married less than a week and he was already wondering if they should get counseling.

The elevator glided to a gentle stop and the doors whispered open, revealing another amber-and-mirrored foyer. A tall fortysomething woman dressed in a formal black suit and a crisp white, immaculately tailored shirt stood waiting to receive them. Her blond hair was pulled back in a tight bun. She had the elegant bone structure, the long legs, and the gravity-defying breasts of a former showgirl.

"Welcome, Miss West. Congratulations on your marriage."

"Thanks, Perkins, but, really, it's just an MC."

"Nevertheless, it's a marriage and, if I'm not mistaken, your first." Perkins looked at Elias. "You must be Mr. Coppersmith."

"That's right," Elias said without inflection. "I'm the husband."

Hannah blushed again and rushed into an apology. "Sorry. I keep forgetting to introduce him."

"Don't worry," Elias said. "I'm getting used to it."

Hannah looked at Perkins. "Our situation is sort of complicated."

"Marriage is always complicated," Perkins said serenely.

Virgil chortled at her. She smiled and gave him an affectionate pat. "Good evening, Virgil. I have a special treat for you tonight. If the three of you will follow me, I'll escort you out to the terrace where Mr. Smith is waiting."

Perkins turned gracefully on her stiletto heels and led the way through another glittering room littered with white leather sofas and draped with swaths of tasseled amber-gold cloth.

The wall of windowed doors at the far end of the room stood open to the warm desert night and a lush, softly lit rooftop garden. A pool ringed with statues glowed with underwater lighting.

A small, round elf of a man waited on the terrace. He wore white trousers and a loose-fitting white shirt stitched with crystal beads. The wide collar of the crisp white shirt was unfastened at the throat. A white silk scarf and white shoes completed the outfit. His eyes sparkled with pleasure at the sight of Hannah.

"Welcome, my dear," he said. "Many, many congratulations to you."

He opened his arms in a paternal way.

Hannah put Virgil down and did a quick air-kiss hug with the casino magnate. Virgil chortled and bustled off in the general direction of the pool.

"Thanks," Hannah said, stepping back. "But it's just an MC."

Smith raised silver brows and gave Elias a speculative look. "Indeed?"

"Don't worry. We'll explain," Hannah said. Belatedly she waved a hand at Elias. "This is Elias Coppersmith."

"The husband," Elias said. He smiled politely. "She sometimes forgets that part."

Smith chuckled. "Give her time. She's still a newlywed."

"People keep telling me that," Elias said.

Smith extended a soft, manicured hand. He wore a ring set with blue amber. Elias was not surprised to discover that there was a lot of power in the elf's grip — power of the paranormal variety. He glanced at the gently sparking blue amber and acknowledged the silent message with a small respectful nod — he was, after all, the younger man and he was on the older male's turf. But he also sent a whisper of

325

energy through his own ring. Smith's eyes narrowed faintly. Then he smiled, as though satisfied.

"Welcome to my home, Elias," he said.

Hannah rolled her eyes. "Men."

Smith turned to her. "You must forgive us, my dear. We have our ways."

"Is that what you call it?" She watched him with knowing eyes. "Looked more like two male specter-cats sizing each other up."

"There is a bit of that in our primitive little rituals," Smith said. "But for what it's worth, I think you chose well, my dear."

Hannah looked startled. She opened her mouth to respond and somehow Elias just knew he didn't want to hear another explanation about the status of their marriage.

He spoke first. "Nice place you've got here, sir."

"Thank you," Smith said. "I enjoy it."

His tone was one of polite modesty, as if they were not standing on top of the gambling and entertainment empire he had built. He did not have to boast, Elias thought. It was a given that no one achieved Smith's level of success without a lot of powerful talent and the ruthless edge required to use that talent in whatever manner best served his objectives.

"I have taken the liberty of ordering some

champagne to celebrate your nuptials," Smith said. "I trust you both will join me?"

"Thanks," Hannah said. "To tell you the truth, I could use a drink. Things have gotten very weird, Mr. Smith — and I'm not talking about my Marriage of Convenience."

"Yes, Clara and Bernice mentioned the problem. I, too, am quite concerned. Can't have out-of-town gangs thinking they can harass the local citizenry. We take public safety very seriously."

Smith nodded at Perkins, who stood waiting beside a silver tray. There was a bottle of champagne and three glasses on the tray. At Smith's signal she went to work opening the bottle.

Elias walked to the waist-high glass brick barrier that surrounded the garden and looked out over Illusion Town. Down below he could see the towering new roller coaster that was being constructed on the grounds of the Amber Palace. According to the sign in front, it was called Alien Storm. It was set to open in a few weeks. Hannah had mentioned that tickets for the first few months had been sold out for ages.

Just one more over-the-top attraction in a town that routinely reinvented the definition of "over-the-top."

The Alien towers at the heart of Illusion

Town were enclosed by a great wall constructed in the shape of an octagon. But unlike the walls of the other Dead Cities, the eight-sided barrier was not intact. There were countless ragged holes, narrow fissures and cracks in the green quartz. Several of the ethereal towers had collapsed into rubble. With his senses only slightly heightened, Elias could see paranormal hot spots scattered around the grounds of the ancient city.

Long ago something had happened here in the desert, something so catastrophic in nature that it had torn open the nearly indestructible quartz walls of the ancient city and left the surrounding landscape much hotter than most of the other aboveground ruins. Even from his lofty vantage point, Elias was aware of the strong currents of energy that shivered in the atmosphere. The paranormal heat within the broken walls of the octagon was as intense as that of the catacombs and the Rainforest and in some places, even hotter.

The eight zones radiated out from the eight ancient walls. The gaudy lights of the grand casinos in the Amber, Emerald, and Sapphire Zones glittered like hot jewels in the night.

Most of the other zones were steeped in

moonlight and the green shadows of the ruins. But two glowed with a peculiar paranormal radiance — the Storm Zone and the Fire Zone. According to Hannah, the psi in both zones was so intense that even the homeless avoided it.

He turned away from the view and re-joined the others. They settled into white leather chairs while Perkins offered canapés and glasses of champagne. There was also a bowl of pretzels for Virgil, who rushed out of some nearby shrubbery to accept the treat. He thanked Perkins by going into full cute mode. Perkins was charmed.

With the champagne served, Perkins dis-appeared into the penthouse. Smith leaned back, hitched up his white slacks with a practiced twitch of his fingers, and crossed his legs.

Virgil, having made short work of the pretzels, bounded off to explore the gardens.

"After I got your aunts' phone call this morning, I consulted with Detective Jensen of the Illusion Town Police Department," Smith said. "I also took steps to inform the other members of the Illusion Club. I can assure you there is considerable concern all around. Action is being taken as we speak to find out as much as possible about the gang that attacked you."

"Good to know," Elias said.

"Unfortunately, by the time the local police got to the location of the ambush, the assailants had disappeared," Smith continued. "Detective Jensen would very much like to get his hands on one of the Soldiers of Fortune so that he could conduct a proper interrogation."

"Why is everyone so sure those bikers are from out of town?" Elias asked.

"Illusion is not without its criminal element," Smith said. "No city can claim to be crime-free. But generally speaking, our local police are well acquainted with the troublemakers in our midst and do a good job of keeping an eye on them. After speaking with my colleagues and making a few inquiries, I can assure you that the gang you describe was not local in origin."

"I didn't think so," Hannah said. "But where does that leave us?"

"I'm still pursuing answers to your question, my dear," Smith said. "But I have a few of my own for your husband."

Elias had been about to eat a canapé. He paused. "Yes, sir?"

"I understand that your family's company recently had some trouble with a rather shadowy organization called Vortex."

"I'm impressed," Elias said. "Your connections are excellent."

"Thank you," Smith said. "My question is, do you think there's some link between what happened at the project Coppersmith is pursuing on Rainshadow and what happened here?"

"Believe me, I've given that a lot of consideration," Elias said. "And I'm almost certain the answer is no. Coppersmith Security and the FBPI are still mopping up that other situation so it's possible that something might pop up that links to our problem but I doubt it."

Smith's eyes narrowed. "What makes you so certain?"

"It comes down to the quality of the hired muscle involved in each case. The bikers who came after us were armed but they appeared to be old-school biker-gang types. The Vortex crowd fielded a much more sophisticated crowd. Gear, transport, outfits — it all had the feel of a well-run, tightly disciplined organization. If there is a connection, Vortex is keeping its affiliation at a very long distance."

Smith nodded. "I understand your logic. As I said, my people will continue to investigate from this end. I will keep you informed of any developments. In the meantime, our good friend Ollie and the police assure me that security has been reinforced in the Dark Zone."

Hannah munched a canapé. "Thank you, Mr. Smith."

"Of course, my dear. You're one of us. We take care of our own."

The sudden splashing in the pool sounded very loud in the hushed atmosphere of the penthouse gardens.

Hannah leaped to her feet. *"Virgil."*

Elias looked at the glowing pool. Virgil surfaced amid a lot of churning water and promptly vanished.

Hannah rushed toward the pool. "He's drowning."

"Be careful, my dear," Smith called after her. "You'll get your dress wet. I'm sure your little pal is just having fun. Any animal with six paws is bound to be an instinctive swimmer."

Virgil broke the surface of the pool again, growled in an agitated manner, and disappeared.

Hannah reached the edge of the pool. "He dropped Arizona Snow into the deep end. He's trying to rescue her. He may be able to swim but he's not made for diving, at least not in such deep water."

"I'll have Perkins fish him out of the water," Smith said. He reached for a discreetly concealed buzzer in the arm of his chair.

"No need to ask Perkins to take a late-night swim," Elias said. He got to his feet. "I've got this."

He looked around for the equipment that was usually located near a swimming pool. As he expected, there was a ring buoy and a long pole with a net attached designed for skimming debris from the pool.

He took down the pole and net and went to the edge of the pool. He arrived just as Virgil surged to the surface again.

"Relax, Virgil," Elias said.

He inserted the long pole into the water, scooped Arizona Snow off the bottom and hauled her to the surface.

Virgil chortled excitedly and changed course. He swam to the edge of the pool. Hannah crouched and plucked him from the water. He immediately wriggled free, paused to shake the water out of his fur, and then, fully fluffed, hurried across the pool deck to collect Arizona Snow.

Satisfied, he chortled at Elias and bustled off for more pretzels.

Hannah looked at Elias. "Thank you."

"Anytime," Elias said.

Smith chuckled. "Obviously there are some advantages to marrying an engineer, my dear. They tend to think pragmatically in a crisis."

Hannah smiled. "Yes. I've already discovered that."

There was, Elias decided, a little heat in her eyes. It stirred his senses and warmed him all the way through.

An hour later Perkins escorted Hannah and Elias back downstairs and bid them good night.

Elias looked at Hannah.

"Mind if we walk for a while?" he said. "I want to do some thinking and I do that better when I'm walking instead of driving."

"Sure," Hannah said.

They went through the glittering casino and outside into the bright, sparkling lights of the Strip. Virgil perched on Hannah's shoulder. He munched the one last pretzel that Perkins had given him and gripped Arizona Snow, who had survived her near-drowning experience with no signs of damage.

The crowds on the sidewalks moved from one casino to another, buzzed on the energy.

Elias's senses were stirring, too, but he knew that the cause wasn't the Illusion Town vibe — it was the woman at his side.

They strolled past the locked gates that

protected the Alien Storm roller-coaster construction site. A number of people had stopped to gaze at the towering heights, chilling twists, and steep loops of the tracks. The sign in front promised that the ride would be the ultimate in roller-coaster rides — the scariest, the most thrilling, absolutely mind-bending.

"Don't tell me you plan to buy a ticket on the Alien Storm," Hannah said. "I would have thought you'd had enough Alien storm energy to last you for a while."

"You can say that again."

She laughed. "Runner and his pals can't wait to get tickets on that monster roller coaster. But it's going to be a while. Like I said, it's been booked solid for months. Who knew so many people wanted to ride a roller coaster?"

"According to the sign it's not just any roller coaster. It's the biggest, the scariest, and the most exciting roller coaster in the four city-states."

"Well, sure, that's how we do things here in Illusion Town. You know the local motto — 'Welcome to Illusion Town. The thrills are real.' "

"Will Runner and the guys eventually get tickets?" he asked.

"Once the initial rush fades the locals will

335

be able to get tickets at the usual half-price discount that the casinos provide for residents of Illusion Town. But judging by the excitement the Alien Storm is generating, it could be months before the bargain tickets become available."

She was silent for a moment. He got the feeling she was trying to figure out how to ask him a question.

"Think you'll be spending a lot of time at the new portal jobsite?" she asked.

She sounded politely curious. He couldn't tell if the answer mattered to her or not.

"The Ghost City is the most unique and possibly the most profitable territory Coppersmith has opened up in years," he said. "There are decades of work ahead and I'm in charge of the R-and-D labs. So, yes, I'll be living here in Illusion Town."

"Okay," she said.

He glanced at her. "Just okay?"

She smiled a little. "Okay, I'm glad you'll be in town for a while."

"So am I."

He tightened his grip on her hand.

"What are you thinking?" Hannah asked.

"I'm thinking that the local cops are even more in the dark than we are when it comes to getting a handle on the Soldiers of Fortune problem," Elias said.

"I'm sure they'll figure it out. It's what cops are paid to do, right? And believe me, the Club makes sure our cops are paid very, very well."

"I believe it. But the guy we're really after is the one who sent those bikers after us. He's desperate. He knows time is running out. He's probably close to full-blown panic."

"There's another possibility," Hannah said. "If he's thinking rationally, he may accept the fact that he failed. Maybe he'll just disappear instead of taking the risk of getting arrested for attempted kidnapping."

"If we're right about him, he's an obsessive collector who has spent a lot of time, energy, and money trying to find the Midnight Carnival. You're the expert on obsessive collectors. Do you believe that he'll give up?"

She hesitated. "No. Not if he thinks there's still a slight chance of achieving his objective."

"We need to draw him out into the open — convince him that there is a chance to grab you."

"How do we do that?"

Elias stopped. "I've got an idea but we're going to need backup."

"Cops, you mean?"

"No. Local DZ talent. People we can trust."

CHAPTER 30

"So this MC was all about protecting Hannah?" Clara Stockbridge studied Elias with a long, cool, assessing look. "That seems like a rather extreme step to take under the circumstances."

"In hindsight, it wasn't necessary," Hannah said quickly. "The problem was that after we came up out of the tunnels that first night we realized we were both going to crash. We knew we'd been hit with some kind of heavy energy. We assumed we might experience some memory loss. We had no way of knowing how much we would recall after we woke up."

They were sitting on loungers on the balcony of her aunts' house. It was the home in which Hannah had been raised and she felt attached to it in some indefinable way. The residence was situated on a gently sloping hillside, close enough to the Wall to soak up the strong vibes of the ruins and high enough to offer a fine view of some of the glowing emerald structures of the Dead City.

Clara and Bernice had bought the property soon after Hannah had arrived on their doorstep. At the time both women had been in the process of crafting what had become a highly successful magic act. Clara had a talent for sleight of hand and Bernice possessed a gift for altering the currents of her aura in such a way that it rendered her invisible to normal human sight, at least for short periods of time.

Their particular paranormal abilities were common enough among the entertainers in Illusion Town, but Clara and Bernice had succeeded in a crowded market by adding a glamorous song-and-dance routine. Any halfway decent magician could make a pretty lady disappear onstage. Two spectacularly dressed women who could do feats of magic while also performing an elegant striptease and singing popular songs had proven to be a surefire formula for filling casino nightclubs for nearly thirty years.

Clara and Bernice had both been stunningly attractive women in their prime but looks alone would not have assured a comfortable retirement. Illusion Town, after all, was filled with beautiful women. But Clara and Bernice had been pragmatic about their futures from the start. They had accepted that the Ladies of High Magic act would not last forever and they had prepared for the transition to private life by investing well. It turned out that, in addition to a talent for sleight of hand, Clara had a gift for playing the stock market. And Bernice had proven to have a flair for buying and selling real estate. The result was a flourishing second career for each of them.

They were both in their fifties now. The years had taken a toll but to Hannah her aunts still radiated glamour, grace, and feminine power. Clara and Bernice were, and always would be, her role models.

"So you got married knowing that, if you did lose your memory, you would at least start asking the right questions when you came out of the crash," Bernice said. She gave Elias an approving smile. "And you hoped that the creeps who were chasing Hannah would think twice about kidnapping the wife of a Coppersmith."

"That was the plan," Elias said. "But the real problem was that we weren't sure at first why someone was after her. It could have been to stop her from opening the gate at the portal. But now we think this is all about her new find in the Underworld."

"And you're gallantly sticking with the marriage until you identify whoever is trying to steal Hannah's find?" Clara asked, her eyes sharp. "How very noble of you."

Hannah winced. "It's not like that, Aunt Clara. Not exactly."

Bernice waved a silencing hand at Clara. "Don't mind her. She's the naturally suspicious type."

"I understand," Elias said. He looked at Clara. "In your shoes, I'd have the same questions."

Clara gave him a chilly smile. "Bernice and I are, naturally, concerned about Hannah's safety. Her uncle Ollie runs that part of the DZ. He tells me he doubled the neighborhood watch and he's making inquiries into what happened the other night. And Mr. Smith assured me he would get to the bottom of this."

"Yes, we know," Elias said. "Coppersmith Security is also monitoring the situation as far as possible from the outside. But there's not much they can do inside Illusion Town."

"That's for damn sure," Clara said. "The Club runs this town, including the police. But the good news is that, generally speaking, the cops do a good job of maintaining law and order."

"I don't doubt it," Elias said. "Coppersmith Security is working with the FBPI on the outside but they are sharing information with the Illusion Town police."

"Which is the same as sharing it with the members of the Club," Bernice said. "You can bet none of them will take kindly to the idea of an out-of-town gang thinking it can just roar into Illusion and try to kidnap a local resident."

Bernice, acknowledged by both Clara and Hannah as the serious cook in the household, served dinner on the balcony. Virgil was provided with a dish of his own at the far end of the table. Unlike the others, who took their time finishing the meal, he made short work of his plate of roasted vegetables and crab cakes. When he had polished off his share of the chocolate-cookie-and-whipped-cream dessert, he grabbed Arizona Snow and hopped up onto the railing. Hannah thought that he appeared to be savoring the DZ night vibe, always stronger after dark. But who knew how a dust bunny interpreted the heavy currents of energy in the atmosphere?

As far as she could tell, Elias had weathered the relentless grilling from Clara with admirable aplomb. It certainly hadn't affected his appetite. He'd asked for seconds on everything, including dessert.

In fact, he gave every indication of being prepared to linger over coffee and discuss the finer aspects of his crystal and quartz research with a surprisingly interested Clara. Hannah decided enough was enough. Her aunts were putting Elias through the sort of ordeal a man expected to endure if he was proposing a full-on Covenant Marriage. But it was understood from the outset that most MCs were fated to be short-term. The operative word in a Marriage of Convenience, after all, was *convenience*.

"Wow, would you look at the time," she said. She gave Clara and Bernice a bright smile. "I'll help with the dishes and then we'll be on our way."

"Don't worry about the dishes, dear," Bernice said. "Clara and I will take care of them later. Why don't you show Elias the garden? It's so pretty at night."

Hannah froze, trying to think of a way to decline. Before she could come up with a response, Elias rose from the table and looked at her.

"I'd like to see the garden," he said.

Bernice beamed.

Clara waved a hand. "Go. We'll deal with the dishes."

Hannah got a small shock of alarm. Clara had as good as given her approval to the marriage. The garden, after all, was her personal passion. Permission to enter it was considered a gesture of welcome.

Hannah drew a breath. "Okay. I guess."

Elias looked amused. "Don't get too enthusiastic."

She glared and turned on her heel.

"Follow me," she ordered.

Sensing an outing, Virgil chortled and vaulted off the balcony railing. He landed adroitly on Elias's shoulder.

Without a word Hannah led the way downstairs to the back door. She opened it and moved out onto the wide porch. Elias followed, closing the door quietly. He joined her at the railing. Together they looked out over the softly glowing wonderland that Clara had created.

Under the influence of the heavy psi currents in the area the leaves and blossoms and vines gleamed and glittered and sparkled like psi-infused gemstones.

"This is incredible," Elias said.

"All the plants and herbs and flowers were chosen for their natural paranormal luminescence," Hannah explained. "They're all attractive during the daylight hours but they really shine after dark. Some people string colored lights around their gardens to celebrate the holidays but Clara's garden glows all year-round."

"My mother would love to see this," Elias said.

For the first time that evening Hannah relaxed a little. "It is pretty amazing, isn't it? Aunt Clara has been working on it for years, developing hybrids that thrive in the atmosphere here in the DZ."

Virgil bounded down off Elias's shoulder. He chortled a cheery farewell to Hannah, and disappeared into the garden with Arizona Snow.

Elias put his arm around Hannah's shoulders. She was very aware of the heat and strength in him. Instinctively she nestled a little closer.

"In addition to my mother, I know some serious para-botanists in the Coppersmith labs who would pay good money for a tour of this place," he said.

"I think Aunt Clara would enjoy showing some real experts around," Hannah said. "She is always conducting experiments with new seeds and cuttings. A few years ago she created an orchid that she named in honor of me. Want to see it?"

"Of course I want to see it."

"It's over there by the little pond. Come on, I'll show you."

Somewhat reluctantly she moved out from

under the comfortable weight of his arm and went down the porch steps. They walked along the gently curving path to the bubbling fountain and stopped in front of a cascade of elegant turquoise blue orchids that glittered like rare jewels in the night.

"This is it, Magic Hannah," Hannah said. "I was thirteen when Clara developed this particular orchid. It was a birthday present of sorts. I was just starting to dream-walk and I had become afraid to go to sleep at night. My aunts had no way of knowing what to expect because they didn't know much about my para-genetics."

"Your brand of talent would be enough to unnerve any teenager," Elias admitted. "To say nothing of her family."

"I thought at first that maybe the dream-walking was some kind of scary magic. Clara and Bernice told me to remember that what looks like magic to the audience always has a logical explanation and that to be a good magician, you have to maintain control of the trick."

"In other words, they let you know that you would have to learn to control your talent."

She laughed. "It was either that or spend a lifetime trying to stay awake. I didn't think that would go well."

Elias studied the waterfall of glowing orchids for a time and then he turned Hannah in his arms. She could see the heat in his eyes.

"I think I know why your aunt named the orchid Magic Hannah," he said.

"Because of my weird talent?"

"No," he said. "Because sometimes the magic is real."

She smiled. "That's funny coming from an engineer. I doubt if you ever believed in magic even when you were a little kid. You're the guy in the audience who can't enjoy the show because he's too busy trying to figure out how the trick works. And once you know, you lose interest in the performance."

"So, when I tell you that some magic is real, you know I'm telling you the truth."

He kissed her then amid the glowing leaves and sparkling flowers. She opened her senses to the night and to the man who held her in his arms.

He was right, she thought. Sometimes the magic was real, at least for a while.

Bernice walked out on to the balcony and joined Clara at the railing. Together they looked down into the radiant garden. Hannah and Elias were at the pond. They were silhouetted in the luminous energy of the glorious cascade of Magic Hannah orchids. The two were obviously lost in each other's arms.

Bernice gripped the railing with both hands and allowed herself to hope. But she was careful not to let herself go too far. There had been other men in Hannah's life, including one or two she feared would break Hannah's heart. But Clara had always been the one who saw the truth behind the brief moments of illusion. So now she waited for the verdict.

"What's your take on him?" she asked softly.

Clara reached out and gripped Bernice's hand. Their wedding rings gleamed in the soft night.

"I think," Clara said, "that he may be the first one to understand why we named the turquoise hybrid Magic Hannah."

CHAPTER 31

"Whew," Hannah said. "Sure glad that's over. Thanks again for being so polite about the whole meet-the-in-laws thing, fake though it was."

Elias tightened his grip on her hand. "Do me a favor. Stop implying our marriage is a fake. It's real. And stop apologizing for the fact that your aunts wanted to meet me. It's natural under the circumstances."

"Sorry," she mumbled.

"Which reminds me, I got a call from Dad today."

They were walking home through the Dark Zone, which, in defiance of its name, was illuminated with the paranormal energy of the ruins. The narrow streets and lanes were infused with a light, gently swirling psi-infused fog. The small casinos and nightclubs were starting to come alive for the evening. Their bright signs and dark entrances promised cheap thrills and exotic

350

mysteries that could not be matched any-where else in town.

"I suppose your father wanted an update on the situation here in Illusion," she said.

"Turns out he had one for me. The FBPI, working with Coppersmith Security, picked up the last pirate this morning. He still had the two Coppersmith keys so there's plenty of evidence to link him to the murders."

"Your theory was that there was a third key — one created by a different lab. Did they find it?"

"Yes. The third key is powered by quartz but it wasn't as stable as the Coppersmith versions. Still, it was damn sophisticated. The suspicion is that it came out of a Vortex lab but there's no real proof."

"But you didn't find the Vortex tattoo on those two dead pirates."

"No. The murderer didn't have the tat, either. Dad says the FBPI thinks that Vortex tried to farm out the operation in an effort to keep some distance from it. But they got double-crossed for their pains. The killer put together a team that included Hank Richman and the others, and then, when the job was done, he got rid of his partners. He planned to sell the two Coppersmith keys on the black market."

"Vortex wouldn't have liked that."

"No," Elias said. "If the FBPI hadn't picked him up, the killer probably would be dead by now."

"Did your father have anything else to tell you?"

"He gave me my new orders."

"Orders?"

"He told me that it was time I introduced you to my side of the family."

"Oh, dear. This is getting complicated, isn't it?"

"I've heard that marriage can be complicated," Elias said.

"It's just an —"

"Don't say it. Repeat after me — an MC is a legal marriage."

She took a deep breath. "An MC is a legal marriage."

Until it isn't, she thought but she decided not to say it out loud. The night was too nice to spoil with an argument about the future of their relationship — especially now that she was allowing herself to hope that there would be a future of some sort. *Don't look behind the curtain. You don't want to know if it's all a trick of the light.*

"So, if Plan A doesn't work out, what's our next move going to be?" she asked.

"I've been thinking about that. You said you filed a claim on the sector of the cata-

352

combs where you discovered the carnival."

"Right. Legally, that should protect me."

"And as I keep reminding you, there's a long history of claim jumping in the mining world."

"Whoever is behind this would have to kill me to make me go away. And if he did that, what are the odds that he could find another dreamlight talent with a para-profile so close to mine that she could unlock the gate?"

"I agree it's unlikely but that doesn't mean one can't be found. After all, he found you, didn't he?"

"Okay, I get the point. But what else can I do to protect my claim?"

"Sell the carnival to Arcane. Fast."

"I told you I need to do a complete inventory in order to establish the value of the find."

"Pick a number, any number. Make it sky-high. Arcane will pay whatever you ask. The sooner they take ownership of the carnival, the sooner you'll be safe."

"All right. But I gotta tell you, the businesswoman in me really, really doesn't like the idea."

"I understand, believe me," Elias said. He tightened his fingers in warning and lowered his voice. "We've got company."

"Runner and his crew?"

"No."

"Cops?"

"Someone else." Elias glanced at his ring. "I'm picking up some low-level psi frequencies. They're being generated by some kind of para-tech. Guns, I think, and phones."

"You were right. The Soldiers of Fortune really are dumb enough to make another try to grab me right off the streets of my own neighborhood."

"Either dumb enough or so sure of themselves that they think they can outgun the local neighborhood watch."

"I don't hear the motorcycles," Hannah said.

"So maybe they've figured out that it would be a little reckless to ride through the DZ again on those big Raleigh-Starks."

"That would indicate that they did learn something last time."

"All we need is one of those bastards," Elias said.

Hannah shot him a sidelong glance. She could tell that Elias was jacked; running hot. Her own senses were flaring in response to the danger.

Fog-muffled footsteps sounded behind them. Up ahead a shadowy figure loomed in the mist.

"They're closing in now," Elias said. "Two of them. One in front, one behind."

"Runner and his crew will have them marked by now," Hannah said. "The cops will be on the way. It's going down just like you planned."

"Maybe not."

"What do you mean? The bikers won't make a move as long as we're in this part of the DZ. Too many tourists."

"And a whole lot of psi fog. They're going to try to use it for cover."

"We can duck into a nightclub or a tavern but if we disappear that way we'll lose our chance to grab one of them tonight."

"I've got an idea."

He stopped abruptly and hauled her into a nearby alley. Hannah realized that the deep shadows and the fog effectively made them vanish.

"Flat against the wall," Elias said. He spoke directly into her ear.

She flattened her back against the old stone wall.

The deliberate footsteps suddenly shifted into a quick trot. And then the two assailants broke into a run.

"Where'd they go?" The voice was male, harsh with temper and a flicker of alarm.

"The alley," the second man said. He

sounded cooler and more in control.

A flashlight beam speared straight down the alley, narrowly missing Hannah and Elias. The ray of light struck the wall at the far end.

"It's a dead end," the coolheaded man announced. He sounded relieved. "They're trapped."

"That's what you said the last time when we ambushed them in that lane. It didn't go well. I'm sure as hell not going into that alley blind. Coppersmith is going to be armed."

"There's plenty of hot psi in the area, enough to pull a ghost. They'll come running out in a minute."

Hannah felt energy heighten in the atmosphere. Cool Head was rezzing his talent, drawing the dissonance energy out of the ambient currents of Alien psi. A storm of green fire took shape midway down the alley.

A brush with hot ghost light was more than enough to cause unconsciousness. Prolonged contact could damage the nerves and destroy the paranormal senses. A truly powerful ghost could kill. Ghost hunters were paid good money to clean the Unstable Dissonance Energy Manifestations out of the Underworld. But in addition to being able to destroy one, they had the ability to create the storms and use them as weapons.

It was, of course, highly illegal to summon a ghost for the purpose of menacing innocent people, just as it was illegal to threaten someone with a mag-rez pistol. But stuff happened in the back alleys of every city, including Illusion Town.

Ghosts were hard to manipulate; the result was that they moved slowly. It was relatively easy to outrun one. But in this case Hannah knew that she and Elias would run straight into the arms of the would-be kidnappers.

Where were the cops? she wondered. Surely by now Runner had alerted them. The plan had been a simple one. But good plans had a way of going bad.

The ghost drifted toward the alley entrance, singeing everything in its path. There was a sudden scurrying and rustling in the narrow space. Several pairs of eyes appeared in the mist. Rats, fleeing from the approaching energy storm, Hannah realized. It was all she could do not to scream when one ran over the toe of her evening sandal. It didn't hang around. It rushed out of the alley together with its friends and neighbors.

Another small creature appeared out of the fog. Four eyes, two of them hot amber, burned in the mist.

"Virgil," Hannah whispered.

He vaulted up into her arms and then onto her shoulder.

"Keep him out of the way," Elias ordered. "I need to get a clear focus."

She reached up to touch Virgil, silently willing him to stay put. He seemed to get the message. He hunkered down, tense and ready to spring.

She thought she heard a siren in the distance but she couldn't be certain because the sparking, crackling ghost fire was so close now it was affecting her normal senses.

In the next instant she felt a rush of energy. She saw Elias's ring flash with dark fire.

"Whatever you do, don't move," he said.

Using normal vision, the two men at the entrance of the alley would have been little more than shadows in the fog. But the paranormal senses made it possible to see in other ways. She could make out the auras of the two bikers. She knew that Elias could see them, also.

A narrow beam of paranormal radiation sparkled from Elias's ring. It arrowed through the fog. There was a grunt from the target. An instant later the ghost winked out of existence.

"Shit." Harsh Voice sounded on the edge of panic. "Gage? What the hell happened —"

The nervous biker broke off abruptly. The sirens were very loud now. Hannah saw the man's aura move in the fog and knew that he was turning around to flee.

But Elias was already in motion. He launched himself toward the shadow. There was a heavy thud. The biker landed hard on the sidewalk.

Runner and his crew arrived first, breathless.

"Hannah?" Runner called. "Where are you? You okay?"

She peeled herself away from the wall and went toward the entrance of the alley.

"I'm fine," she said.

Elias was crouched beside the two fallen bikers. He went swiftly through their pockets. The one he had taken down with his ring was starting to stir. The other man had been winded by the fall. He was struggling to catch his breath.

"I called the cops when I saw that you and Coppersmith were being followed but we lost you for a bit when the fog started to get heavy," Runner said. "Then I realized you'd gone into this alley. But it's a dead end."

"We noticed," Hannah said. "But it's all right. You and your guys did great. Here come the cops. Thanks, Runner." She looked at the four other young men hovering in the shadows. "Thanks to all of you."

"Yeah, sure, anytime, Finder," Buddy said. He looked at Elias. "What'd you use on that guy?"

"Some new experimental tech from a lab," Elias said.

"Worked pretty good," Buddy allowed. "Nice. I don't suppose — ?"

"Sorry. Not ready for market yet," Elias said.

Runner nodded. "Right. But when it is market ready you're gonna need a delivery crew that knows how to deliver tech like that in the DZ. Keep us in mind."

"I'll do that," Elias said.

Runner looked at Hannah.

"Cops will be here in a minute," he said. "Need anything else?"

She looked at Elias. "Your call."

Elias got to his feet and looked at Runner and his crew. "We're good. Thanks. Couldn't have done it without you. I owe you. Pizza at Ollie's is on me when this is all over."

"Yeah, sure," Buzz said. He sounded like he didn't expect to collect the pizza reward.

"You gonna show up to eat it with us?"

Sam asked. "Or just pay the tab?"

It struck Hannah as an odd question. It was as if Sam was laying down a marker, daring Elias to show up at Ollie's for pizza with Runner's crew. And then she got it. Sam and the others weren't used to hanging with men from Elias's world. They didn't expect him to actually break bread — or pizza — with them.

"I'll be there," Elias said. "I'll give you a full report on what we learn from these two."

"High-rez," Sam said. "See ya."

The sirens grew louder.

"We'd better get moving," Runner said. "We've got what you might call an understanding with the cops but we try to stay out of each other's way, if you know what I mean."

"Understood," Elias said. "See you at Ollie's."

The DZ Delivery Service crew disappeared into the fog.

Hannah looked at Elias.

"You used your ring to take down one of these men, didn't you?" she asked.

"Like I said, I've been on a steep learning curve with this crystal ever since you located it for me. I didn't know what it could do until my intuition told me to try to generate some energy through it tonight."

"So, it's a weapon of some kind?"

"It's power, Hannah. Power can be used in a lot of different ways. But yes, it looks like in this case it can be used as a psychic weapon."

CHAPTER 32

The flash of knowing — the sense that they were closing in on the answers — shivered through Elias's para-senses with such force, his physical senses reacted. His ring heated a little and his hand jerked ever so slightly, just enough to send a few drops of coffee over the rim of the delicate china cup.

"What the hell?" he said very softly.

"Elias?" Hannah looked at him, alarm in her eyes. "Everything okay?"

The spilled coffee wasn't the most awkward part about his reaction. His talent had flashed for a couple of beats and Hannah had sensed it. He knew Maxwell Smith and Detective Jensen had picked up some of the vibes, too.

"We're close," Elias said. "I can feel it."

"How close?" Jensen asked.

He was in his forties, with a sturdy, stocky build, thinning hair, and cop eyes. He also had some talent, enough that Elias could sense it in his energy field. Probably a hunter. They were naturals for police work. They also made very good criminals. The skill set required for success in both professions was virtually identical. The chief difference between the two professions was a sense of right and wrong, a conscience.

It wasn't entirely clear which career path Jensen had chosen. Maybe he had started out as an idealistic officer of the law, determined to serve and protect. But somewhere along the line he had seen a little too much of the worst of human nature. Or maybe he didn't like knowing that he was a professional law enforcement officer in a city that was run by a consortium of powerful casino magnates who considered Illusion Town their personal fiefdom. That had to make for some difficult moments in police work. Whatever the case, Elias was pretty sure that Jensen was not a glass-half-full kind of guy. But he seemed to be a good cop.

The call from Smith had come just as Hannah had opened Visions for the day. Elias, under Virgil's supervision, had been repairing a broken display cabinet. Hannah had locked up the shop immediately and they had driven to the Amber Palace, where Detective Jensen had been waiting to brief them.

Now they were gathered in Smith's private office located on the executive-suite floor of the casino. On the way down the hall from the reception lobby Elias had glimpsed the usual array of corporate management departments — Accounting, Human Resources, Marketing, and all the rest of the divisions associated with any big business enterprise.

There had also been an impressive amount of state-of-the-art security and communications equipment. Screen after screen displayed live video feeds from the countless cameras scattered throughout the hotel and casino.

But Smith's office was surprisingly old-fashioned. It looked more like a wealthy man's private study. *Like my father's study,* Elias thought.

Smith glanced at the drops of coffee splashed across the papers spread out on his gleaming desk.

"Don't worry about the spill," he said. "No harm done." He turned back to Jensen. "You were saying, Detective?"

"Right," Jensen continued. "The motorcycle gang. The two perps who attacked Miss West and Mr. Coppersmith last night do belong to that gang of bikers called the Soldiers of Fortune. Used to be known as the Emerald Ruin Riders, a small-time operation that was into the usual biker-gang businesses, mostly drugs and prostitution. The guy at the top was old-school and smart — at least smart enough to stay out of this town."

Hannah looked at him. "I take it the situation has changed?"

"Six months ago the leader of the Riders suffered a heart attack brought on by an overdose of a new street drug," Jensen said. "He collapsed and died."

"Can we assume the overdose was not accidental?" Elias asked.

Jensen snorted softly. "Let's just say that everyone I know in law enforcement is going on that assumption. For a while there was some vague hope that without a strongman at the top the Riders organization would disintegrate. But that's not what happened. Someone stepped into the power vacuum. There's a new guy in charge, Felix Cordas, a small-time career criminal who rode with the gang for the past year. He appears to have developed illusions of grandeur."

"A new name for the gang and a new business model — is that it?" Elias asked.

"Now, that's interesting," Smith said. He lounged in his chair and put his fingertips together. "How do you change up a biker-gang business model?"

"By diversifying," Elias said. He looked at Jensen. "The Soldiers of Fortune are hiring out as mercenaries."

"That's what it looks like," Jensen said.

Hannah looked at him. "Who hired the SOF to grab me?"

"Unfortunately, the two we interrogated don't know much about the client who commissioned the *mission,* as they called it," Jensen said. "They were just following orders and the orders were to get you out of the picture, Mr. Coppersmith, and pick up Ms. West. But I'm almost positive that the person who contracted with the SOF for the kidnapping is either local or has a good local connection."

Elias looked at him. "Because the intel on Hannah that they used to track her was so good?"

Jensen shrugged. "They were operating in the Dark Zone. You've spent some time there. You know what it's like."

"A maze," Elias said. "But we know how they kept tabs on Hannah. There was a tracer frequency on one of the crystals in her necklace. I neutralized it after your people arrested the two bikers last night."

"Huh." Jensen gave Hannah's necklace a

curious look. Then he turned back to Elias. "A tracking crystal would explain how our unknown perp was able to find Miss West but what made him target her in the first place? Let's face it: no offense to the lady, but she's not exactly a major player in the antiquities market."

"We've been working on that problem," Elias said. He met Hannah's eyes across the vast desk. "We need to talk to the one person in this thing who has been there all along; the one who knows all about your para-psych profile."

"Grady?" she said. "He's not on my list of favorite people but I really can't see him hiring a bunch of bikers to kidnap me. Grady Barnett is all about becoming famous in the para-psych world."

"How did Barnett find you?" Elias asked.

"He didn't," she said. "I found him. I needed a comprehensive para-psych profile. He was local and convenient and cheap so I hired him to test me."

"Why did you choose him?"

"It's not like there are a lot of qualified para-psych researchers who specialize in my kind of talent and who are also affordable," she said.

"Barnett gave you a deal, didn't he?" Elias asked gently.

"Yes," she said.

"How did you know he was both qualified and inexpensive?" Elias asked.

Comprehension lit her eyes. "Oh, crap."

Smith and Jensen looked at her.

"What are we missing here, Hannah?" Smith asked.

She drew a deep breath. "Professor Paxton Wilcox, the genealogist I hired to research my family tree sent me to Grady. Wilcox said Grady was an expert who was qualified to prepare a good para-psych profile on a dreamlight talent and he also happened to be local and affordable."

Smith looked troubled. "You must have seen Wilcox's prints at some point, my dear. Was he the intruder?"

"That's just it," Hannah said. "I've never actually met Wilcox — not in person. He doesn't live here in town — at least I didn't think so. All my communication with him has been online. According to his website, his office is in Resonance."

"I've got a contact on the Resonance force," Jensen said. "I'll give her a call and ask her to pick up this Dr. Wilcox for questioning."

"Forget it," Elias said. "Wilcox may have an address in Resonance but he won't be there. I think you're right, Detective. He's somewhere here in town."

Smith's brows rose. "Why would he take the risk if he can track her from afar?"

"Because he's an obsessive collector and he's very close to getting what he wants," Hannah said. "Elias is right. He's somewhere nearby. He won't be able to stay away, not now."

"Got any idea where to start looking?" Jensen asked. "It's easy to hide under a fake identity in this town."

Elias heard his phone ping. He set his cup down on the desk and took the device out of the pocket of his jacket. He smiled when he saw the familiar code on the screen.

"We may have a starting point," he said. "Grady Barnett."

"What makes you think he can lead us to Wilcox?" Jensen asked.

"I asked Coppersmith Security to run a background check on Barnett." Elias opened the report and read through the summary. "Here we go. Grady Barnett was once a rising star in the para-psych department at the University of Resonance. But he was fired after he was caught falsifying some of the data in two of his papers that were published in a major journal. He maintained his innocence but the university let him go. He left Resonance and set up his own lab here in Illusion Town."

"On his website, Paxton Wilcox claims that he did some consulting work for the University of Resonance's antiquities department," Hannah said.

"Maybe his website is not a complete work of fiction," Elias said. "They say if you're going to tell a lie, try to use as much of the truth as possible. Less chance you'll trip yourself up that way."

Mr. Smith tapped his fingers together twice. "It appears that there may, indeed, be a connection between Paxton Wilcox and Grady Barnett."

Jensen rocked on his heels a little. "I can have Barnett picked up for questioning but I won't be able to hold him for long."

Smith gave him a benign smile. "I'm certain we can find charges, should they be needed, Detective."

Jensen grunted. He did not look happy but he did not protest.

"I think Hannah and I might get more out of him if we pay a call on him ourselves," Elias said.

Hannah smiled grimly. "Oh, yeah."

CHAPTER 33

The Office of the Barnett Research Institute
was housed in a gloomy Colonial-era building at the edge of the Dark Zone. The
neighborhood was poised on the precarious
knife-edge between shabby-but-respectable
and going-to-seed. The neighboring businesses consisted of a lawyer who specialized
in slip-and-fall work, a palm reader, a
tawdry gentleman's club, and an all-night
convenience store. It was common knowledge that the Hot Rez Grocery survived by
selling cheap liquor out the front door and
assorted drug-laced snacks via the alley
door.

"Gosh," Elias said. "What was your first
clue that you might not be dealing with a
high-end dreamlight research lab?"

"Hey, the Barnett Research Institute came
highly recommended," she said.

"Yeah, by Paxton Wilcox, the guy who's
trying to steal your big find."

"Okay, I get the point." She shifted Virgil to her left arm and started to rez the intercom. She hesitated. "Do you really think that Wilcox referred me to Grady because he knew he could bribe Grady to give him confidential information about me?"

"You said you never got your complete file."

"Grady insists that was because I walked out before it was completed."

"What do you want to bet Wilcox did get your file?"

"That bastard," Hannah said.

"Which one?"

Hannah rezzed the intercom button.

"The Barnett Research Institute," Kelsey announced in a liquid accent.

"Hannah West to see Grady," Hannah said. "Tell him it's urgent."

"What is this about, Miss West?" Kelsey asked, her tone plunging several degrees.

"You can tell Grady I want to talk about the details of that job he offered to broker for me."

"There's someone with you," Kelsey said. "I can see him on the camera."

"My husband," Hannah said.

"You've got that little rat with you, too."

"Virgil is not a rat, you dumb —"

A scratchy sound on the intercom interrupted her. Grady's voice came through the speaker.

"Hannah? Is that you? About time. Come on up. I think there's still time to salvage the deal. The collector is desperate. I guarantee you that you won't regret taking this commission. Like I said, you can name your own price."

There was a click as the door unlocked.

Virgil growled.

"What did you say, Miss West?" Kelsey asked sharply. "Is there a problem with the door?"

"No problem, Kelsey."

Hannah pushed the door open and walked into the tiny, dimly lit lobby. Automatically she kicked up her talent the way she always did when she entered a space. There were two hundred years of psi-prints layered on the floor but the older ones had faded into a murky sea of energy. Only the more recent tracks were easily distinguishable. She could see Kelsey's and Grady's but there were no other new ones.

"Evidently business has not been brisk," she said, speaking over her shoulder to Elias. "The only new prints are Kelsey's and Grady's."

"That doesn't mean Barnett and Wilcox

aren't in this together," Elias said.

"And possibly the lovely Kelsey, too," Hannah said grimly.

"Why do I have the feeling that you two really don't like each other very much?" Elias said.

"You must be psychic."

Halfway up the stairs, Virgil made a low rumbling sound and opened all four eyes. He wasn't sleeked out but it was clear he was not happy about the visit to the Barnett Research Institute.

"Don't worry," Hannah said. "We're not spending the night this time."

The stairs were old. They creaked. Like the vast majority of the First Generation structures, the building was designed primarily to be functional. After the Curtain had closed the colonists had been focused on survival. There had been little time or energy to spare on such frivolous things as architectural adornment. And the Barnett Research Institute had not put much money into remodeling.

At the top of the stairs Virgil wriggled free of Hannah's arm and made his way up onto her shoulder. He growled again.

"I'm not looking forward to seeing Grady and Kelsey again myself," she assured him. "But this is important."

"Maybe he's trying to tell us something," Elias said. "Let me go first."

She glanced back and saw that he had his flamer in his hand.

"I really don't think that's necessary," she said.

"It makes an impression."

He motioned for her to move to the side so that he could go past her. There was no point arguing. Besides, it would be interesting to see the expressions on Kelsey's and Grady's faces when they saw the flamer.

She paused on the landing.

"Grady's office is to the left," she said. "Down that hallway."

"Stay here while I check out the hallway and the office." Elias moved cautiously around the corner.

"Hannah?" Grady's voice sounded from inside his office. "Is that you? Coppersmith? What in green hell? Put that damn flamer away. There's no need for violence. I just want to chat with Hannah. This is a business matter, nothing more."

A woman's high-pitched scream reverberated through the building. Hannah winced.

"Are you crazy?" Kelsey yelped. "What do you think you're doing? It's illegal to carry a flamer aboveground."

"Must have slipped my mind," Elias said.

"Hannah, it's okay. There's no one else here, just a couple of lab rats."

Hannah kicked up her talent and went around the corner.

She froze.

Hot psi-prints burned on the old floor-boards of the hallway. They came from the far end of the corridor. The man who had left them had entered the building through the alley door and used the back stairs to climb to the second floor. That was why she hadn't sensed them in the front hall or on the main stairs.

The dreamlight currents were shot through with a dark, disturbing tension. She had seen similar prints before — on the white quilt she had been forced to discard.

She could feel Virgil's claws digging into her shoulder. He was in full attack mode now. Elias was standing in the doorway of Grady's office. He had not put the flamer away but he held it alongside his leg, pointing toward the floor.

"Hannah?" he asked. "What is it?"

"The man who ruined my new quilt and trashed my shop," she said. "He was here. And quite recently."

CHAPTER 34

"I can explain everything," Grady said. "This isn't some kind of sinister conspiracy." He shot Hannah a reproachful look. "Frankly, the fact that you're trying to make it look that way indicates a degree of paranoia. It's another sign of instability in your aura."

"Oh, shut up," Hannah said. "I don't want to hear another word about my para-psych instability. Just answer my questions."

Elias suppressed a groan. They were gathered in Grady's office. Kelsey Lewis sat stiffly in a chair, and he had to admit that she did, indeed, look quite attractive in a chilly, dominatrix sort of way. Her red hair was cut in a sleek wedge that angled down to her sharp chin and she had the body and the sculpted features that would have made it possible for her to apply for a position in an Illusion Town chorus line. She lacked the height, however. She was not nearly as tall as the average showgirl. At the moment her pretty face was tight with anger.

Grady was in his chair, his hands folded on top of his desk. Hannah was seated in one of the two padded chairs in front of the desk. Virgil was perched on the back, hovering in a protective manner. Only his baby blues were open now but the way he watched Grady would have made any smart man nervous. Grady appeared to be smart enough to be nervous.

Elias had one shoulder propped against the doorway where he could keep an eye on the hall as well as the tense scene inside the office.

The biggest problem at the moment was restraining Hannah. She was in a fine rage. He didn't blame her but he knew it wasn't the best way to get answers.

"If you don't want to answer our questions, Barnett, you're welcome to go downtown to police headquarters and answer Detective Jensen's questions," Elias said.

"The cops can't arrest me," Grady announced. "They've got nothing on me because I haven't done anything illegal."

"How about unethical?" Hannah said fiercely. "You set me up for a lying, thieving bastard who wants to steal something I discovered in the Underworld."

"I swear, I didn't know that Wilcox was planning to steal anything," Grady said. "He contacted me about a month ago."

"Right after I bought my crystal at an online auction," Hannah snapped.

"I don't know anything about a crystal. I did know Wilcox. We met while I was affiliated with the University of Resonance. But it's not like we were good friends. He had retired from the faculty but he had the usual academic privileges that retired professors get. He spent a lot of time in the para-psych library doing his own research. I knew he was interested in using para-genetic profiles as a tool for genealogical research. He came into the lab a few times. We had some conversations about my dreamlight work. But that was the end of it."

"Until you got fired," Hannah snapped.

Grady looked deeply offended. "I was not fired. I left the university to pursue other career opportunities. I've always wanted my own research lab."

"You were fired because you faked the data you used on some of your published papers," Hannah said.

"It was a matter of interpretation," Grady said coldly.

Elias held up one hand, palm out. "We're going way off topic here. Let's get back to

Wilcox. You said he contacted you about a month ago."

"Yes." Grady inhaled slowly and exhaled with control, regaining his composure. "He said he wanted to refer a client to me for a complete dreamlight workup."

"Me," Hannah said.

"Yes. You showed up and I agreed to perform the analysis at a discount. You were an extremely interesting subject."

Kelsey smiled an icy smile. "But quite unstable."

Hannah rounded on her. "You want unstable? I'll give you unstable."

"Hannah," Elias said gently. "Let's try to stay focused here."

Hannah gave him a bright, ominous smile. "Oh, you mean on having these two arrested for fraud? Sure. By all means let's stay focused."

"We haven't committed fraud," Grady roared.

"Let me see if I've got this straight," Elias said. "You got a call from Paxton Wilcox informing you that he was referring a client to you for testing. When Hannah arrived you began analyzing her para-psych currents. Right so far?"

"Right," Grady said forcefully.

"When did you realize that you could use

her for your own personal research purposes?" Elias asked.

"The day she walked into his office."
Kelsey gave a little snort of disgust. "Grady
was so excited. He couldn't wait to get to
the sleep tests. All he could talk about was
how badly he wanted to hook her up to his
machines."

"But all I wanted was a basic para-psych
profile," Hannah said. "I didn't want to be
a research subject."

"Which is why he didn't tell you after that
night in the sleep lab that the para-psych
profile was complete," Kelsey said. "He
knew you'd quit the testing process as soon
as you had that profile. He had to find a
way to keep you coming back for more tests.
That's why he tried to seduce you."

Hannah smiled coolly. "Well, that didn't
go well, did it? Thanks to you. I really owe
you, Kelsey. If I hadn't overheard that
conversation between the two of you and
caught the two of you having a good time
in the supply closet, I might have stuck
around to finish the profile. Yes, indeed, I
am truly grateful to you."

"Once again we are straying from the
subject," Elias said. "All right, here's what
I've got so far, Barnett. Correct me if there
is any misunderstanding. You prepared a

para-psych profile on Hannah but you lied to her and told her that it was not complete."

"I wanted to recheck some of my findings," Grady muttered.

"But you sent that profile to Wilcox, didn't you?" Elias said.

"Wilcox was a colleague," Grady said stiffly. "He offered to consult on Hannah's profile."

"He offered to pay you a nice fat bribe for a copy of that profile," Elias said.

"It wasn't a bribe," Grady snapped. "And it wasn't unethical. After all, Hannah had commissioned the profile with the intention of sending it to Wilcox herself."

"The money you got from Wilcox was a bribe," Elias said. "And, yes, what you did was unethical."

Hannah smiled at Grady. "But that's nothing new for you, is it, Grady? You've got a history of unethical behavior."

Grady propped his elbows on his desk and dropped his head into his hands. "What do you want from me, damn it?"

"We know Wilcox came to see you recently," Elias said. "When was the last time you met with him?"

Grady scowled. "How did you know he was here?"

"My unstable talent tells me he was standing right here in this office," Hannah said very sweetly. "I can see his footsteps. He came up the back way. Used the alley entrance. Guess he didn't want to take a chance on being seen with you."

Grady shrugged. "Fine. He was here this morning."

"Where is he now?" Elias asked.

"How should I know?" Grady said.

"Got an address for him here in Illusion Town?" Elias asked. "Does he have an apartment? Is he staying in a hotel room?"

"I don't know, damn it." Grady raised his head. "I didn't ask for details. He was in a raging temper, if you must know. Something about having spent years searching for some lost artifacts and that he was so close he could almost touch it, whatever that means. He claimed I'd screwed up everything and that our deal was off the table if I didn't get you to cooperate by five o'clock today."

Hannah's eyes widened. "Wilcox was the mysterious collector you claimed to be representing, wasn't he? The one you said wanted to hire me to find a lost artifact. That was the deal you were so eager to broker."

"Yeah, well, you can forget it now," Grady said. "You blew it for both of us. You could have made a lot of money and I could have had a new lab. But thanks to you, it's all gone to green hell. I hope you're satisfied."

Hannah looked at Elias. "Wilcox had no intention of hiring me to find a lost artifact. He already knows where it is. He just can't get to it."

"It was yet another desperate plan to grab you," Elias said. "He probably figured he might have a shot at it if you accepted the bogus job he was offering through Barnett."

Grady looked at Elias and then he glared at Hannah. "I don't know what you're talking about."

She sighed. "Oddly enough, I believe you."

Elias straightened away from the door-jamb. "Time to go talk to Detective Jensen. We know Wilcox is somewhere in Illusion Town. He's a stranger. Doesn't know the territory. We've got a good description. Shouldn't take too long to find him."

Kelsey cleared her throat discreetly. "I might be able to help you speed up the process."

They all looked at her.

She raised one shoulder in an elegant shrug. "Professor Wilcox made me a little uneasy." She gave Hannah a thin smile. "I do have some talent, you know. He arrived in a cab. He was afraid he wouldn't be able to get another one to pick him up in this neighborhood so he instructed the cab to wait."

Elias looked at her. "You made a note of the number of the cab, didn't you?"

"Yes," she said. "I'm sure the police can persuade the cab company to tell them where the cab took Wilcox."

"Wow," Hannah said. "I'm impressed. Just how much do you want in exchange for the number of the cab that picked up Wilcox?"

"A lot," Kelsey said. She gave Elias a glowing smile. "But I'm sure that it will be petty cash to Mr. Coppersmith."

"Always happy to pay for good information," Elias said.

Detective Jensen phoned Elias twenty minutes later.

"I'm standing in room 118 at the Glowing Ruin Inn," Jensen said. "Wilcox was here, all right. Registered under another name but the front desk clerk recognized him from a photo. He checked out a few hours ago. Now that we have a lead on him it shouldn't take us too long to find him."

"We've got another problem," Elias said. "A few minutes ago Wilcox contacted Hannah. This is now a hostage situation."

CHAPTER 35

"I got your message, Professor Wilcox," Hannah said. "I'm here and as you can see, I came alone. Let Runner go. He's not a threat to you."

"All in good time, Miss West, all in good time."

Paxton Wilcox was standing a respectful distance from the powerful dreamlight gate that sealed the entrance to the Midnight Carnival. He looked exactly like the photo on his website — a middle-aged academic complete with wire-rim glasses, a scruffy beard, and a crumpled jacket with leather patches on the elbows. The only thing unscholarly about him was the flamer he held in one hand.

He was not alone. Two beefy men dressed in the leathers and colors of the Soldiers of Fortune stood nearby. One had a long, graying braid secured with a leather thong. The other had shaved his head and tattooed it with the image of a skull. Both held flamers but in a rather casual manner.

Ghost hunters gone rogue, Hannah thought, just as Elias had said. Although they were armed, their real weapon in the Underworld was their talent for working the dangerous, volatile currents of dissonance energy that flowed through the psi-heavy atmosphere.

Runner, his hands bound behind him, was sitting on the floor of the tunnel, slumped against the wall.

"Hey, Runner," she said gently.

"Hey, Finder," he muttered. "You shouldn't have come."

"What else could I do?"

He didn't answer. They both knew that if the situation had been reversed, he would have been standing where she was. *Family.*

She realized he was staring at her with a bemused expression. He opened his mouth to say something and closed it just as quickly.

She knew that he had just realized that Virgil was not with her. She thought she saw a spark of cautious hope in his eyes. He quickly veiled it.

"Why in green hell did you fall for this bastard's threats?" he asked instead. "You know he's lying. He can't afford to let either one of us live after he gets what he wants. He's gonna send us both on a long walk through the tunnels without good amber."

Which was, Hannah knew, the equivalent of a death sentence.

"You know me, Runner," she said. "Ever the optimist."

Wilcox snorted in disgust. "There was never any question but that Miss West would show up, provided she had the right incentive."

"What made you so sure?" Hannah asked.

"I've studied your para-psych profile," he said. "At least as much of it as Barnett was able to assess before you walked out. I also have his notes. There was more than enough material to confirm what I suspected when I sent you to him for testing. It's the profile of a fragile, off-the-charts talent."

"I'm not fragile," she said. "And by the way, that profile was supposed to be confidential. I never authorized Barnett to send it to you."

"Money talks very loudly to people like Grady Barnett. I realize that you're a little annoyed with him at the moment but rest assured, I didn't have to study his para-psych profile to know that he would be open to a business arrangement involving your profile."

"Yeah, I gather you two were BFFs from the old days at good old University of Resonance."

"I have no idea what a BFF is but I can tell you that any researcher who is willing to falsify his data in order to get published is a researcher who can be manipulated with the promise of grant money," Wilcox said.

"Out of curiosity, did you ever intend to actually pay Grady?" she asked.

Wilcox shrugged. "I'm sure that one small artifact from the treasure trove on the other side of this dreamlight gate would have been more than enough to keep him quiet."

"You shouldn't have kidnapped Runner," Hannah said. "We don't have a lot of rules in the DZ. But we enforce the ones we do have. Rule Number One — you don't get away with threatening friends and family."

Wilcox grunted. "Young Runner here is hardly a friend. He's a petty criminal. And you don't have any family, remember?"

"Runner is not a criminal," Hannah said. "He runs a delivery business. And just so you know, you dumbass genealogist, I do have a family. You just kidnapped my brother and you're going to regret it."

Wilcox chuckled. "It was so simple to manipulate your misplaced sense of family loyalty."

"I'm guessing you're not close to your own family," Hannah said. "Or maybe your relatives prefer not to get too close to you? It's not like they can count on you to bring a lot of honor and respect to the family name, can they?"

Rage flashed briefly in Wilcox's eyes. "You do realize that your need to create a fake family composed of the riffraff of the Dark Zone is just another example of your para-psych fragility, don't you? It's the reason I've been able to control you from a distance ever since you showed up at my website." He relaxed slightly. "I had almost given up, you know."

"Given up on what?" Hannah asked.

"A couple of years ago I put up that website advertising myself as an expert genealogist who specialized in dreamlight para-genetics. I knew that the orphaned daughter of a cheap Illusion Town showgirl and a third-rate magician had to be out there somewhere." Wilcox smiled. "Sooner or later every orphan goes looking for her family. I baited my trap very carefully and finally, *finally* you showed up."

"But you had to be sure that I had the necklace so you put that crystal up for auction and waited to see if I would grab it. How did you get that ultraviolet stone, by the way?"

"I picked it up in a genuine estate sale years ago. I traced the rest of the crystals to your mother. But your father had a duplicate made and palmed it off on me. He thought he could get rid of me that way."

Shock whispered through Hannah. Fury followed in its wake.

"You're the one who murdered them, aren't you?" she said. "You shot my parents."

"Your father tried to cheat me," Wilcox bellowed. "Now shut up and open that damned dreamlight gate."

The two Soldiers of Fortune exchanged glances. Hannah realized they were starting to get a little worried about the mental state of their employer.

She took a deep breath. "Just so you know, those of us who live in the DZ are pretty good at protecting what's ours. Isn't that right, Runner?"

"Yeah," Runner said. "Won't be long before this idiot figures that out."

The Soldier of Fortune sporting the graying braid aimed his flamer at Runner in a threatening manner.

"That's enough, kid," the man said. "I'm getting tired of listening to you."

"I think we're done with the question-

and-answer portion of the program," Wilcox said. "I'd rather not hang around this town any longer than absolutely necessary."

"I'll bet you don't," Hannah said. "You've made some serious enemies, including my husband. As soon as he realizes I'm gone, Coppersmith is going to come looking for me."

"I don't think I'll need to worry too much about your Marriage-of-Convenience husband. Coppersmith got what he wanted from you when you opened that dreamlight gate at the portal and led him to the pirates. Haven't you asked yourself why he's still hanging around? The sex may be good but a man in his position can easily replace his bed partners. No, Hannah, he's sticking close to you for the same reason I've been keeping tabs on you for a month. You've got one irresistible quality — you're the key to the Midnight Carnival."

"You're wrong about Elias," she said quietly.

"You're a very foolish woman but that is no longer my concern. I'm out of time. *Open the damned gate.*"

"Okay, if you're sure that's what you want. But Runner comes with me. I'm not leaving him behind."

"Don't worry. We're not leaving that little

tunnel rat behind. He'd make a break for the surface the second I turned my back on him." Wilcox motioned to Runner. "On your feet."

Runner scrambled upright and moved to join Hannah in front of the gate.

She put her hand on his shoulder in what she hoped looked like a reassuring gesture. The reality was that she needed the physical contact to protect him from the full force of the powerful dreamlight.

She was so close now that the energy stirred her hair and excited her senses. A sea of nightmares beckoned, promising hellish visions and senses-crushing sensations.

Under her palm she felt Runner shiver. Even though she was shielding him from the worst of the effects, she knew that some of the nightmares were getting through.

"Man, this is so high-rez," he rasped.

"Tell me about it," she said. "But I can handle this stuff."

"Sure. You're Finder. You know dreamlight."

"Yes," she said. "I do."

She rezzed her senses and began searching for the core frequencies. Small flashes of paranormal lightning sparked off the gate.

The dreamlight currents began to wail, faint and audible only on the paranormal end of the spectrum at first but they increased rapidly in volume. She knew that the men behind her could detect them now.

In such an environment even normal dreamlight took on added dimensions that affected different people in different ways. There was nothing normal about the dreamlight in the gate. She knew that Braid Dude and Skull Head were very much on edge now.

"Shit," Skull Head muttered. "What is that weird noise?"

"Just a side effect of the dreamlight," Wilcox said.

He sounded impatient but Hannah thought she caught an edge of nervousness in his voice.

"Just one more question before I do this," she said. She had to raise her voice to be heard above the eerie howling of the fierce currents. "What happens after I open this gate? You can't possibly imagine that you'll be able to steal every artifact in the Midnight Carnival. I've been in there. It's huge. There are hundreds of hot relics inside. Some of them are dangerous. Once they start hitting the underground market, rumors will fly. Half the collectors in the four city-states will be looking for the source, not to mention Arcane."

Wilcox gave her a thin smile. "Rumors won't be a problem if everyone keeps quiet. It will be in your best interests and the best interests of your so-called brother to keep your mouths shut. Get the gate open."

She glanced at Runner and knew from his grim expression that he understood the situation as clearly as she did. They had both grown up in the DZ. They knew how to get to the bottom line in a hurry. Once Wilcox gained access to the carnival he would buy the time he needed to transport the relics to another location by getting rid of the only two people in the vicinity who could not be counted on to keep silent — Runner and herself.

And then there were the Soldiers of Fortune, she thought. They gave the situation an intriguing twist.

She glanced back at them. "Hey, guys. Keep an eye on Wilcox. After all, he'll have to murder you two, as well. It's either that or risk losing the Midnight Carnival to your boss. I understand that Felix — that's his street name, right? Felix is the ambitious type. He'll probably want to grab the carnival artifacts for himself."

Braid Dude exchanged another uneasy glance with Skull Head.

"Shut up," Wilcox snarled. He aimed the

flamer at Runner. "If you don't stop talking, I'll set the tunnel rat's shirt on fire. You can watch him burn alive."

Runner rolled his eyes, unimpressed with the threat.

Hannah turned back to the gate and concentrated on de-rezzing the tightly oscillating currents. The psi-lightning flashed more violently and the energy levels in the tunnel grew more intense. The wailing and howling of the nightmare currents shuddered through the atmosphere.

"How long does this take?" Skull Head hissed.

"Shit," the other one gasped. "What is that energy?"

Runner snorted. "Thought those guys were supposed to be tough."

"They're not from around here," Hannah said. "They don't know tough."

"Nope."

"Hurry, damn it," Paxton ordered.

"Yeah, sure, whatever," Hannah said.

Gently, she manipulated one last frequency, allowing it to flatline.

In the next instant the energy gate winked out.

The sudden stillness caught Wilcox and the bikers by surprise. It took them a few seconds to recover from the shock created by the sudden cessation of the nerve-rattling nightmare energy.

Hannah used the moment to urge Runner into the chamber.

Heavy currents of psi shuddered and shivered through the atmosphere. The attractions of the Midnight Carnival glittered and dazzled, promising thrills and chills and great secrets.

"Wow," Runner whispered. "What *is* this place?"

"Long story," she said softly. "Tell you later."

Skull Head and Braid Dude walked hesitantly into the chamber and stopped a short distance inside the gate. They both looked stunned.

Wilcox moved slowly through the hot space, enthralled by the artifacts.

"So this is the Midnight Carnival," he said. "To think that all these years it's been hidden down here, right below Illusion Town."

"Just to be clear on the technicalities," Hannah said. "It's my find. I filed a claim to this whole sector a couple of weeks ago."

"That won't be a problem," Wilcox said. "You are going to sign the papers that will transfer the claim to me. I have them with me."

"Not a chance," Hannah said.

Paxton sighed. "I see we must negotiate. Here is my position: Sign the papers or I'll start making the members of your Dark Zone family disappear, one by one, starting with young Runner."

An eerie music floated across the chamber. The carousel with the dangerous clockwork toys and miniatures began to revolve.

"What's going on?" Skull Head asked sharply.

The carousel continued to rotate at a leisurely pace. The odd melody got more disturbing. One of the figures — the Old World queen — came into view. She got a fix on Skull Head. Energy shifted in the atmosphere.

"Unnh." Skull Head clutched at his chest. "Can't breathe."

The slow rotation of the platform took the queen out of view, breaking the focus. But now the black glass windows of the fairy-tale carriage flashed with power.

Braid Dude staggered. "Wha— ?"

Skull Head stumbled quickly back toward the gate. "That statue on the merry-go-round. It did something to me."

Braid Dude swung around to confront Wilcox. "What in green hell is this place?"

It was Elias who answered.

"Welcome to the Midnight Carnival." He shut down the carousel, walked out of the control booth, and stepped off the platform. He gripped a flamer casually in one hand. Virgil was on his shoulder. "Have you seen and heard enough, Detective Jensen?"

Jensen, accompanied by three uniformed officers, emerged from behind an arcade machine.

"More than enough," Jensen said. "Got it all recorded — sound as well as video. We've got a list of charges that run all the way from kidnapping and extortion to drugs and reckless driving."

Virgil chortled and bounded down to the ground. He scurried toward Hannah, Arizona Snow clutched in his paw.

"I missed you, too," Hannah said. She scooped him up and kissed his scruffy head somewhere between his ears.

She plopped him down on Runner's shoulder. Reaching down, she took a small utility knife out of the sheath inside one of her boots and went to work cutting through the ties that bound Runner's wrists.

Runner reached up to pet Virgil. "Good to see you, pal."

Virgil waved Arizona Snow, bounded down to the floor, and scurried toward the arcade machine that was filled with toys and stuffed animals. He paused to chortle encouragingly at Runner.

Intrigued, Runner trailed after him.

Hannah looked at Jensen.

"Don't forget breaking and entering," she said, jerking a thumb toward Wilcox. "And attempted claim jumping."

Jensen smiled, startling her. It was, she realized, the first time she had seen him smile. He looked almost happy. Okay, maybe *happy* was too strong a word. More like quietly satisfied. Evidently, this was a good day for Detective Jensen.

Wilcox stared at Elias. "It's not possible," he gasped. "How did you get in here ahead of us?"

"Turns out there are at least three gates," Elias said. "We used one that can be accessed inside the Shadow Zone. Hannah and I found it the night your bikers chased us through the tunnels. Hannah reopened it for us this afternoon before she went to meet you at the first gate."

Braid Dude and Skull Head recovered from their shock. They evidently made the executive decision not to waste any time trying to fight an obviously lost battle. They turned and ran for the open gate.

Hannah released the psychic grip she had been using to hold the gate open. The

401

nightmarish currents roared back in a torrent.

The gate slammed shut just as the bikers reached it. They were so close the shock wave struck them with lightninglike ferocity. The men jerked and stiffened, their bodies twisting in painfully unnatural postures. Their faces were frozen masks of panic.

In the next instant they fell unconscious to the floor and lay very still.

For a second or two, everyone stared at the fallen men.

Everyone except Paxton Wilcox.

Moving with surprising speed, he locked an arm around Hannah's throat and put the barrel of the flamer to the side of her face.

"You bitch," he hissed. "You've been nothing but trouble. Worse than your mother and that bastard magician. But now you're my ticket out of here. Open that damned gate."

"You murdered them," Hannah said. "It was you. My parents didn't die in a drug deal gone bad. You shot them both."

"I told you, they tricked me. Your father was a very, very good magician, I'll say that for him."

"They died to protect my inheritance."

Everyone else in the chamber went very still.

"Let her go," Elias said, his voice lethally quiet.

"We both know that's not going to happen," Wilcox said. "Open that gate, Hannah, or I'll rez this trigger. At the very least one half of your face will be ruined. You'll probably lose your eye."

Virgil raced out from the direction of the arcade booth. He was all teeth and eyes. He was not growling. He was closing in for the attack.

Wilcox tightened his grip on Hannah's throat.

"Make that creature stop or I'll burn him," Wilcox said.

"Virgil," she said quietly. "That's far enough. I've got this."

Virgil seemed to understand. He halted a few feet away, crouched on his hind legs, ready to spring.

"You know what really pisses me off, Wilcox?" Hannah said. "What pisses me off is that you murdered my parents and you kidnapped my brother today. No one gets away with harming a member of my family."

"You really don't know when to shut up, do you?" Wilcox said. "Open that gate."

He had her tightly pinned against his chest. She had all the physical contact she needed. She rezzed her talent, found a focus, and generated enough energy to overwhelm him in nightmares.

Between one breath and the next he was plunged into the ultimate private horror show. At first she had no idea what he saw — no one could view another person's dreams, just as no one could actually read another person's mind.

"No," he whispered. He gazed, transfixed, at a vision only he could see. "No. You're dead. You're both dead." His voice rose. "You're nothing. Just a cheap Illusion Town whore and a third-rate magician. You're both dead."

The flamer dropped from his hand. His arm fell away from Hannah's throat. He staggered backward, transfixed by the visions his mind had conjured.

And then his eyes locked with Hannah's one last time.

"You look just like her," he rasped. "Just like your mother. Tell her to leave me alone. Tell the magician to leave me alone. It wasn't supposed to end like this. You're just a bastard. No family. No trouble."

"You got that wrong," Elias said. He pulled Hannah into the circle of his arm.

"She's got a lot of family, including a hus-band."

"And a brother," Runner added.

Virgil chortled, fully fluffed once more, and once again vaulted up into Hannah's arms.

"And Virgil," Hannah said. "And a couple of aunts. And parents who died trying to protect my inheritance. Got anyone you can trust, Wilcox?"

He did not answer because he was rapidly losing consciousness. He fell to the floor without a word.

"That's what I thought," Hannah said.

CHAPTER 36

The dream started the way it always did. The doppelgänger rose from the bed and looked down at the dreamer and the man sleeping beside her. The man had one arm around the dreamer in a way that suggested tenderness and intimacy. He stirred a little when he felt the energy shift in the atmosphere.

The dust bunny at the foot of the bed opened his baby blues and fixed his attention on the dreamer.

"What's the matter now?" the dreamer asked in the silent language of dreams. "It's been a long day."

"This is important," the doppelgänger said.

"Yeah, yeah. With you, everything is important."

The doppelgänger looked at the man. "We're talking about your future."

"I've been trying to avoid that topic."

"That works with some things. But not with this. You love him."

"I know."

"What he feels for you is real."

"But is it love?"

"I don't know. Why don't you ask him?"

The dreamer got the impression that the doppelgänger was smiling, as though certain of the answer the man would give. But she could be hard to interpret.

In any event it was too late to ask for clarification. The doppelgänger was already fading rapidly.

Hannah came awake but there was no sense of disorientation this time. No panic. No feeling that time was running out.

This time she understood her intuition's message. She did not have all the answers but she had the one she needed. She loved Elias.

She opened her eyes and turned onto her side to look at him. He was awake, watching her.

A deep sense of certainty settled on her.

"I love you," she said.

He smiled a slow, compelling smile. "Took you long enough to figure that out."

"You were so sure?"

"No, but I come from a family of incurable gamblers, remember? We've got a long history of playing for high stakes. We've also got a long history of winning."

She touched the hard, determined line of his jaw. "You bet on us?"

"I didn't have a choice. I started falling in love with you back when our only connection was online. The minute I walked into your shop I was ready to ask you to marry me."

She smiled. "Which is exactly what you did that very first night. And I said yes."

"Because I convinced you an MC would buy you some protection."

"No, that was just a convenient excuse. I said yes because I fell in love with you online, too."

His eyes heated and his energy stirred the atmosphere.

He threaded his fingers through her hair. "Is that right?"

"I didn't put a name to what I felt because I was afraid to believe my own doppelgänger — my intuition. But the truth is, I had begun to dream about you — serious dreams, *dream-walking* dreams — before we met face-to-face. I couldn't see your face in my dreams, but when you walked into my shop, I knew who you were before you said a word."

"Will you marry me again, my love? A real, forever Covenant Marriage? Will you create a family with me?"

"Yes, oh, yes, my love."

He drew her into his arms and she went to him on a tide of joy.

Virgil chortled a cheery farewell. There was a small thump when he hopped down off the bed. He headed for the stairs with Arizona Snow. Hannah knew he was on his way outside to join his dust bunny pals and do whatever dust bunnies did when they gathered at night. He would be back for breakfast.

Meanwhile, everything she wanted was right here in her lover's arms.

CHAPTER 37

Ollie's House of Pizza was crowded when Elias, accompanied by Virgil, arrived. But he had taken care to reserve a table that would accommodate the entire DZ Delivery Service team. Runner and his associates were waiting. Buddy looked surprised to see him but he nodded once, satisfied that Elias was a man of his word.

"Told you he'd show," Runner said.

A number of pizzas were ordered, including an extra one for Virgil — and conversation turned to business. Elias explained that the Arcane Society had paid a fortune for rights to the Midnight Carnival and that Hannah planned to give each member of the DZ Delivery Service a share of the profits. That news had such an impact that Runner and the others actually stopped munching pizza for a few seconds.

When they managed to recover from the shock, murmurs of amazement rippled around the table.

"That is so high-rez," Runner said. "With that kind of money, I could open a real office."

The other deliverymen looked equally thrilled.

"And we could get serious delivery bikes," Buddy said.

Elias ate some pizza while the news settled around the table. When the group stopped talking about what they would do with the money, he continued.

"You'll be getting formal invitations to our wedding," he said. "But I wanted to invite you all personally, just so you'd know that Hannah and I really want you there. Also, I've got a little surprise for you. No big deal compared to the money from the sale of the carnival but I thought maybe you guys would like these."

He took the envelope from the inside of his jacket and put it on the table.

"Courtesy of Mr. Smith," he said.

When they saw what was inside the envelope, Runner and his crew got excited all over again.

CHAPTER 38

The formal, hour-long Covenant Marriage ceremony was solemn and heavily freighted with traditions and rituals that went back two hundred years to the founding of the colonies. The service was held in a chapel in the Dark Zone — the same chapel in which Clara and Bernice had been married.

There was a standing-room-only crowd because this particular wedding had a couple of attractions going for it. The first and most obvious was that the bride and groom were, once again, briefly famous. After all, one of the heirs of the legendary Coppersmith clan was marrying the woman who had discovered Arcane's long-lost museum.

The second reason so many of the DZ residents were in attendance was because the bride and groom had let it be known that they would be making their home in the Dark Zone. They were both officially members of the close-knit community now. Family.

Invitations had been coveted by every high-ranking member of the Arcane Society as well as various para-archaeologists and museum officials from the four city-states. The experts were given a carefully supervised tour of the carnival the day before the wedding. Several had declared it almost priceless. The bride, however, had managed to find a price and Arcane had paid it without quibbling.

Runner sat in the row reserved for family. His crew was seated directly behind him. All of the members of the DZ Delivery Service were spiffed up for the occasion. Their hair was slicked back, their jeans were new, their boots were polished, and the hardware on their leather jackets gleamed.

Ollie closed the House of Pizza so that he and his staff could attend. Hannah's friends and neighbors, the people who had known her all of her life, filled up the rest of the seats.

The groom's side of the chapel was also filled to capacity.

Elias's brother, Rafe, was best man. Rafe's wife, Ella, was in the front row with the rest of the family on the Coppersmith side.

There had been a special note on the

invitations — *Dust Bunnies Welcome.* The result was that about a half dozen were in attendance. Among them was Elvis, the companion of the star reporter from the *Curtain,* Sierra McIntyre. His small white crystal-studded cape added some extra glitz to the occasion. Sierra was there as a guest — she was married to John Fontana, the boss of the Crystal City Guild — and also in her professional capacity. She was covering the wedding for her paper.

Marlowe Jones, the director of the Frequency City office of Jones & Jones, and her husband, Adam Winters, the chief of the Frequency City Guild, brought Marlowe's dust-bunny pal, Gibson.

And of course, Lorelei, Ella Morgan Coppersmith's dust bunny companion, was there perched on the back of the family pew and carrying her own wedding veil.

There were a few others but Virgil looked particularly dashing in a black bow tie. He was on the back of the bride's family pew, clutching his prized Arizona Snow doll.

The musical cue sounded, reverberating throughout the chapel. The crowd got to its feet and turned to watch the bride come down the aisle.

Hannah and her small retinue emerged from the dressing room and paused at the back of the chapel. The bridesmaids made last-minute adjustments to the train of the white gown.

Clara, dressed in a tuxedo, took Hannah's arm.

"Nervous?" she whispered.

"Excited," Hannah said. "Thrilled. Happy. And, okay, maybe a little nervous."

"Everything is going to be just fine," Clara said. "In fact, the future looks wonderful."

"You sound very sure of that."

"I am." Clara looked down the aisle at Elias, who stood waiting at the altar. "After all, you're marrying the man who knows why Bernice and I named the Magic Hannah orchid after you."

"Because my talent looks a bit like magic?"

"No," Clara said. "Because you are magical."

Hannah smiled. "Thanks, but we both know I never had the talent to go onstage like you and Aunt Bernice."

"You weren't born to be a professional stage magician but you changed our lives. Bernice and I are very different people now than we would have been if you hadn't wound up on our doorstep. We stopped the wild partying and got married because of you. We settled down, created a home, and made plans for a future all because of you. And now you're going to bring a little magic into Elias's life. He knows that. He understands how fortunate he is to have found you. That makes him the right one for you."

"Aunt Clara, I'm going to cry and ruin the makeup that the nice cosmetician just spent half an hour putting on my face."

Clara laughed. "Don't you dare. Remember the old stage motto: Never cry in front of an audience unless it's part of the act."

Hannah sniffed. "Okay."

"Ready?"

"Ready."

The music rose to a joyous level.

Clara tightened her grip on Hannah's arm and escorted her down the aisle.

Elias never took his eyes off Hannah. In that moment she saw the promise of a lifetime of love and knew that together she and Elias would create some real magic — a new family and a future.

The reception was held in the glorious rooftop gardens of the Amber Palace. Maxwell Smith had insisted on hosting the event. In Illusion Town you didn't turn down such a gracious offer from one of the members of the Club. And there was no denying the venue made a spectacular setting for a party.

There were the usual toasts with Smith's very fine champagne and various and assorted traditions were honored.

A hush fell over the crowd when Elias led Hannah out onto the dance floor that had been set up in the middle of the garden. When the music came to an end he pulled her into his arms and kissed her. There was a round of applause.

And then the fun really got started.

If there was one thing Illusion Town knew how to do well, it was throw a party.

A good time was had by all, including the dust bunnies who, after stoking up on the special wedding cupcakes that had been made for them, headed straight for the glowing pool.

Perkins served as lifeguard. Some of the guests were secretly disappointed when the frolicking in the water did not result in any emergencies requiring the butler to strip out of her elegant uniform.

Sometime after midnight the bride and groom took their leave. Everyone assumed they were headed for one of the opulent honeymoon suites in the Amber Palace. But the truth — later reported in the *Curtain* — was that they spent their second wedding night in the bride's little apartment above

417

her shop. When asked for a comment, the couple had explained that the apartment felt like home.

CHAPTER 39

With the bride and groom gone, the rooftop party wound down. But the night was far from over. The human guests headed for the bright lights of the Strip where the glittering casinos and exotic shows awaited.

The dust bunnies allowed themselves to be hauled out of the pool but their fun was not yet over, either. Runner and his crew were waiting for them. They collected Virgil and his pals and headed for the newest attraction on the Strip.

The Alien Storm roller coaster was officially open for business. Tickets for the first couple of months had been sold out for ages. But the bride and groom knew some important people in town. The envelope that Elias had presented to Runner and his crew had contained passes for the night of the wedding. Management had agreed that dust bunnies could ride for free.

The night was still young and the tickets

were good for an unlimited number of rides. As luck would have it, dust bunnies and humans had a few things in common when it came to the definition of a good time. Both groups liked their fun spiked with a few thrills.

In Illusion Town, the thrills were real.

ABOUT THE AUTHOR

The author of a string of *New York Times* bestsellers, **Jayne Ann Krentz** uses three different pen names for each of her three "worlds". As Jayne Ann Krentz (her married name) she writes contemporary romantic-suspense. She uses **Amanda Quick** for her novels of historical romantic-suspense. **Jayne Castle** (her birth name) is reserved these days for her stories of futuristic/paranormal romantic-suspense. She earned a B.A. in History from the University of California at Santa Cruz and went on to obtain a master's degree in Library Science from San Jose State University in California. Before she began writing full time she worked as a librarian in both academic and corporate libraries. She is married and lives with her husband, Frank, in Seattle, Washington.

The employees of Thorndike Press hope you have enjoyed this Large Print book. All our Thorndike, Wheeler, and Kennebec Large Print titles are designed for easy reading, and all our books are made to last. Other Thorndike Press Large Print books are available at your library, through selected bookstores, or directly from us.

For information about titles, please call:
  (800) 223-1244

or visit our Web site at:
  http://gale.cengage.com/thorndike

To share your comments, please write:
Publisher
Thorndike Press
10 Water St., Suite 310
Waterville, ME 04901